Unmistakable Identity

With a twinge of regret, Mara pushed away from the bedpost. But when she turned to leave the antique shop, she slammed into a wall. A solid, well-muscled male wall. Quite possibly the most beautiful man she had ever seen.

His intensity wrapped around her, dark and seductive, his deep-seeing gaze seeming to burn away her clothes until she felt fully exposed. Naked. Perhaps even a bit . . . tingly. After all, it wasn't every day a man's mere gaze seared her into feeling devoured, and in the most rousing, delicious ways. She bit her lip before she could sigh and risk revealing her weakness.

More than his strapping build and handsomeness, it was the draw of his incredibly intense eyes that captivated her. Sea green eyes a woman could drown in.

But now his burning gaze held only arrogance. Annoyed, Mara drew a tight breath. He glowered at her as if she had the pox. Perhaps he'd heard her talking and didn't like Americans? If so, there was an easy remedy: she'd smother him with charm.

"Hi," she said, flashing her best smile. "I'm Mara McDougall."

He remained stony faced.

"Look, I'm sorry I bumped into you," she said. "It won't happen again."

"With surety, it shall not," he agreed. "The bed is mine, wench. Begone."

There was that accent again. Warm, rich, and buttery smooth. And so annoyingly sexy, just listening to him sent another rush of desire curling though her.

But *wench* and *begone*?

He narrowed his eyes. "You are a MacDougall. No one of that ilk will ever sleep in my bed. I forbid it. . . ."

Highlander in Her Bed

Allie Mackay

A SIGNET ECLIPSE BOOK

SIGNET ECLIPSE
Published by New American Library, a division of
Penguin Group (USA) Inc., 375 Hudson Street,
New York, New York 10014, USA
Penguin Group (Canada), 90 Eglinton Avenue East, Suite 700, Toronto,
Ontario M4P 2Y3, Canada (a division of Pearson Penguin Canada Inc.)
Penguin Books Ltd., 80 Strand, London WC2R 0RL, England
Penguin Ireland, 25 St. Stephen's Green, Dublin 2,
Ireland (a division of Penguin Books Ltd.)
Penguin Group (Australia), 250 Camberwell Road, Camberwell, Victoria 3124,
Australia (a division of Pearson Australia Group Pty. Ltd.)
Penguin Books India Pvt. Ltd., 11 Community Centre, Panchsheel Park,
New Delhi - 110 017, India
Penguin Group (NZ), cnr Airborne and Rosedale Roads, Albany,
Auckland 1310, New Zealand (a division of Pearson New Zealand Ltd.)
Penguin Books (South Africa) (Pty.) Ltd., 24 Sturdee Avenue,
Rosebank, Johannesburg 2196, South Africa

Penguin Books Ltd., Registered Offices:
80 Strand, London WC2R 0RL, England

First published by Signet Eclipse, an imprint of New American Library,
a division of Penguin Group (USA) Inc.

ISBN 978-0-7394-7426-6

Printed in the United States of America

With much love and affection,
for Pat Cody and Karen D. Stevens,
sister authors, the greatest of travel
companions, and fellow paranormal
enthusiasts. You are dear friends of
immeasurable worth, and I wouldn't want
to explore haunted places with anyone else.
For all the ghosting good times we've had
stateside and across the Big Pond—
I thank you with all my heart.

ACKNOWLEDGMENTS

Scotland is the wellspring of my inspiration, and on every visit there I am impressed anew by the beauty of the land and the ever-present pulse of its deep, ancient history.

Beguiling and magical, Scotland stirs passion with its misty hills, silent glens, and romantic castle ruins. Such passion runs deep in the blood of those of Scottish descent. There is always an ache, an irresistible pull to return. I know this yearning well: the great joy of being there and the sadness of having to leave.

This book allowed me to indulge two of my own fondest fantasies: to someday be able to stay in Scotland, and to have a yummy medieval Hottie Scottie materialize out of the mist at one of the remote castle ruins I so enjoy exploring.

Three women helped make this book possible, and I owe them my heartfelt gratitude: agent Karen Solem, for finding Alex the perfect home; agent, best friend, and personal champion Roberta Brown, for reading every line almost as soon as it was written and cheering me on; and my wonderfully skilled editor, Anne

Bohner, for loving Alex as much as I do and giving him this chance.

Also a loving nod to the real "Dottie," my friend Anne MacDougall Bryant's late springer spaniel, Dorothy Joy. A true MacDougall heroine, Dottie was a very special girl, gentle and precious. She lives on in our hearts, never to be forgotten.

Above all, my unending love and appreciation to my handsome husband, Manfred, for his support and unflagging enthusiasm, and to my own wee sweet muse, my little dog, Em. He is spoiled beyond measure and rightly so; I do not think I could write a single line without him.

Prologue

West Highlands, near Oban, 1312

He'd known not to trust MacDougalls.

Would that he'd calculated their number.

Now, in the gut of a deep ravine, the most harrowing way into their benighted territory, Sir Alexander Douglas and his entire array faced their respective ends.

They were caught in the thickest of fighting, surrounded by dying, cursing men and screaming, frightened horses; their fate stood clear. Sealed by both ill fortune and poor judgment. His surety that none would suspect he'd choose such an ambush-prone defile as his path.

That, and the honor that forbade him to refuse a king's orders.

Furious, he swung his horse round, his blade arcing without cease, run red with blood and dripping.

And still it wasn't enough. Trapped indeed, he cursed every MacDougall to come at him, cutting down as many as he could, and glaring at the steep-sided gorge that had so quickly become a whirling turmoil of death and destruction.

On and on they came. An endless torrent of MacDougalls, streaming out from every hidden crevice and surging down the braeside in a savage, killing flood the likes of which he'd never seen.

And although his men were every bit as fierce, even superbly armed and accoutred, they did not stand a chance.

In only a few chaotic moments, a journey that should have held such promise came to a dizzying, brutal end. All around him, his entourage lay smashed and shattered, the lot of them unable to withstand the crushing ferocity of hurtled boulders, the MacDougalls' wild downhill charge.

Those who yet stood or sought to fight from the backs of their steeds knew well who'd won the day.

Then, from the midst of the sword-swiping clangor, a proud-faced MacDougall came spurring to within a few yards of Alex, a handful of hot-eyed, pike-bearing clansmen close at his heels.

"Hah, Douglas! I greet you!" the man called, his eyes flashing scorn. " 'Tis a fine day to die, is it not?"

"You do your line no service, Sir Colin," Alex shot back, recognizing the man from the bargaining table that had brought him to this wretched pass. "Rather death than to see my name sullied as you have now soiled yours."

Coldly arrogant, the MacDougall flicked a glance

at Alex's sword, his sneer indicating without words that he'd not missed that the great brand's tip had snapped off.

"Drop your blade, man. 'Tis now as useless as your life," he scoffed, nodding approval when his henchmen advanced on Alex, pike shafts lowered, swords at the ready. "A pity you didn't know better than to come riding hotfoot into our territory."

Tight-lipped, Alex scowled defiance. They could slice him to ribbons before he'd reveal he'd known indeed. 'Twas his king, the Good Robert Bruce, who'd hoped for the MacDougalls' honor. A forgiving monarch, he'd trusted the querulous clan to grip a hand extended in peace and put an end to the long-running feud between the two great houses.

"Your error in judgment has sold your men's lives dearly," Colin taunted him. "Your own as well."

"And you shall suffer for your treachery, that I promise you!" Alex jerked, well aware of the growing silence and its foul portent.

There would be no winning away, no unexpected turning of his fortune, and, the Almighty as his witness, no yielding, either.

A Douglas stood until he fell.

" 'Tis you who shall regret!" One of the lance bearers urged his horse closer, jabbed his spear tip into Alex's thigh.

Ignoring the pain, Alex focused on their leader, meeting Colin's glare with a scalding stare of his own. A circular ruby brooch gleamed at the man's shoulder, its glittering gemstones the same deep red as the stain spreading down Alex's leg.

"With such fine plunder lying about, I dinna think we'll be a-bothering with much suffering." Colin gestured at the blood-soaked hillside, the deep ravine now littered with the corpses of Alex's men, the shattered remnants of his baggage train. "Aye, right good pickings."

Alex bristled, swallowed the bile in his throat. "Too good for the likes of you."

Already men scavenged, bands of them moving amongst the fallen to search for spoils worth harvesting. Rich booty indeed, much of it gleaned from the unwieldy cargo Alex had insisted on bringing despite the perilous journey.

The greatest prize, a magnificently carved four-poster bed, carefully dismantled for the journey and packed with all its luxuriant trappings.

His wedding gift to a bride he'd never see.

A token offering of goodwill for a wife he hadn't wanted but had given his oath to claim.

Gall near choking him, he flung away his tipless brand and made to hurl himself upon the MacDougall, ached to curl his hands around the other's neck, but a ringed phalanx of steel-headed pikes stopped him. In particular, the one pressing into the hollow of his throat.

Anger burning hot within him, he drew himself as upright as the thrusting spear heads allowed. "Your Lady Isobel sought this union, wished to see your house in the king's grace."

The men encircling him smirked at each other.

"So you say?" Colin raised his brows. " 'Twas her da who favored such an alliance, and he, God rest his soul, is no more. Besides, the Lady Isobel has been sweet on me since we were both in swaddling. 'Twas her own good self sent us to intercept you."

The back of his neck blazing, Alex fought to keep his wits, a near impossibility with the twisted body of his youngest squire sprawled not far from the MacDougall's feet, the poor lad's eyes staring unblinking at the sky.

Others of his retinue lay nearby, some heaped in mounds, all equally still. Good and proud men, slain in their dozens.

Alex shuddered, his stomach churning. "King Robert will see you swinging from the nearest gibbet," he swore, his voice sharp enough to cut granite. "Every last one of you."

Colin gave an exaggerated shrug. "That remains to be seen, but I think not. See here, this is the Bloodstone of Dalriada," he boasted, rubbing his knuckles over the brooch at his shoulder. "A sacred relic passed down from Kenneth MacAlpin, first King of Scots, and wrest from your own Bruce's cloak in a struggle at Dalrigh. Its possession is the pride of all MacDougalls."

Alex narrowed his eyes, his gorge rising. "I have no interest in your brooch, however it came into your hands."

"Och, but you should." The other's lip curled with malice. "See you, with you dead and no witnesses to naysay us, we will claim you absconded with the Bloodstone of Dalriada on the eve of your wedding. Not even your upstart king will avenge a man who'd so shame his bride."

"God's curse on you!" Alex cried, knowing the truth of the man's words.

Colin hooted a mirthless laugh, waved a hand at the growing pile of plunder. "Ahhh, Lady Isobel will be mightily pleased with your bride gifts," he jeered, a wolfish smile spreading across his face. "Yon bridal bed looks to be a fine piece. We shall use it well."

"You will not spend a single night in my bed," Alex hissed, rage surging in his chest. "Not in bliss. That I swear on my mother's grave."

Unfazed, Colin removed his brooch and tossed it to Alex. "Something better than a light-skirted bitch to swear upon."

His fury now white-hot, Alex snarled, "Were you man enough to fight me one-on-one, I'd tear out your tongue for that, MacDougall."

But Colin only curled a hand around his belt and rocked on his heels. "The Bloodstone of Dalriada is magical," he crooned, clearly enjoying himself. "Some say it contains the blood of Saint Columba. Others swear the brooch came to MacAlpin by way of the fey ones. *Fairy folk,* who promised to grant the bearer three wishes so long as a year and a day passed between summons."

A red haze clouding his vision, Alex stared hard at the man he knew to be his murderer, his fingers clasped so fiercely around the brooch, its pin sank deep into his palm.

Ignoring Alex's glower, Colin rumbled on, his tone almost jovial, "If the tradition is true, mayhap you might attempt a last wish of your own."

"I'll see you in hell first," Alex growled, struggling

against the men forcing him to the ground, but all his might and anger proved no match for the jabbing spear heads.

"Dastards," he seethed, casting a furious look around him. "You'll not get away with this."

"Some would say we already have." Colin stepped closer and raised his sword. "I shall pray for your soul before I take Isobel to your bed this night."

"You will rue the hour you e'er laid eyes on my bed," Alex vowed, glaring at his death. "I shall haunt you and your issue until the end of all days, that I swear."

"We will see," Colin said, and took a swinging blow.

"Bloody MacDougall bast—" Alex began before sinking down beneath a hail of flashing steel, his last mortal words forever silenced.

His curse on the MacDougalls etched onto eternity.

Chapter 1

London, the Present

Bloody MacDougall bastards.

Mara McDougall jumped at the angrily whispered slur. Her pulse racing, she spun around, but saw . . . no one. Nothing but clutter and dust stared back at her. A musty shop room brimming with other people's castoffs, each supposed treasure as silent as the grave.

Yet she would've sworn someone had hushed the words just behind her ear.

A masculine someone with a very deep voice.

A voice with a rich, curl-a-girl's-toes accent she couldn't quite place.

Pressing a hand to her breast, she strove for calm and hoped she wasn't becoming as unhinged as the characters she'd been escorting all over the English countryside for the past two weeks.

The longest two weeks of her life.

With a fortitude she hadn't known she possessed, she'd herded the group of would-be ghost hunters through more castles, stately homes, and supposedly haunted pubs than she could count. She'd sat through nonsensical discussions about cold spots, gray ladies, and things that go bump in the night. For the sake of her business, she'd even feigned interest.

And now she was hearing voices that weren't there.

Her preciously seized alone time was rapidly deteriorating and even though this particular trip had landed her one-woman touring company, Exclusive Excursions, a handsome profit, enough was enough.

This was not amusing.

She had neither the time nor the inclination to start hearing things, and if her current clients posed a sampling of the kind of people who did, she didn't want any part of such dubious capabilities.

Shuddering, she became aware of the faint throbbings of an approaching headache and reached to rub her forehead. Soon she'd part company with the ghost busters. One more day, a too-long plane ride across the Atlantic, and she'd never have to see them again, wouldn't have to listen to any more of their outlandish stories.

Still, the real-sounding slur had her peering into every corner of the dimly lit back room of Dimbleby's Antique and Curio Shoppe.

A simple precautionary measure, just to be certain that nothing but disorder and a few very good dust-covered pieces shared the room with her. Satisfied she'd scrutinized every possible hidey-hole, she turned her attention back to the unusual four-poster bed she'd been examining.

Never in all her travels had she seen anything as remarkable. The bed was fashioned of fine old oak, smooth and blackened by age; its sheer presence dominated the room.

The bed had to be old . . . *really* old.

Drawing an awed breath, she trailed her fingertips down one of the richly carved posts. Cool and satiny to the touch, the ancient wood sent a tremor of excitement rippling through her.

How many centuries had it taken to create such a patina? Whose skilled hands had so lovingly crafted the intricate design of thistles and oak leaves adorning the bed's massive headboard and ceiling?

She sighed, a wistful smile curving her lips. Who had been born, died, or made love in such a regal bed? The possibilities were as endless as her imagination.

"Magnificent, hmmm?"

Once more, Mara jumped, her eyes flying wide. And for the second time that day, a chill sped down her spine. But this time the male voice behind her did not sound angry.

And certainly not as smooth and deep.

Merely very *English,* and overlaid with the slight touch of superiority inherent to antique shop owners.

Straightening, Mara took a deep breath and squelched the flare of self-consciousness such haughty individuals sometimes roused in her.

Then she turned around and her flash of insecurity slid away.

The highly cultured voice belonged to a rather nondescript man somewhere in his fifties. Of slight build, he wore a rumpled suit of light gray and had carefully combed his thinning hair across a bald spot on the top of his head.

And even though he was standing as erect as if he'd swallowed a broom, she topped him by a good three inches.

For once glad of her height, Mara nodded agreement. "Yes, it is amazing. I've never seen anything like it." She glanced at the bed. "Is it Tudor?"

The man rubbed his chin. "Could be, but I suspect it is much older, perhaps fourteenth century. I wouldn't be surprised if it dates back even earlier. It's most unique, the finest piece of medieval furniture you'll find outside a museum."

He studied her with sharp blue eyes. "I'm afraid it's quite dear."

"Oh, I don't want to *buy* it," Mara said, wishing she could. "I was just admiring it. Do you know its history?"

"Only what I can surmise, Miss . . . ?"

"McDougall. Mara McDou—" A resounding crash snatched her words, the loud *bang* reverberating through the room and jarring the glass and porcelain antiques.

Mara froze. Her nerves sprang to life again, and icy little prickles broke out all over her. She looked at the Englishman, but he appeared totally unperturbed.

"It's only the window." He indicated a milky double-hung affair across the room. "It's a bit dodgy and sometimes slams down on its own," he added, arching a brow at her. "I trust it didn't alarm you?"

"No-o-o, not at all," Mara fudged, not about to admit that the noise had set her reeling.

Rubbing her arms, she regretted not wearing a sweater. A *jumper* as the Brits called it. Sheesh, all of a sudden, she was freezing. Enough that she could hardly believe her teeth weren't chattering.

She hoped she hadn't caught Nellie Hathaway's cold. The ghost-hunting bookkeeper from Pittsburgh had been sneezing without cease ever since they'd spent the night in a cemetery outside Exeter.

"It's a bit cold in here," she said, still trying to rub away her gooseflesh.

"Cold?" The man gave her a quizzical look. "But it's quite stuffy, my dear." As if to prove it, he produced a white linen handkerchief and dabbed at his brow. "Word is, this is the hottest June we've had in decades."

Mara bit her tongue. Something was seriously wrong. It was so cold, she could hardly think straight. Only an Eskimo would consider the room even halfway warm.

"Allow me to introduce myself," the man was saying, clearly oblivious to her discomfort. "Donald Dimbleby, proprietor, at your service. It is a pleasure to see a young American interested in antiques."

Mara blinked, determined to focus on him and not the room's iciness. "A lot of Americans like antiques."

Donald Dimbleby sniffed. "Ah, but are they interested in a piece's origin and history or merely wanting a quaint bit of Merry Olde to take home with them?"

"I couldn't take home this bed even if I could afford it. I'd have no place to put it," Mara said, thinking of her minuscule Philadelphia apartment.

The massive bed wouldn't fit into her living room and bedroom combined—even if she threw out everything else to make room for it. A pang of pointless regret shot through her at the thought, but she shoved it aside and smoothed her hand along the bedpost again.

To her surprise, it now felt warm beneath her touch.

Slightly heated, and somehow charged . . . as if a strong electrical current sizzled and leapt beneath the wood's smooth surface.

"You don't know the bed's history?" she asked the proprietor, her fingers tingling.

"Unfortunately, I have not been able to trace its origin. A great pity, as I am certain it has a fascinating background." He pulled a pair of glasses from his pocket and donned them before moving to the elaborately carved headboard.

"Take a look at this." He touched a finger to the graceful swirls of decorative leaves. "These are oak leaves. They represent valor. Such symbols were chosen with great care because the qualities depicted were directly related to the bearer. Therefore, we can assume the bed belonged to a baronial family or perhaps a knight."

A knight. Mara's heart jolted, the very word setting her insides aflutter. "You can tell that by the design?"

A pleased blush colored Mr. Dimbleby's face.

"Heraldry is a hobby of mine," he said and cocked a speculative eye at the headboard. "Now, the thistles might mean the bed came from—"

"Scotland?" Mara supplied, certain of it.

After all, her genealogy-obsessed father had embarrassed her often enough by filling their modest suburban home with plaid and thistles, even once bribing her with a spring break trip to Fort Lauderdale if she'd stencil thistle borders around the bathroom ceiling.

The proprietor lowered his glasses a notch and looked at her over the rims. "Quite right," he agreed. "The thistle represents Scotland. But even though I acquired the bed at an Edinburgh antique show, I tend to believe it has its origins in England."

Mara ran a finger across one of the oak leaves. "Why? Because the oak is associated with England?"

That, too, she knew. From her passion for medieval history and also from having escorted so many tours through English country manors.

But Donald Dimbleby shook his head. "Could be, but I would say because of the bed's fine craftsmanship." His voice took on a slight edge of condescension. "Nothing against our northern neighbors, but in those days, I'm afraid the English would have been far more advanced in creating such pieces. For instance, this bed can be completely dismantled and put back together with surprising ease. The Scots would not have been so skilled at that time."

"My ancestors came from Scotland," Mara said, and a blast of Arctic air hit her full in the face. "I've never been there, though."

Mr. Dimbleby gave her an indulgent smile. "With a name like McDougall and hair such a lovely shade of copper, I'd already guessed you'd have Scottish roots. I—" He broke off at the shrill of a telephone.

"If you'll excuse me," he said, already heading toward an opened door on the far side of the room, which he closed firmly behind him.

Left alone, Mara turned back to the bed.

It fascinated her. Grasping one of the posts with both hands, she rested her cheek against its solidity and closed her eyes, tried to envision the bed as it must have been centuries ago.

Blessed with a vivid imagination, she soon conjured a dashing knight in a mailed hauberk carrying a fair-haired maiden up a winding turret stair, then gently lowering her onto the sumptuously dressed bed.

Chill bumps rose on her arms again, but this time her shivers had nothing to do with the cold.

These were *delicious* shivers, accompanied by a quickening of her breath and hot little rushes of sheer delight. To a lover of old things, such as she was, almost orgasmic.

If only she had lived in the age of romance and chivalry.

Instead, she was Mara luckless-in-love McDougall, fated to run a business that, at times, stretched her nerves just so she could catch occasional whiffs and glimpses of the long-ago world that so fascinated her.

She let out a heavy sigh. Like it or not, she lived in the here and now. And if she wanted to see England again after this trip, she'd better not indulge in flights of fancy. A combination of hard work and creativity had allowed her to build Exclusive Excursions into a semithriving business.

Not mooning over what-ifs and might-have-beens.

Somehow she'd survive this last evening of playing mother hen to the proud cardholders of the Society of Intrepid Ghost Hunters. And, as always, she'd pass the months until the next tour with a flurry of industrious advertising and planning. Then, before she knew it, she'd be back on the next London-bound plane.

Little else mattered.

With a distinct twinge of regret, she pushed away from the bedpost. She had just enough time to catch the Tube to Victoria Station, dash the few blocks to her bed-and-breakfast, then ready herself for the night's festivities.

No more time to fantasize about mail-clad knights with slow, lazy smiles and heated glances.

But when she turned to leave, she slammed into a wall.

A solid, well-muscled male wall.

Quite possibly the most beautiful man she had ever seen. And without doubt the tallest. Faith, she had to tilt back her head to look at his face. Something she'd done fewer times than she cared to admit, not being exactly a petite miss.

Mara stared at him, her heart making embarrassing little flip-flops. He wore close-fitting brown hose and a long-sleeved tunic of the same shade, with a wide leather belt slung low around his hips. Fine brown boots finished his outfit, and for one startling moment Mara imagined she'd caught the flash of a long sword at his side.

But she blinked and the sword was gone, leaving only him and his masculine beauty. His intensity wrapped around her, dark and seductive, his deep-seeing gaze seeming to burn away her clothes until she felt fully exposed.

Naked.

Perhaps even a bit . . . tingly.

After all, it wasn't every day a man's mere gaze seared her into feeling devoured, and in the most rousing, delicious ways. *Titillating* things she'd best not dwell on, so she bit her lip before she could sigh and risk revealing her weakness.

How easily her long-neglected femininity could grow hot and achy if he did not soon stop looking at her in a way that made her feel as if he'd stepped right out of her most heated dreams to tempt her—and knew it!

Trying not to blush, she eyed him as well, her own measuring stare sliding over him with equal daring.

Not only much taller than any man she'd ever seen, he was simply beyond perfection. Full magnificent, he even looked like a knight with his rich chestnut brown hair skimming his broad shoulders and such an indescribable air of power thrumming through him that she could hardly breathe.

Forcing herself to do just that, she resisted the urge to reach out and twine her fingers in his hair. Just to see whether it was real. With shimmering highlights the color of sun-warmed honey and every strand gleaming with such a lustrous sheen, his hair really did give him an uncanny resemblance to a dashing hero in some fusty old museum portrait.

But more than his strapping build and handsomeness, it was the draw of his incredibly intense eyes that captivated her.

Sea green eyes a woman could drown in.

She could see forever in them.

Unfortunately, he did not appear equally enamored. Animosity poured off him, and he crossed his arms in an unfriendly posture. Worse, now that he'd practically melted her, he wasted every hunky inch of his appeal by pinning her with a frigid stare.

No more hot, body-roaming glances to beguile her and send long, liquid pulls tingling through her darkest, most secret places.

Now his burning gaze held only arrogance.

Perhaps even fury.

Annoyed, Mara drew a tight breath. His looks didn't matter at all so long as he glowered at her as if she had the pox. Her heart pounding, she swept her hair over one shoulder, her agitation growing. Maybe she could lose a few pounds, but she wasn't *that* bad.

Or perhaps he'd heard her talking and didn't like Americans?

If so, there was an easy remedy.

She'd smother him with charm.

"Hi," she said, flashing her best smile. "I'm Mara McDougall."

He remained stony faced, not even bothering to acknowledge the gesture. If anything, his frown deepened.

Mara swallowed, moistened her lips. Maybe he expected her to apologize? After all, she had plowed into him, and with considerable force.

Yes, that was surely his problem.

He wanted an apology.

"Look, I'm sorry I bumped into you," she said, happy to give him the boon. "It won't happen again."

"With surety, it shall not," he agreed, stepping closer. "The bed is mine, wench. Begone."

Mara's heart froze. There was that accent again. Warm, rich, and buttery smooth. The purest Scottish burr she'd ever heard, now recognizing the musical cadence she'd only caught a hint of before. And so annoyingly sexy, just listening to him sent another little rush of desire curling through her belly.

But *wench* and *begone*?

Not to mention *bloody MacDougall bastards.*

Bristling, she took a few steps backward. "Good looks aren't a license to be rude," she said, giving him a look she hoped would say even more.

She wouldn't have thought it possible, but his scowl darkened. Reeking hostility, he drew himself to his full height, threw back his shoulders, and glared at her.

Squaring her own shoulders, she stared back. "And the bed isn't yours. It belongs to Mr. Dimbleby and it's for sale. Maybe I'll buy it."

He narrowed his eyes. "You are a MacDougall."

"So? What's my name got to do with it?" Mara's foot began tapping. "I already know you don't like McDougalls."

"No one of that ilk will ever sleep in my bed. I forbid it."

"*Of that ilk?* And you forbid it?" Mara could feel her jaw dropping. "What is this, some kind of joke?"

He stalked to the headboard. "I jest you not," he said, his green gaze leveled on her in clear menace.

Mara shook her head. "You jest me not? What kind of English is that?"

"The king's English," he declared, his gaze burning her. "At least when he deigns to speak that foul tongue."

"The *king's* English?" Mara echoed, placing her fingertips on her temples and pressing hard. Either she was imagining this conversation or one of them was not quite right, and she hoped it wasn't her. "What happened to Queen Elizabeth?"

To her surprise, he blinked and an expression very close to perplexity crossed his face. But the slightly dazed look disappeared in a heartbeat, quickly replaced by another fierce scowl of displeasure.

A look scathing enough to send her on her way, and good riddance. She'd had her share of fruitcakes lately. She didn't need an encounter with another, especially an ill-mannered one. Whether he had an irresistible something about him that made her think naughty thoughts or not, it didn't matter. He was lucky she had enough restraint not to tell him to *bugger off.*

Determined to leave before her temper could activate the tic beneath her left eye, she whisked past him and made it halfway through Dimbleby's before she stopped in her tracks.

The black-frowning hunk had ruined the only free afternoon she'd had on this tour from hell, and she shouldn't let him get away with it.

She might have been pushed to her limits, but she *was* a McDougall.

And McDougalls weren't cowards.

So she waited just long enough to set her face in her best don't-mess-with-someone-from-Philadelphia expression, then whirled around and returned to the back room.

But hunky was gone.

Vanished as if he'd never been.

Her indignation swinging into something that felt annoyingly like disappointment, she scanned the cluttered room, even dropped to one knee to peer beneath the massive four-poster bed. But the effort only served to prove how well dust bunnies flourished in dark, protected places.

The hottie Scottie with his yummy accent and dark scowls was nowhere to be seen.

Equally strange, the room was warm and stuffy.

Not a trace remained of the bone-numbing chill of only moments before.

Common sense told her that this couldn't be happening, but a cascade of shivers spilled down her back all the same—until she spied the closed office door at the rear of the little room.

Relief washed over her, swift and sweet.

She wasn't losing her grasp on reality.

The lout had only slipped into Mr. Dimbleby's office and as far as she was concerned, he could merry well stay there.

For one tempting moment, she considered marching up to the door and yanking it open, but she dismissed the notion as quickly.

The handsome devil wasn't worth the energy.

Especially since he'd reminded her of how long it'd been since a man had made her melt and tingle, or had caressed and savored her curves before sliding deep inside her in a fine, slow electra glide.

How long it'd been since she'd yearned.

Yes, she'd simply remember him as the perfect ending to a less than stellar day and head back to her bed-and-breakfast. If she hurried, she'd have time to shower and change before she had to escort her ghost busters to Berkeley Square for their gala farewell dinner and séance.

But a short while later, her fortunes took an even wilder turn as she stood in the lounge area of the Buxton Arms and read the scrawled message the front desk clerk had handed her when she'd picked up her key.

Please call Mr. Percival Combe, Solicitor. Urgent.

Mara's brows drew together. The message gave a London listing, but who was Percival Combe? And what could a solicitor possibly want with her?

And the message couldn't have been for someone else. How many Mara McDougalls of Exclusive Excursions could be staying at the small inn?

Only one, and well she knew it.

Puzzled, she climbed the steep, carpet-covered stairs to her third-floor room. Not surprisingly, the phone rang the moment she opened the door. And as she sank onto the edge of the bed and reached for the receiver, her every instinct warned that something significant was about to happen.

"Mara McDougall," she answered, shutting her eyes.

"Ahhh, Miss McDougall," came a very distinguished reply. "Percival Combe here, with Combe and Hollingsworth. I'm so glad to have caught you."

Mara's eyes snapped back open. "There must be some mistake," she said, not at all sure she cared to be *caught*. "If this is about my current tour . . ."

She tailed off, her palms dampening. No way did she wish to discuss her England: The Uncanny and the Inexplicable tour with a London solicitor.

"This has nothing to do with your business," he was saying, sounding all business indeed. "At least not directly. And you are the young woman I've been seeking. Your father was kind enough to give me your itinerary."

Mara's stomach began to feel queasy. If a solicitor had gone to the trouble of contacting her father—in Philadelphia—then something must be seriously wrong.

"Miss McDougall, would it be convenient for you to dine with me at the Wig and Pen Club this evening? I have something quite important to discuss with you."

Mara's heart skittered with apprehension. "What sort of something?"

"I'd rather not say over the phone, but you can be assured it is nothing bad. Quite the contrary, in fact." He paused to draw a breath. "A driver can be at your hotel at half past six, and he'll also return you safely after we've had dinner and discussed the matter."

"Ah . . ." She hesitated, curiosity getting the better of her. And an evening at the exclusive dining establishment on the Strand sure beat attending a dinner séance with fifteen would-be psychics.

Besides, they'd be too busy looking for spooks to care whether she was there or not. Even so, she'd have to do some quick thinking. She couldn't just take off without ensuring that their evening ran smoothly.

She couldn't afford disgruntled clients.

Not even wacky ones.

Mr. Combe cleared his throat. "I hope you will not mind, but I've arranged for a friend of mine from the British Tourist Authority to accompany your . . . eh . . . charges to the dinner and séance in Berkeley Square this evening."

Heat shot up the back of her neck. "You seem to have thought of everything," she stammered, her pulse pounding with embarrassment.

"It is crucial that I speak with you; therefore, it was necessary to be certain you could get away." He waited a beat. "I am also aware this was to be your last evening in England."

Was to be her last evening?

Mara blinked. He'd said that as if she'd be staying on.

As if she wouldn't be flying back to Newark the next morning.

At once, a good deal of her mortification evaporated, replaced by a surge of fluttery excitement. If whatever he had to say would allow her to spend a few extra days in London, she was all for it.

"Can you be ready at half past six?" Percival Combe prompted.

Mara almost laughed out loud.

Visions of Harrods and Covent Garden and long strolls through Hyde Park danced through her head. Mercy, she'd sell her soul for a few extra *hours* in London.

"Miss McDougall?"

She tightened her fingers on the receiver, her decision made. "I'll be ready, yes."

I'll be ready with bells on.

Chapter 2

"I what?"

Mara stared at Percival Combe with disbelief. Her fork slipped from her fingers and clattered onto her plate, her clumsiness sending two spring peas sailing through the air. "A whole castle?"

She swallowed at the solicitor's nod, her face flaming as shocked silence swept the hallowed Wig and Pen Club and fellow diners swiveled their heads to stare. Not that she cared. Such news was well worth a few raised eyebrows.

If she could believe it.

With her luck, she'd probably misunderstood.

Sheesh, she hadn't even managed to find someone willing to invest in Exclusive Excursions when she'd hoped to find a partner not so long ago.

So who would leave her a castle?

Not even halfway convinced anyone would, she curled her fingers around her chair's armrests and leaned forward. "Would you repeat that, please?" she asked, hoping she didn't have suspicion written all over her.

But Percival Combe only smiled. "With pleasure," he obliged, sounding as if such astounding disclosures were the merest commonplace. "My late client has bequeathed her holding, Ravenscraig Castle, to you."

Looking at him, Mara chewed her lip. Something bothered her, and not just the improbability of becoming an overnight heiress. "This is extraordinarily hard to believe," she said, wishing her doubt weren't so palpable. "Where I come from, people just don't go around inheriting castles."

"No, I don't suppose they do," he agreed.

"That's right, and if anyone ever did, I can't imagine a more unlikely candidate." Skepticism beating all through her, she searched his face for a sign she'd fallen prey to someone's warped sense of humor.

But there was nothing.

Far from it, he appeared the epitome of sincerity. Kindly faced, graying, and with startling blue eyes, the sixty-something solicitor looked anything but the bearer of falsehoods.

Even so, she had to know. "Are you sure this isn't a joke?"

"You have my solemn word," he assured her. "Lady Warfield was most determined to see Ravenscraig go to you."

Mara's brows lifted. "Lady *Fiona* Warfield?"

He nodded.

"Oh, dear," Mara gasped, and struggled for something better to say.

She knew Lady Warfield.

The eccentric old woman owned—no, apparently *had* owned—Wychwood Hall in the Cotswolds and had graciously allowed Mara to escort tours through her home. She'd sometimes even accompanied the groups, claiming a fondness for Americans.

And she'd always been especially nice to Mara.

"I'm sorry to hear she passed away," she said, remembering the woman's sprightly walk and sparkling eyes. "I didn't know. Wychwood wasn't on my current itinerary. How—I mean . . ."

"She slipped away in her sleep a month ago yesterday," the solicitor said, understanding her unspoken question. "Quite peacefully, I was told."

Mara nodded her thanks. "She was a remarkable lady. A bit unconventional, but I liked that." She swallowed against the sudden heat in her throat. "We got on well, but I can't imagine why she'd remember me in her will."

"She had her reasons," he said and took a sip of wine. "You might be surprised to learn she believed she knew you quite well."

Mara's brows knitted. "I don't see how."

"Ah, but you said yourself that she was unconventional. Is it then so surprising to learn that she saw the same trait in you?" he asked, smiling at her.

No, that, at least, made sense.

And Mara knew exactly what he meant.

Glancing aside, she noted more than the well-laid

tables with their flickering candles and gleaming silver, the brilliance of crystal. Her inner eye caught the airs and undercurrents, the constant posturings of the hoity-toity as each one vied to outdo the others' nonchalance.

Though she'd definitely been at home in such circles, Lady Warfield would have taken wry amusement in the long-nosed looks still aimed at Mara's table.

"Is that why she did this?" Mara fixed her most direct gaze on the solicitor. "Because we shared a few worldviews?"

"Among other things." Percival Combe angled his head, his expression as serious as her own.

Enough so to give her a jolt of apprehension. "What kind of *other things*?"

"Nothing unpleasant, I assure you."

Mara lifted a brow. "Maybe I'd prefer to judge that myself," she said, shivering in reaction.

She knew what was coming.

The catch.

There had to be one. Nothing came without strings. And she smelled a stipulation as surely as she'd known her mushy vegetables would taste like boiled cardboard even before she'd tried them.

"So what do I have to do?" She sat back to wait for the blow. "What's the real reason I am a beneficiary?"

Percival Combe sighed. "Lady Warfield liked you. There was, however, more to her decision. It was your name, Miss McDougall. Quite simply your name."

"My name?"

"Were you aware Lady Warfield was a Scotswoman?" he asked, peering intently at her.

Mara's eyes widened. "I had no idea." She shook her head, genuinely bewildered. "She never once mentioned Scotland and she spoke with such an English accent."

"A cultivated accent," the solicitor said, watching her over the rim of his wineglass. "She came from Oban in the West Highlands, though not many knew. She was born a MacDou—"

"MacDougall?" Mara near choked on her astonishment.

Percival Combe set down his glass and nodded.

Mara's face grew hot. Now she knew why the name Ravenscraig had bothered her.

It was the ancestral home of her clan.

Leastways the seat of the lesser chieftain her branch of the MacDougalls hailed from.

Her father even kept a faded photo of the castle framed above his desk. A photo carefully clipped from a Scottish magazine, not one he'd snapped himself, much to Hugh McDougall's regret. No one in her family had ever been able to afford to make the trip, and in recent years her father's health had proved too poor to risk the transatlantic flight.

The closest they'd come was buying a house, albeit humble, at One Cairn Avenue. And even with such a Scottish-sounding name, the street was in a blue-collar corner of Philadelphia, not Scotland.

"Sadly," the solicitor was saying, "Lady Warfield's husband, Lord Basil, did not share her great love for her homeland. Out of devotion to him, she allowed him to anglicize her. A decision she regretted in later years."

Mara shifted uncomfortably. She didn't harbor any great affection for tartan and pipes either, preferring London with all its fascinations to peat bogs and sheep.

Her nerves began to tighten. "Surely she didn't think we were related?" she asked, her voice sounding a shade higher than usual. "My father spends all his time researching our ancestry. He would swoon over a direct blood tie to the MacDougalls of Ravenscraig, but our line goes back to John the Immigrant, an impoverished crofter who left Scotland in the mid-eighteen hundreds."

"Lady Warfield knew that," the solicitor admitted, looking slightly chagrined. "We did a background investigation on you, hoping to discover a connection, however remote. Yet when our efforts failed, she still wanted you to have Ravenscraig."

"But why?" Mara puzzled. "There had to be a deeper reason."

The solicitor let out a sigh. "If you were as familiar with Scotland as your father appears to be, you would know family is everything to a Scot," he said, his expression bitter earnest again. "The clan system is generous, accepting a wide variety of name spellings. Each clan has members scattered across the globe, yet the bond remains powerful."

"I know," Mara agreed, for a moment seeing her father bent over his papers and books, a plaid across his knees and zeal in his eye. "The Scottish Diaspora in their millions, each one proud to the bone and ever yearning for their home glen."

Percival Combe inclined his head. "Such a pull is strong, Miss McDougall. Even now, centuries after their day, the clans evoke deep emotions. To Lady Warfield, you were family. A MacDougall."

Mara touched her fingers to her temples, her mind still flailing. "But surely she knew someone more appropriate?"

"You were her choice." The solicitor leaned toward her, his blue gaze capturing her, roping her in. "She was the last surviving descendant of the clan's original chieftain, and she died childless. Under other circumstances, she would have surely selected a suitable heir from her family's clan society. But through her marriage to Lord Basil, she'd alienated herself from the lot of them."

He sat back. "And that, my dear, is where you come in."

"You mean what I must do to make this happen."

"A stipulation, yes." He cleared his throat. "You must fulfill a goal she wasn't able to accomplish."

Mara's heart plummeted.

She let out a windy sigh. Of course, it'd been too good to be true.

"Please don't tell me I have to spend the night in a haunted dungeon or try out medieval torture equipment," she said. "I've had all the spooks and weirdness I can handle lately."

The solicitor shook his head, warmth lighting his

face. "Nothing quite so adventurous. In fact, Lady Warfield was confident you were the best-suited person for the task."

Mara lifted a brow. "How so?"

"She felt your organizational talents would help you coordinate her wish to erect a MacDougall memorial on the castle grounds."

Mara sat up straighter, a surge of hope strengthening her. This wasn't as bad as she'd thought. And if the castle came along with funds, such a task didn't sound so difficult at all.

Still, there had to be more.

Certain of it, she tilted her head. "So what else must I do?"

"You must reunite the clan," he said, watching her. "That, and make certain as many MacDougalls as possible attend the memorial's unveiling ceremony."

Mara reached for her wineglass and drained it. Her benefactress had chosen unwisely. She was the last person who'd know how to bring a family together, much less mend a clan-sized rift.

An only child, she knew solely about *small* families.

Small, dysfunctional families, since her mother had run off when she was two, and with his nose always buried in genealogy records, her father hadn't exactly invited interaction with the handful of relatives they did have.

Mara sat back in her chair. "And if I fail?"

The solicitor drew a deep breath. "If, after the monument's completion and a fair attempt to establish good relations between the clan members and yourself as new chatelaine of Ravenscraig, the hard feelings toward my late client haven't been resolved, you must leave."

"I see," Mara said, surprised by the depth of her disappointment. "And what would happen to the castle then?"

"Simply put, you would retain half of the fortune Lady Warfield is leaving you and Ravenscraig would go to Scotland's National Trust, the same as Wychwood went to the British National Trust."

Mara looked aside, astonishing herself even more because her eyes were misting. She rarely got emotional, prided herself on keeping her feet firmly on the ground and making sure her only hopes and dreams were attainable ones.

But neither had she ever run from a challenge.

In fact, she thrived on them.

"Miss McDougall?" Percival Combe's voice came edged with encouragement, as if he sensed her capitulation.

And she was surrendering, her determination to succeed mounting with each indrawn breath.

"You can be assured I will help you in every way I can." He spoke again, the possibilities behind his words wooing her. "Anything you—"

"Anything?" Mara's heart gave a lurch, a wild notion beginning to spin inside her.

Percival Combe smiled. "The smallest detail."

"Well," she began, "there *is* something."

"No need to be hesitant, my dear."

"It's about a bed . . ."

* * *

Much later, in the small hours of the same night but on the other side of London, Sir Alexander Douglas suppressed a yawn with all the noble dignity he possessed. Seldom had he been so weary. Or more resentful of not being allowed to succumb to the long sleep of centuries.

Instead he'd spent his evening striding about *her* bedchamber, hoping in vain that his spurred footsteps would clank loudly enough to wake her, but the wretched inn she'd chosen for lodgings kept *tapestries* on the floor!

Flexing his fingers, Alex glared at the offensive flooring. A full-caparisoned destrier could thunder across such thickly woven cloth and make nary a stir.

Aye, he'd done his utmost and still the wench slept.

His ire rising, he stopped his pacing and, if only to fuel his gall, once again surveyed this new MacDougall's lavishly outfitted sleeping quarters.

THE BUXTON ARMS, the establishment's signpost proclaimed, the Englishness of the name darkening his mood. As did the room's trappings. And not just the arras-laid floor. That particular affront was but a small portion of the decadency. Saints, the wee chamber brimmed with more luxury than Robert Bruce's entire royal court.

A fine cushioned chair, infinitely sumptuous, earned his especial wrath. The piece stood near the foot of the bed, and, och, but it beckoned. Alex folded his arms, his resolve granite hard. He'd sooner stand naked in a patch of stinging nettles than sink into a MacDougall chair.

Aching limbs or no.

His brows snapping together with displeasure, he glanced at his reflection in the mirror, scowling not at his own formidable appearance but at the smooth perfection of the mirrored glass.

The MacDougalls' fortunes clearly hadn't lessened over the centuries if a member of their dastardly number could afford to lodge in such splendor.

"Tapestried floors, indeed!" he snorted, turning away.

Silence and shadows greeted him, the drip-drip of rain and the sighing of the night wind increasing his weariness. Not to mention the weight of his mailed shirt and other knightly accoutrements, all donned expressly to strike terror into the MacDougall lass should she waken and glimpse him looming over her, but alas . . .

He risked another glance at the chair, considered continuing his watch from its well-padded depths. After all, no one would know, and surely it wasn't beneath his dignity to allow himself a wee respite?

The MacDougall chit hadn't stirred in hours.

Besides, he was a seasoned warrior, greatly respected in his time and with no need to prove his prowess or stamina.

Neither was there any cause for caution.

Not because of *this* MacDougall.

Alex's lip curled with derision. While she had the distinct look of a bawd about her, the only sharp object she seemed in possession of was her tongue.

And such a small indulgence as whiling a few moments in comfort was the least the MacDougalls owed him.

His decision made, he lowered himself into the chair, almost letting out a sigh of pleasure. Instead, he unsheathed his sword and rested it across his knees.

For effect and good purpose.

A battle-clad knight with a gleaming brand at the ready made a more intimidating appearance than a bone-weary one sagged into a chair!

But as soon as he struck a comfortable and sufficiently daunting pose, the wench moved.

And in such a way that instantly banished his exhaustion. Indeed, his every nerve leapt to high alert as she twisted and writhed beneath the bed coverings. Practiced movements, to be sure, and calculated to make a man admire her wantonness, even harden with the urge to possess her.

To sink himself deep inside her until her writhings and moans were caused by his rhythmic in-and-out glides and not the simple vagaries of sleep.

Banishing the fool notion at once, Alex glared at her, determined not to harden no matter how provocatively she tossed and stretched beneath the coverlet. Indeed, as if she sensed his ill ease, she stilled suddenly, appearing to have turned onto her side, but he couldn't tell her exact position for certain because she'd pulled the coverlet to her chin.

Only her hair identified her as the MacDougall spawn determined to claim his bed. And what hair it was, too. *Temptress* hair, all flame-bright curls and tousled waves. The kind of hair that made a man ache to bury his face in its richness and just inhale until he drowned in its swirling, silken strands.

The dark, sensuous scent of her.

A fearsome scowl threatening at the thought, he tried to look away and found that he couldn't.

MacDougall or no, she *did* have glorious hair.

Great, glossy skeins of red-gold streamed across her pillow in a blaze of color sure to bewitch the susceptible. And for one crazy-mad moment, even he wondered whether such bounty would feel as silky as it looked. Especially how such lusciousness might feel sliding across the bared flesh of his chest or certain other sensitive places.

Not that suchlike interested him!

The passing of so many centuries must've pickled his brain for such foolishness to even cross his mind. But then she moved again, the slight shifting only emphasizing the ripe fullness of her body, and even worse thoughts assailed him.

Not that he could help it, for she'd rolled onto her back and stretched her arms above her head in a lascivious pose surely designed to take unfair advantage of centuries of agonizing abstemiousness.

Feeling bedeviled indeed, Alex squirmed, his annoyance mounting when the coverings slipped to reveal twin mounds of the creamiest, most perfect breasts he'd ever seen. Full and luscious they were, and topped with deep rose-colored nipples that puckered under his stare.

And the wench still wasn't through with her trickery!

As if she knew she had a captive audience, she began inching her right foot up the calf of her left leg, her raised knee lifting the bedding just enough to reveal a part of her that no red-blooded man could resist gazing upon.

And perturbed or no, Alex leaned forward, as close as he dared.

Near enough to see quite plainly that not the barest slip of modesty shielded her secrets from view. Clamping his jaw lest he disgrace himself by groaning, he stared at the triangular thatch of red-gold curls.

Stared, and used every shred of his willpower to remain . . . *unaffected.*

Or at least not rage so hard he forgot his purpose.

Blessedly, she soon lowered her knee again, and with it, the covers. So he returned his attention to her breasts, not surprised to discover them still fully bared, their peaks still puckered and thrusting.

Heat flashing all through him, he tried to ignore the tautness in his vitals and concentrated on stifling all thought of what it might be like to graze those hardened peaks with his teeth. Suckle them until she arched her back and cried out her need for deeper, more intimate ministrations.

Throbbing pleasures he had no business thinking about.

And certainly not involving a MacDougall!

His frown growing blacker by the moment, he swiped the back of his hand across his forehead. If the wench meant to tempt or shock him with her wanton display, it would not do to have her catch him with beads of perspiration misting his brow.

" 'Tis not sitting and scowling I'd be doing in the face of such temptation," came a deep voice from the shadows.

"And just what *are* you doing here?" Alex whirled around, the shock of his friend's untimely arrival making his heart plunge. "Have you naught better to do than spy on me, you black-hearted varlet?"

"Something better to do?" Hardwin de Studley of Seagrave lounged against the doorjamb, a look of high amusement on his aristocratic face. "Nay, my friend, I cannot say that I do."

"So I see," Alex shot back, anything but pleased.

He should have known the womanizing scoundrel would make an appearance.

Warring companions and friends in life, they were now assured a continuing relationship through an odd twist of fate. Like Alex, Hardwick, as the dark-visaged knight was commonly known, had also fallen victim of an enchantment.

Or a curse, depending on how one looked at it.

A notorious wencher, Hardwick was bound by a traveling minstrel's spell to spend eternity pleasing women yet nevermore to attain his own release. For the minor slight of refusing a night's lodging to the wandering bard, the *sennachie* reversed their roles, binding Alex's friend to roam the earth, doomed to satisfy a different woman every night for all eternity.

Alex's lips twitched and his vexation began to ebb. At least he need only guard his bed, keeping it free of MacDougalls. Even MacDougalls who roused unwanted urgings in him and stirred his deepest senses. An existence such as his friend must endure did not bear contemplation.

"Be that the latest MacDougall?" Hardwick changed the subject, his glance on the bed.

"So it would seem," Alex confirmed, careful not to let his gaze dip to the thrusting evidence of Hardwick's affliction. "And a pricklier female ne'er walked the earth."

"Indeed?" Hardwick's eyes glinted with interest. "Shall I soften her *disposition* for you? The task would be a pleasure."

"No doubt." Alex frowned, his expression darkening even more upon following the other's gaze.

Saints, he'd forgotten the wench's exposed bosom!

A lush feast for manly eyes, her breasts rose and fell with the rhythm of her sleep, their rounded swells beckoning.

"Leave her be, Seagrave. She deserves no such attention."

Hardwick took a step toward the bed. "Ah, but her loveliness begs to be—"

"Ignored!" Alex shot to his feet and used the tip of his sword to flick the coverlet into place.

But not before Hardwick burst out in broad, raucous laughter.

"So that is the way of it," he hooted, scarce containing himself.

Refusing to be baited, Alex returned to the chair. "Nay, that is not the way of it," he denied, slapping his blade back across his knees. "Beshrew me for caring, but I only meant to shield you. I strongly suspect—"

"Shield me?" Hardwick's jaw dropped. "And from such a sweetmeat?"

"I strongly suspect she is of the fey," Alex finished with a glare.

Truth be told, he was certain of it.

But his friend only grinned and folded his arms. "Your sour countenance doesn't fool me."

"Be that as it may," Alex said, returning his stare to the slumbering wench, "you would be wise to think for once with your head rather than your—"

"My tarse?" Hardwick laughed. "If my poor, accursed *condition* makes you uncomfortable, then I shall leave you to seek my pleasure elsewhere. But one question before I go: Why did you cover the maid's breasts?"

Alex flashed a hot glance at him, but the other knight was already gone. Melted into the air before Alex's irritation could scorch him. Only his laughter remained, echoing in the darkness until the last of Hardwick's chuckles faded to silence and Alex was alone once more.

Alone with the MacDougall witch-woman.

A spell-casting enchantress whose dark tricks sent shivers clear through his marrow.

So why *had* he covered her breasts?

And why did he sit here still, watching her sleep, rather than return to the relative peace of Dimbleby's back room and his own empty bed?

The answer came in one last disembodied chuckle, floating to him from the shadows near the door.

An answer so unappealing, he would almost rather change curses with his mirth-filled friend.

Almost.

He'd simply have to do everything in his power to ensure that he never had to make such a choice.

Chapter 3

Oban.

The long train journey from London behind her, Mara stood in the middle of the waterfront promenade of the West Highland capital and took a deep breath of Scotland, and then another and another. Clean, cold air, rain fresh and brisk, smelling slightly of the sea and proving everything her father had ever said about even the air of Scotland being different.

Special.

He'd sworn it would be so, and now that she was here, a scant month after her fateful dinner with Percival Combe at London's posh Wig and Pen Club, she surprised herself by having to admit that there really was something almost intoxicating about inhaling so much good, clean air.

Good, clean Highland air, the increased thumping of her heart reminded her. And with enough of a jolt to make her straighten her back and square her shoulders against the unexpected swell of emotion Hugh McDougall would insist came from setting foot on Scottish soil.

The earth of home.

And Mara supposed it was—for her long-dead ancestor John the Immigrant. Him, and the countless Scotophiles like her father whose throats thicken at the first skirl of pipes and flash of kilted plaid.

She had a cooler head on her shoulders, recognized the tightness in her chest for exactly what it was: simple regret that her father's health had kept him from sharing this moment with her.

"But you're here, aren't you, Ben?" She reached down to stroke the aged border collie's head, found comfort in his dark, heart-melting gaze.

An accepting gaze, laced perhaps with a touch of gratitude, for Ben was Lady Warfield's living legacy, and the gentle old dog seemed to know that his new mistress's great affection for canines had spared him spending his twilight years in some loveless London dogs' home.

Eager to see her new home, Mara scanned the crescent-shaped promenade, searched the bustling throng for Malcolm, the driver Percival Combe had assured would meet her. A young man she'd supposedly recognize not only for his great height and fiery red hair, but also for his engaging smile.

A meaner feat than she would have believed, for Oban seemed filled with tall, reddish-haired men. And each one her gaze happened to fall upon grinned back at her! There were the two standing outside a fish-and-chip shop, happily munching their lunch, and the really cute one who'd winked at her before disappearing into a butcher's shop.

Even Oban Bay, with its stunning views of the Inner Hebridean skyline, teemed with them, for she spied a red-haired fisherman industriously working on his boat, and others stood at the rail of the large Caledonian MacBrayne ferry just maneuvering into place at the pier.

Her heart beginning to flutter with nerves and a mounting sense of hilarity, Mara blew her own coppery red bangs off her brow. How, in a maze of smiling, redheaded men, was she supposed to find just one?

Half afraid they might all be Malcolms as well, she tightened her grip on Ben's leash and started down the pavement. But before she could decide where to search for her Malcolm, someone plucked her carry-on bag off her shoulder.

"Hey!" She swung around, ready to give chase, but stopped short when she saw the culprit.

He stood not a pace away, six foot four inches of beaming exuberance, not a day past twenty, and with a shock of the brightest red hair she'd ever seen.

Her Malcolm.

Mara smiled, extended her hand. "You must be—"

"Malcolm." His smile deepened to reveal a dimple in his left cheek. "That's myself, true as I'm here."

He reached to take her hand, but before he could, Ben shuffled forward and thrust his head between them to nose the young man's pockets.

"Ben! Sto—"

"Ach, never you mind, Mara McDougall." Malcolm laughed and reached down to scratch behind the collie's ears. "He'll only be a-smelling the mackerel I had in the car boot," he explained in a butter-smooth burr. "Had 'em in just this morning and brought 'em along for selling at one or two of the hotels."

"Mackerel?" Mara blinked, not sure she'd heard him correctly.

But apparently she had, for his dimpled smile spread into a full-fledged grin. "Fetched a fine price, they did," he told her, glowing with satisfaction. "My mum's fresh-made butter, too."

Mara looked at him in amazement, his soft, musical voice reminding her of *another* deep Scottish accent she'd heard not so long ago. One that, unlike this young man's, had not flowed with friendly Highland sibilancy but thrummed with barely restrained animosity.

But mackerel and fresh-made butter?

Mara glanced aside, at the busy little bay with its sun shadows and silver-flecked water, the young man's words and his gently lilting voice painting funny images in her head and, oddly enough, making her heart do silly little flip-flops.

For one crazy moment she imagined a small white croft house, low and thatched, with a plume of peat smoke rising from its single squat chimney. A rosy-cheeked woman sitting beside the hearth, a butter churn gripped between her knees as she furiously worked the plunger up and down.

Scenes from another world, her father would have enthused with a dreamy smile. A forgotten simplicity sadly set aside in favor of today's hectic lifestyle.

Celtic whimsy, she called it, catching herself before she, too, succumbed to Brigadoon fever.

"How did you know who I am?" She sought neutral ground, a safe place far from such foolish notions and how they could set a vulnerable heart to thinking.

Dreaming.

"I could have been anyone," she persisted, nodding at a young woman leaning against the harbor rail not far from where they stood, an overstuffed rucksack at her feet. "Her, for instance."

Malcolm's eyes lit with merriment. "Not a chance, Mara McDougall." He dismissed the possibility with a toss of his bright head. "That one doesn't have the look, see you?"

"The look?" Mara swallowed. "I don't think I know what you mean."

"Och, nay?" Malcolm peered at her, his expression saying so much more than the two oh-so-Scottish-sounding words. "I mean the look I saw on you when you gazed out over the pier, out toward the isles."

Mara's face heated. "So?"

"So?" Malcolm the Red lifted a brow. "You belong here, Mara McDougall," he said simply, his wonderful burr daring her to claim otherwise.

And, heaven help her, but her mouth suddenly felt way too dry, her tongue too clumsy, for her to form even the weakest denial.

Not as foolish as she felt standing on the pavement looking at him with a dumbstruck stare.

Ben suffered no such inhibitions. Still snuffling around the Highlander's legs, the dog used a tongue-lolling grin and a few energetic tail swipes to convey his enthusiasm.

Malcolm smiled, too, and produced something edible from a pocket, much to Ben's tail-thumping delight.

"Aye, it's *the pull* that came o'er you when you looked at the Hebrides just now," he told her, something in his eyes as he said the words making her almost believe it. "No true Scot, no matter where he was born, can come here and not feel it."

And she did feel it.

Or felt *something.*

Something indefinable and just a tiny bit . . . daunting.

An uncomfortable awareness that things she'd cringed at in her father's plaid-hung, thistle-bordered house, like the doorbell playing "Scotland the Brave," didn't seem so outlandish here in this little Highland town with its scores of soft-voiced, red-haired men and the surrounding hills rising so clear against a blue summer sky.

The young Highlander was watching her again, and closely, but before she could open her mouth to speak, he flashed another of his full-of-charm smiles and picked up her suitcase, hefting it easily under his arm.

"Come, I'm after getting you out to Ravenscraig. They'll have a nice fire waiting on you, and tea," he promised, already heading for a small car parked a distance down the curb.

"There's something you should know," he announced a short while later as they turned north onto the coastal road. "The good folk at Ravenscraig might seem a bit—"

"A bit what?" Mara snapped to attention, shot him a quick, wary glance.

She'd been staring out the window at the ghostly wisps of mist drifting down the sides of the hills and thinking about sitting in a comfortable wingback chair before a crackling fire in the hall, sipping a good lager or stout, Ben curled on a rug at her feet.

Maybe even a tartan rug.

But the thought failed to bring the chuckle it would have any other time, for something about the young Highlander's tone gave her the distinct impression that he'd been about to say the people at Ravenscraig were . . . *odd*.

Suppressing a shiver, she gave him her most encouraging smile, but the moment had passed and he didn't seem willing to divulge more, his concentration now focused on the winding thread of road and the numerous lambs and their mothers who seemed determined to stray onto the asphalt.

Mara resisted the urge to question him, choosing instead to smooth the wrinkles in her skirt. Feeling better already, she pushed her hair back over her shoulder and returned her attention to the mist-hung hills.

As anyone from Philadelphia would know, there was much to be said for curbing one's curiosity.

Suicidal sheep and a castle staff that were a bit *something,* indeed.

Besides, whatever oddities might await her at Ravenscraig, she had the feeling she'd soon discover them.

Whether she wanted to or not.

Ravenscraig Castle.

Alex ground his teeth on the name, half surprised his glowers didn't singe the bloody walls. Truth be told, he found himself with a fearsome urge to do more than scorch the wretched castle's stonework. Much more, as his rising gorge and the tightened muscles in his jaw indicated.

He began pacing, his hands curled into hard fists. That his bed should find its way to the very lair of his enemies was more than even his benighted soul should have to bear.

His bed landing in a chamber assigned to *her,* a fouler fate than he deserved.

Dangerous, too, because just the thought of her, of how his gaze had traveled over her sleeping nakedness, delving her every fragrant secret and, saints preserve him, finding himself *bestirred* by her, was enough to curdle his wits.

Besides, he'd suffered trials enough when the bed had rested, dismantled and forgotten, in a dank room in one of Edinburgh's stinking tenements. Saints, he'd lost count of the centuries he'd spent in that hellhole.

Just remembering sent a shiver through him.

And what blessed relief it'd been to awaken and find himself in airier surrounds not too long ago.

Even if Dimbleby's had been on English soil.

At least the occasional shaft of sunlight had seeped in through the grimed windows. And the visitors who'd sometimes ooh and aah over his bed had proved far more agreeable time passers than the gutter rats and damp he'd shared his days with in Edinburgh.

But *this*—he seized a fistful of one of the silk wall tapestries and shook it—landing here, was insult enough to vex a saint.

A vile deed calling for immediate retaliation, and he knew exactly who would be the recipient of his wrath. He clutched the tapestry, the urge to wield the cutting edge of his blade on its exquisite threads nigh overwhelming him.

Indeed, he was so sorely tempted, his fingers itched!

He'd known the witch-woman lusted after his bed, but he hadn't expected her to taunt him by having it returned to the scene of his betrayal.

But she had, and just thinking about her perfidy made his ears burn and his hand reach for his dirk.

He harrumphed just as quickly, though, and thrust the jeweled blade back under his belt. Keeping his wits had seen him through many troublous times, and any knight worth his spurs knew hotheadedness was naught but a quick path to misery. So he quashed his vexation and resumed his pacing, a slow smile curving his lips.

A wicked smile, tempered with a small measure of satisfaction.

After all, the long wait for her arrival had afforded him ample time to devise numerous and delightful ways to spoil her pleasure in his bed.

Soon she would be there.

He could smell her.

She had the scent of infidel whores about her. A dark and heady musk designed to make a man believe he could feel the heat of her body even from across a room.

Not that it mattered. She could bathe in the bewitching scent for all he cared—its seductive powers would prove useless on him.

He would remain unaffected, stronger than he'd been in London. No thoughts about lush, warm curves or soft, hot breath whispering across naked skin would cross his mind.

Raising his arms above his head, Alex set his jaw and cracked his knuckles, readying himself.

Aye, her arrival was imminent.

And the moment night fell and she sought the comforts of his bed, he would treat her to an appropriate welcome.

One she'd not forget for the rest of her days.

CEUD MILE FAILTE!

"A Hundred Thousand Welcomes!" proclaimed a large banner stretched across the entrance to Ravenscraig's gatehouse. A warm-hearted Gaelic hello, fastened with a flourish to the raised portcullis, its unexpected appearance making Mara's breath catch and her heart thunder.

She stared at the sign, surprise and delight whirling inside her. A giddy blend of emotions promptly followed by a hot rush of self-consciousness when Malcolm gave her a quick, audacious wink and slowed the car to a snail's pace.

Not that she would have missed the flapping streamer.

Indeed, with its bright blue lettering, each word at least a foot tall, the thing quite caught her eye. And the closer they came to it, the huge block letters staring right at her, the more difficult she found it to breathe.

Speaking was out of the question.

"They've been in fine fettle about your arrival for days," Malcolm declared, saving her the trouble as they passed beneath the banner and through the tunnel-like interior of the gatehouse. "True as I breathe, they'll be gathered in front of the castle, waiting."

Mara swallowed, the image only increasing the fluttering in her stomach. "But how—"

"How will they ken we're almost there? Ah, well, I could say they've been waiting since daylight, but, truth is, every croft we've passed will have rung up to report our progress." He slid a glance at her. "Did you know this is the first time the lady of the castle has been at Ravenscraig in over twenty years?"

Mara's jaw slipped. "Lady Warfield didn't visit?"

Malcolm shook his head. "Never came back save once or twice after she married. Lord Warfield didn't much care for Scotland. Folk say he fussed he could ne'er get warm, and that he despised the mist."

But Mara scarce heard him, for they'd left the deepest part of the wood, and Ravenscraig Castle was coming into view through the trees.

Tall, parapeted, and more impressive than any likeness she'd ever seen, her ancestral home stood on the far side of a wide, emerald green lawn, and its appearance presupposed everything she'd ever heard about the romance of medieval Scotland.

More startling still, the castle seemed perched on the edge of the world, the lawn ending abruptly behind, with nothing beyond but a huge swath of endless blue sky.

"Oh-my-gosh," Mara gasped, staring.

Malcolm chuckled. "A bonnie sight, no?"

She glanced at him, a ridiculous sense of unreality snaking round her ribs and squeezing so tight, she wondered her heart still had room to beat. She certainly couldn't find words.

A nod was the best she could do.

Her father would have been much more eloquent, his eyes growing as round as saucers, and just imagining his eye-popping delight sent a flood of bittersweet warmth to join the constriction in her chest.

Nothing in her wildest dreams had prepared her.

She doubted anything could have.

And although her nerves were a bit frazzled, the dryness of her mouth and her skittering pulse assured her she wasn't spinning fantasies.

Ravenscraig loomed as solid as day before her, complete with two rounded towers flanking a massive iron-studded door, above which she could just make out the MacDougall coat of arms carved in stone.

Not a dark, scowling pile, forbidding and mysterious, but a turreted wonder of pink sandstone, where, true to Malcolm's prediction, a knot of people stood waiting.

One of them, a bandy-legged old man in a kilt, came strutting forward the moment she stepped from the car. He made a grizzled appearance with his lined face and faded blue eyes, but his gaze was alert and his expression friendly.

"Hah! The lady herself—at long last," he greeted her, his voice ringing, but softened by the same musical lilt as Malcolm's. "Welcome to Ravenscraig. I am Murdoch MacEwen, house steward."

Mara blinked, tried hard not to stare. But everything about him from his jaunty sporran to his gray-tufted brows made him look as if he'd just stepped away from a Victorian house party.

Or meant to escort her into one!

Incredulity tingling up and down her spine, she opened her mouth and closed it again before she could find her voice. "Thank you, Mr. MacEwen," she managed, holding out her hand. "I'm so pleased—"

"Och, well, Murdoch will do fine." He clasped her hand briefly before snatching up her bags. "I'll just be taking these up to your room—you can meet the others meantime," he added, his shoulders bowed by the weight of her luggage.

Her own shoulders aching from just looking at

him, she reached to take back her suitcase, but he was already striding away, his crooked legs carrying him up the castle's broad stone steps with surprising agility.

Indeed, he disappeared into the darkness of the entry hall before she could even splutter a protest, and as soon as he did, the others came forward. A genial lot, croft bred from the looks of them, their faces lit with warmth and goodness. And, true to Malcolm's insinuation, they did seem a bit . . . different.

But not in the way she'd feared.

She smiled her relief, her heart lightened as they gathered round. The first to reach her, Gordie, the one-armed gardener, beamed with goodwill but appeared too tongue-tied and abashed to say a word, while twin girls, housemaids by their pert white-aproned uniforms, bobbed their heads in welcoming unison.

"Good day to you, Miss McDougall," the first twin said, and blushed to the roots of her carrot-red hair. "I'm Agnes, and she's Ailsa," she added, nodding at her sister, who, like the one-armed gardener, seemed to have lost her tongue.

"And this is Innes." Agnes turned to a tiny, white-haired woman hovering on the edge of the group. "Innes makes beeswax candles and herbal soaps for the tourist shops in Oban. We use them here, too, don't we, Innes?"

But Innes ignored the girl and focused on Mara. "Mercy me, is it yourself?" She peered hard at Mara. "Are you for coming back to us, then, *mo ghaoil*?

And without Lord Warfield?" she asked, the faraway sweetness of her smile explanation enough for the strange questions.

"It's the Gaelic for *my dear,*" Agnes solved the other riddle, her voice dropping to a diplomatic whisper. "Innes lives in the past and forgets the present. She thinks you are—"

"Lady Warfield," Mara finished for her, the awkward moment saved by the barking arrival of two Jack Russell terriers, their excited circling and snuffling of Ben drawing all eyes.

"Dottie and Scottie," Malcolm supplied the little dogs' names, his face brightening when Ben thumped his tail and seemed to smile at the young terriers' yappy attentions.

Mara smiled, too, her earlier jitters fading like mist beneath the morning sun. Ravenscraig's staff *were* eccentric, some of them clearly peculiar, but so long as no one mentioned ghosts, everything would be fine.

Or so she thought until a look almost verging on alarm suddenly crossed Malcolm's face. "Where's Prudentia?" he wanted to know, his gaze flitting over the little group.

At the mention of the name, Dottie and Scottie stopped racing around Ben, their perked ears and eager expressions indicating they knew Prudentia well, and liked her.

But of their two-legged companions, only Innes reacted.

She teetered.

And in a way that made Mara's nape prickle.

"Who is Prudentia?" she asked, certain she didn't want to know.

"Prudentia MacIntyre, the cook." Ailsa finally spoke, her voice edged with embarrassment. "She's inside somewhere, *feeling* the atmosphere. She thinks Ravenscraig is full of ghosts and insists a new one arrived just the other day. She's been nosing about ever since, trying to make contact with the poor soul."

"Ghosts?" Mara's stomach plummeted. "What kind—"

"No kind at all—save maybe rats, draughts, and hot-water pipes," Murdoch boomed, rejoining the group. "Dinna you worry, lassie. I've ne'er seen a bogle hereabouts, and I've been at Ravenscraig since I was a wee lad."

With a sharp look at the others, he placed a hand on Mara's elbow and propelled her up the castle steps. "Come away in now, and dinna let these blethering fools bend your ears," he said, leading her into the entrance hall.

A fine, dark-paneled passage, filled with old family portraits and tapestry hangings, and smelling faintly of wax furniture polish, chilled stone, and age.

"Prudentia fixed a fine tattie soup for you," the steward was saying as he escorted her through the dimness. "That's *potato* soup if you didn't know. After you've eaten, I'll take you to your room. Your fine bed arrived a few days ago and has been made up nice and fresh."

"Thank you, that sounds heavenly," Mara agreed,

her stomach growling in anticipation. She hadn't realized how hungry she was.

And she was tired, too.

Far too weary to ponder the cook's preoccupation with the supernatural, or her own unsettling notion of how easy an impressionable mind could imagine one of her tartan-wrapped, fierce-staring ancestors stepping down out of his portrait frame at the stroke of the midnight bell.

No, she wouldn't think of such absurdness.

Besides, too much else claimed her interest.

Glancing round, she drew a quick breath, that strange tightness filling her chest again. No matter where she looked, Ravenscraig's vastness swallowed her whole, its treasures seeming to wink at her as if they'd been waiting for this moment just to enchant and dazzle her.

Impressed indeed, she admired the standing suits of armor placed at intervals along the walls and gazed with awe at a collection of medieval swords and targes, promising herself she'd examine both the swords and shields more carefully later.

A spacious open staircase swept up into shadow at the rear of the passage, but rather than mount its age-smoothed steps, the steward turned left, leading her into what could only be the great hall.

But Mara froze on the threshold and . . . gasped.

Not at the sweeping sea vista visible beyond a wall of tall, arched windows, nor at the beautiful painted beamed ceiling.

No, it was the strange-looking woman in the middle of the room who stole Mara's breath.

Plump, frizzy haired, and middle-aged, the woman looked more like she should be stirring the kettle in a gypsy camp than standing beside a dining table set for one in Ravenscraig's quiet great hall.

Bohemian looking indeed, her eyes were tightly closed and she held her arms out to the sides, her fingers wiggling as she rocked from side to side.

"I feeeel your presence," she called in a low, keening voice. "I know you're here."

"Mrs. Mac-Intyre!" Murdoch's face turned beet red. "Do you want our new lady to think you're daft?" he scolded, falling into a rich burr. "Get ahold o' yourself and say good day to Miss McDougall."

Prudentia MacIntyre snapped out of her trancelike state immediately. "Communing with the spirits is important, as you'd be wise to appreciate," she charged, her dark eyes flashing annoyance. "Lost souls need compassion."

The old man drew back his shoulders. " 'Tis you who'll be the lost soul if you dinna stop such nonsense."

Ignoring him, the cook turned to Mara. "There's a new presence here," she announced. "A man. He is very angry, and I think it has something to do with you."

"Hell's bells and damnation!" Murdoch shook a fist at her. "Out with you now, and dinna show your face again until you've come to your senses!"

"I only wanted to warn the miss." Prudentia scalded him with an indignant look before she sailed from the hall, her apron straps flapping behind her.

"*She* is Ravenscraig's incubus, that one," Murdoch

muttered as he pulled out Mara's chair. "She's for hearing a ghost's wail in every curlew's cry. Pay her no mind."

And Mara didn't. Especially not when, a short while later, Murdoch returned to escort her to her room. Pleasantly full after her dinner of soup and oatcakes, she pushed to her feet, the cook and her rantings forgotten.

She was already drowsy from the long journey, and the hearty soup had soothed her nerves. The two drams of fine Talisker whisky she hadn't been able to resist had her yearning for bed.

Her bed.

The wonderfully romantic medieval four-poster she'd fallen in love with in London. She smiled as the steward led her up a winding turnpike stair and then through a maze of dim, musty corridors.

On and on they went until, at last, he stopped before a gleaming oak door. "Nights can be cold here," he said as he opened it. "One of the maids will have put a goonie and a hot-water bottle on the bed for you."

Mara started, hearing only one word. "A *goonie*?"

"A long flannel nightgown," Murdoch translated.

"Oh." Feeling a bit foolish and more relieved than she cared to admit, Mara stepped into the room.

A surprisingly icy room.

Not that its cold mattered, with her new bed standing against the far wall, beautifully dressed and turned down in welcome. She could see the promised hot-water bottle making a lump beneath the covers and a carefully folded white gown waited for her on top of the bed's richly embroidered covers.

Murdoch came in behind her. "We call this the Thistle Room because of the thistles decorating the ceiling."

Mara nearly choked, her glance shooting upward. Sure enough, thistles were everywhere. But the intricate plasterwork looking down at her had nothing in common with her carefully stenciled thistles back home at One Cairn Avenue in Philadelphia.

"You'll have the best view of the sea from here." Murdoch indicated a row of tall windows to the left of her bed. "And you'll have a fire every night," he added, glancing toward a fireplace across the room. "We use wood fires in most of the castle, but, as an American, we thought you'd enjoy the smell o' peat?"

Too cold to think straight, Mara just nodded. "It does smell nice—dark and sweet, exactly as I imagined."

The peats glowed a fine, cheery red, too. But to her shivering regret, the fire's warmth seemed too feeble to dispel the room's cold.

Already chill bumps were rising on her arms.

"I can douse the fire if you prefer?" Murdoch cocked a brow. "It does make the room a bit overwarm."

"No-o-o, I'm comfortable," Mara lied, declining his offer.

What she needed was about a wheelbarrow more peat tossed onto the hearthstone.

Trying not to let her teeth clatter, she rubbed her arms. If the steward didn't soon leave to let her crawl into her bed, she'd grow icicles.

Silently willing him to go, she glanced at the four-poster, pleased to see that the night table held an electric tea maker and a plate of shortbread. She smiled. A steaming cup of tea would be just the thing to warm her.

"If there's nothing else you'll be needing, I'll be leaving you," Murdoch said, moving at last toward the door. "Sleep well."

"I'm sure I will," Mara told him, hoping her relief didn't show.

Or her great weariness.

Half afraid she wouldn't even make it to her bed before sleep overcame her, she closed the door behind him and turned around.

Then she screamed.

The hottie Scottie from Dimbleby's lounged upon the bed!

Some ancient-looking plaid slung over his shoulder, he lay back against the pillows, his long, muscular legs crossed at the ankles.

And, if it were possible, he regarded her with an even more insolent smirk than he'd worn in London.

The smirk made her mad. Angry enough to overlook his incredible masculine beauty, the way her knees turned to water despite her shock and annoyance.

She glared at him. "What are *you* doing here?"

"Guarding my bed—as I told you I do."

"The bed is mine," she objected, disbelief coursing through her. "I bought it and you can get yourself out of it. Now!"

But he only folded his arms behind his neck and stared back at her. "I think not, wench."

"*Wench?*" Mara's face grew hot. "I am not any such thing, and you are mad. Stark raving mad!"

A muscle jerked in his jaw and his expression darkened, but he did not seem inclined to let her rile him.

Nor did he budge.

Quite the contrary, he appeared annoyingly comfortable.

"We'll see about this, you . . . you! O-o-oh, there aren't words!" Spinning around, Mara yanked open the door. "Murdoch!" she cried, her heart hammering. "Please—come back here!"

But the old steward had already disappeared.

The corridor stretched dark and deserted. She'd have to deal with the dolt herself. More angry than afraid, she whirled to confront him, only to find him gone.

The room was empty.

Except for a jeweled dagger pinning the white flannel nightgown to the bed.

Shaking, Mara crossed the room and stared down at the medieval-looking weapon. She needed all her strength to pull its blade from the mattress. When she did, she tossed the thing as far away from her as she could and sank onto the bed, the ruined goonie clutched to her breast.

Laughter, rich and masculine, filled the chamber then, the bone-chilling sound sending her diving beneath the covers.

Next time, wench, the deep Scottish voice whispered near her ear, *it will be my sword and you will be wearing the gown.*

Chapter 4

Mara awoke to the skirl of bagpipes. "Highland Laddie," she recognized, blinking the sleep from her eyes. No tap-tapping drums accompanied the lively tune, but the stirring tones sounded so Scottish, so right, she couldn't help but smile. Nor suppress a little thrill of excitement. Her heart began to beat faster and she tilted her head, listening.

The pipes sounded so real.

No, they were real, she amended, her pulse quickening.

And nothing at all like the cheap CDs her father played in his tartan-hung house at One Cairn Avenue. Bought secondhand at Highland Games, the drone and wails of Hugh McDougall's beloved pipe music blared daily in the narrow Philadelphia brownstone, each ear-splitting note shaking walls and offending ears, terrorizing the neighbors.

These pipes warmed and welcomed.

Especially with such clean, exhilarating air pouring in through the tall, opened windows. Scottish air, pure and sweet. And invigorating enough for her to slide a glance across the room, something deep inside her softening and warming as she caught a glimpse of sparkling blue water, a swath of cloudless summer sky. The morning smelled of pine, new beginnings, and the sea, and she didn't want to miss a moment of it.

Feeling content, she puffed a strand of hair out of her face and stretched beneath the covers, eager to enjoy her first morning as "lady of the house." Chatelaine of her own Highland castle. A notion that still boggled her mind, but a status she suspected she'd like very much.

Until she remembered last night.

The shock of finding *him* in her bed.

At once, any remaining traces of sleep vanished. The sexy Highlander's image filled her mind, his stunning good looks making her heart pound, his rudeness and daring sending hot jolts of indignation streaking all through her. She sat up, clutching a pillow to her breast as she scanned the room. The innocent-looking windows staring back at her from three sides and the nearest wall with its heavy oak dressing table and wardrobe, a huge gilt-framed mirror.

Not wanting to peer too deeply into the mirror's polished depths, she let her gaze flick past an antique writing desk, graced now by an age-worn china bowl and matching jug. As swiftly, her attention moved to the splendid hearth. The faint scent of peat still rose from the long-cold embers, and its white marble mantelpiece gleamed in the morning sun.

She released a pent-up sigh.

Everything looked harmless.

But then she peered into the corner where she'd flung the medieval-looking dagger. And just as she'd suspected, it wasn't there. Nor anywhere else she could see.

She blinked, the back of her neck prickling.

That part of her tingled, throbbed with delicious molten heat. Despite her aggravation. The dark-frowning scoundrel was simply that gorgeous, his deep Scottish burr that potently seductive.

Mara frowned, bit down hard on her lower lip.

Could she have imagined the whole thing?

The sinfully handsome Highlander she'd caught lounging in her bed? His bold and *sexual* stare?

The way his heavy-lidded gaze had slid over her body? Arrogant and knowing, each assessing, intimate sweep across her breasts or down her legs outraging her and making her feel . . . naked.

Undressed and exposed.

As if he knew how long it'd been since she'd enjoyed an orgasm. Maybe even that she'd never even had a real one. The world-stopping, heart-pounding, and rollicking release she suspected he gave every female he treated to the erotic thrills of his hard, beautiful body.

Yes, that was it.

The true reason for his searing, soul-piercing stare.

He'd not only wished to lay claim to her bed; his indecently brazen perusal declared he could have her as well.

In his bed, and beneath him.

Any way he wanted her.

Mara shuddered and touched cold fingers to her brow, pressed hard against her temples. No, he couldn't have been real. Hadn't been there one moment only to vanish the next. Truth was, she'd been through a lot lately. After all, it wasn't every day that a girl from Philadelphia inherited a castle.

Especially a girl from the *wrong* side of Philadelphia.

Frowning, she plucked at a loose thread in the bed coverings. Then, ready to blame the disturbing episode on exhaustion or an overactive imagination, she blew out an irritated breath and leaned back against the pillows.

Unfortunately, her gaze fell upon the nightgown.

The goonie.

A trickle of apprehension slid down her spine. If she'd imagined the incident, there wouldn't be a rip in the nightgown. A careful inspection of the material would prove whether or not the hottie Scottie from Dimbleby's back room had or hadn't been in her bedchamber.

Slowly, as if the crumpled white gown might turn into a snake and bite her, she inched her hand across the bedcovers, reaching for the goonie before she lost her nerve.

Then she pulled the thing onto her lap for a thorough examination.

Her probing fingers didn't have far to seek.

Four two-inch rips marred the gown. Two slashes at chest level, one on the front and one on the back, and two at thigh level, also on the front and back.

And the tears matched perfectly, as if a dagger had been thrust right through the folded gown.

Mara felt a stab of panic. She stared at the goonie, the morning's brightness spiraling away. Even the piper ended his jaunty tune, the lively skirls fading to nothingness as hot and cold chills swept her.

She swallowed hard, her heart thumping. She shouldn't be surprised. She'd known the dagger wouldn't be there. Just as she'd known the rips in the nightgown would be. But she also knew she'd be damned if she'd spend the day hiding under the covers.

She certainly wouldn't cower.

There had to be a logical explanation.

But without her morning coffee, she could think of only two possible courses of action.

First she'd search the room. If she found the dagger, she'd have to admit that hunky had been there.

If not, and she liked this idea best, the goonie was already torn before someone placed it on her bed. In that case, she'd simply ask the maids to verify the gown's condition.

That decided, she sent another glance into the corner and slipped from the bed. She made straight for the oaken wardrobe, but her eyes widened the instant she opened the double doors. Someone had arranged her things. Everything had been painstakingly folded or hung on padded hangers.

The scent of heather streamed out from the tidy shelves, and on closer inspection she saw tiny sachets tucked between her clothes. Like the padded hangers, the sachets boasted the MacDougall colors.

Staring at the familiar tartan pattern, a never-before sense of ancestral pride filled her. Ravenscraig was her new home. She belonged here and she wasn't going to let some darkly irresistible lout from a backwater London antique shop ruin it for her.

Six foot four inches of hunky Highland manhood or not.

Soul-melting stares and butter-soft burr or otherwise.

Blessedly, thoughts of the ill-humored Scotsman reminded her of her mission.

She had to find the dagger.

Her pulse racing, she rummaged in the wardrobe, snatching the first clothes her fingers encountered and donning them. Black stretch pants and a black top edged around the neck with a wide white band. She ignored her new waxed and waterproofed Barbour jacket and slipped her feet into flat black loafers, arranged her hair in a quick French twist, securing its unruly thickness with a wide tortoiseshell clasp.

Without even bothering with makeup, she began scouring the room, not leaving one inch unchecked. She even lifted the edges of the fancy Turkish carpet. But the mystery dagger remained elusive.

"It *has* to be here," she vowed, dropping to her knees and glaring under the bed. Regrettably, nothing but highly polished floorboards greeted her.

Not even a stray dust bunny.

Worst of all, someone chose that moment to knock on the door, opening it almost before she caught the soft rapping. Grimacing at the timing, she scooted out from under the bed and scrambled to her feet.

"Good morning." She forced a smile for the pink-cheeked maid hovering on the threshold, a heavy silver platter in her hands.

"And a fine one to you, miss. Cook thought you might prefer breakfast in your room." The girl came forward, set the tray on a table near the windows. But then she hesitated, the color in her face deepening. "I can take it away and come back later if you're busy."

"No, it's all right. I was just looking for my earring. It rolled under the bed," Mara improvised, her mouth watering at the smell of bacon and golden-brown Lorne sausages.

"I'll look for it later," she added, eyeing the food.

"It's a full Scottish breakfast," the girl told her, pride in her voice. "Crisp streaky bacon, sausages, black pudding and haggis, mushrooms, tomatoes, and beans." She paused to pull back Mara's chair. "There's mixed toast, too, and a large pot of tea."

Mara gave the girl a smile she hoped was appreciative. She also bit back a request for coffee. She needed strong, black American java to think straight, but the heavenly aromas rising from the breakfast platter more than made up for the tea.

Even so, she wouldn't be able to swallow a bite until she got a few answers. So she ignored her hunger and took a deep, silent breath.

"Who was playing the pipes just now?" She angled

her head, hoped the harmless query would ease her way into asking what she really wanted to know. "It was 'Highland Laddie.' I recognized the tune."

The girl blinked. "Pipes? 'Highland Laddie'?" She looked at Mara, her brow knitting. "Begging your pardon, miss, but you must be mistaken. No one here plays the pipes."

The prickles at the back of Mara's neck turned cold. "No one? But I heard—"

"Och, Murdoch's a piper, that he is. Since he was a wee laddie. But he hasn't played in years. He says his lungs are too auld and weary." The girl glanced at the breakfast tray. "If you aren't hungry, I can—"

"No, leave it, please. I'm starving and this smells very good," Mara blurted, scarce aware of what she'd said. "Thank you for bringing it, Agnes . . . or is it Ailsa?"

"I'm Ailsa." The girl dipped a quick curtsy. "Agnes is cleaning the library this morning."

"Wait, please." Mara lifted a hand when the girl turned to leave. "I'd like to ask you something else."

"Aye, miss?"

Mara took the goonie from the bed and held it out before her. "Do you know if these rips were in this gown before last night?"

The girl's eyes widened. "Oooh, nay, that's impossible. I brought the gown up here myself. I would've noticed."

Mara's heart plummeted. "What about a jeweled dagger?"

"Sorry, miss, but I don't know what you're talking about."

"A gem-encrusted dagger . . . a dirk, you call them. A medievaly looking one. Have you ever seen anything like that in this room?"

"Crikey, nay." Ailsa shook her head. "There might be a few dirks in the hall, along with the other medieval weaponry on display, but none of them are jeweled. Even if they were, they wouldn't be in this room."

"Are you sure?" Mara could feel her heart beating madly, her face growing hot. "Maybe someone accidentally brought one up here? One you've never seen before?"

"That's not possible. I dust in the hall every day. I'd know if there was a jeweled dirk about." The girl lowered her voice, cast a glance over her shoulder. "Murdoch would have our hides if we so much as moved one of those old relics. He even stands watch when we polish them."

"I see." Mara stiffened.

She saw indeed.

The hottie Scottie *had* been in her bedchamber. And the lout had purposely tried to frighten her. "One more thing," she added, keeping her voice level. "Is there another way in or out of this room besides that door over there?"

Ailsa smiled. "Oh, aye, through the windows. One of them is a door that opens onto the battlements. Didn't Murdoch show you?" She shot a look in that direction. "There's even a way from there straight down the cliff. The steps are cut right into the rock. They lead to the sea dungeon."

Mara swallowed. "Sea dungeon?"

She shivered and rubbed her arms. Heavens, *sea dungeon* sounded like something out of a Scottish medieval romance novel!

But Ailsa was bobbing her head. "Och, well, it's actually a sea cave, but it used to be a torture chamber." She paused, her voice taking on a conspiratorial tone. "I've ne'er been down there, but the older folks hereabouts are e'er saying a crack in the cave floor opens into a lower chamber. Supposedly that was the dungeon. See you, when the tide comes in, anyone caught down there would drown."

"How gruesome."

"It's only a legend." Ailsa shrugged. "Besides, even if the stories are true, it hasn't been in use for centuries. I doubt anyone has even climbed down the cliff in years. The steps are too slippery and steep to be safe. No one would dare use them."

Hah! Mara almost snorted.

She knew exactly who'd use those steps, and had.

She waited until Ailsa left before she sat down to eat her breakfast. Although the hearty-looking feast had grown a bit cold, she'd clean her plate. Her morning plans had changed, and she'd need the extra fortification to see them through.

Instead of exploring the interior of Ravenscraig Castle as she'd intended, she'd acquaint herself with its dungeon.

She let out a deep breath. Something told her that's where she'd find last night's uninvited visitor. When she did, she'd show him two could play his game. Feeling better already, she poured herself a cup of lukewarm tea.

This time it would be hunky's turn to be caught off guard.

And she meant to enjoy his misery.

Bracing his hands against the crenellated wall of Ravenscraig's battlements, Alex leaned forward and watched the MacDougall wench's tedious progress down the jagged cliffside. She picked her way carefully, seeming aware that one falsely placed foot could send her slip-sliding down the damp-slicked steps. Plunging to certain death on the razor-sharp rocks below, making a watery grave with naught but seabirds and drifting mist wraiths to mourn her.

He certainly wouldn't.

And with good reason. So he narrowed his gaze on her, feeling nary a shred of pity.

Indeed, he almost hooted with derision.

Only a MacDougall could be so foolhardy as to descend treacherous stone steps wearing such ridiculous footgear.

If such flimsy black bits of nothing could even be called footgear.

"Devil take her," he fumed, scowling at her back.

Even her dog had more sense.

The wretched beast, Ben, Alex thought his name was, had refused to follow her through the opening in the parapet walling. But neither had the dog left the wall walk. Instead, he planted himself in front of one of the crenel notches and stared after the she-witch.

Nay, the dog was *mooning* after her.

Worse, he'd cast a few moon-eyed glances at Alex,

too, even once wagging his plumy tail—until Alex glared back at him.

Truth be told, the dog was staring at him now. But Alex ignored him, setting his jaw and keeping his attention on the beast's mistress. Once, in another life, he'd loved dogs. Even had a special one, Rory, who'd followed him into every battle and even given his life protecting Alex's own.

But now he avoided dogs.

It hurt too much when their short lives ended and his lingered on.

Nor was it easy to bear how many dogs now feared him. That a MacDougall dog should prove one of the few in centuries to show an interest in him galled to the bone.

Even so, the old dog had something of Rory about him, and whate'er it was pinched Alex's heart more than was good for him.

"You bide there," he warned when Ben started toward him. "I want naught to do with you."

Or your hell-spawn mistress.

That last he left unsaid, the dog's trusting brown eyes making it impossible for him to speak ill of the wench within the beast's hearing.

"Curse Colin MacDougall, and for all the days of yonder," he growled, wondering why such dastards seemed e'er blessed with the devil's own luck.

And of all the MacDougalls he'd encountered, *she* was the worst of the lot. The flame-haired lass possessed the face of an angel, the mouth of a fishwife, and the body of a siren.

And her soul was surely blacker than a witch's bottom!

Equally irksome, the exquisitely formed lassie knew he was watching her. Now, this very moment. Why else would she twitch her hips in such an indecent manner lest she meant to unnerve him?

Make him run as hard as granite with the need to possess her? Sink deep inside her, plunging in and out of her succulent female heat until he'd quenched every last one of her most lascivious wants and desires.

Not to mention his own.

"Damn a woman's slippery heat and the tight, velvety lure of her . . . *charms*." Alex hissed the words, pressed his hands against the cold, grainy stone of the merlon. His frown turned darker than the lowering clouds gathering on the horizon. "I-do-not-desire-the-MacDougall-she-wolf."

"So you say," a familiar voice crooned behind him, "but mayhap you've forgotten the simplest codes of chivalry? Or do you not care if the maid loses her footing and plummets to her death?"

Alex whirled around. Hardwin de Studley stood not two paces away, a look of mock distress on his handsome face.

"Maid?" Alex near choked. His brows shot upward. "I vow the wench doesna ken the meaning of the word."

"Say you?" Hardwick clucked his tongue. "Some would claim you condemn her too strongly, my friend."

"Harrumph." Alex narrowed a glare on his friend. He wouldn't demean himself by commenting on such a ludicrous notion.

A disgusted grunt sufficed.

His gaze flicked to his friend's *problem*. Though it was truly lamentable, Hardwick no doubt suffered a softening of his brain due to his nightly escapades.

Alex, however, possessed a much sturdier constitution.

And restraint.

He would not be influenced by the tilt and sway of a plump, well-curved bottom. The teasing bounce of lush round breasts. Full, hard-nippled MacDougall teats and sure to be filled with poison—if e'er he was foolish enough to suckle them!

Hardwick looked ready to sample her nipples and more. "Ahhh, to bathe in such tresses," the blighter declared on an appreciative sigh. "To sink to the—"

"You are worse than a rutting stag." A hot spark of anger flared inside Alex. "Nay, a full score of the lecherous beasts," he added, following his friend's stare.

A folly he immediately regretted.

The wench stood in profile halfway down the cliff-side steps. She'd unclasped her hair, allowing it to tumble in burnished copper waves around her shoulders. More vexing still, she was running her hands through the gleaming tresses, letting the silken-looking strands spill from her fingers like pure molten gold.

Then, as if aware of her audience, she refastened

her hairclip with a slowness surely meant to seduce. And she did her work well. Each careful movement of her fingers caused her skimpy, sheathlike top to ride upward, freeing glimpses of taut, creamy-looking skin. Saints, even the dimpled indentation of her navel popped into bold, wanton view!

Alex groaned.

Then he swore beneath his breath.

Her clinging garments left little to the imagination. The thin black material of her top clung indecently to her breasts, clearly displaying their ripeness, while her skin-hugging hose drew attention to the sensuous curve of hips, her round and well-made bottom.

The sweetest he'd e'er seen.

At once, he recalled his quick peek at the luxuriant red curls between her thighs, how she'd inched her foot up her leg, giving him an ever-better view. Alex's heart began a slow beat and his mouth went dry, his entire body tightening.

A condition he refused to acknowledge.

He'd sooner suffer a second death than admit the MacDougall bawd enflamed his desire.

Blessedly, a hearty chuckle cooled his ardor.

"Hah, Douglas—you letch!" Hardwick thwacked him on the shoulder. "Your need is writ all o'er you. Mayhap now you'll answer my question?"

Ignoring him, Alex peered over the edge of the parapet, watched the lass reach the bottom of the steps. He waited until she disappeared behind a bend in the cliff before he turned to face his friend.

So soon as he did, he folded his arms and summoned his fiercest scowl. He knew exactly what question Hardwick had in mind and he wasn't about to answer it.

Not even to himself.

"Do not think your silence fools me." Hardwick looked amused. "Too many are the lasses we've shared. Yet ne'er have you begrudged me the pleasure of gazing on the bared bosom of a comely wench."

Alex stiffened. "So?"

Hardwick's face lit with mirth. "Indeed, 'tis more than naked breasts we've feasted upon together."

Alex pressed his lips in a hard, tight line.

His friend howled with laughter.

"You have turned into a jester," Alex flashed. "And your tongue runs more than an old woman's."

Ignoring the barbs, Hardwick hitched his hip on a merlon. "Do not fear I'll pluck your sweet bloom e'er you admit to wanting her," he said, studying his knuckles. " 'Tis raven-haired wenches I find that I fancy these days. Even so, a tumble with—"

"The only tumble you shall take is from your perch on that wall if you do not stop spouting such foolish prattle."

"Prattle?" Hardwick stood, brushed at his snug-fitting hose. "Since you are in such a foul temper, I shall take my leave."

Alex nodded, his gaze fixed on the horizon.

" 'Tis good that you watch the sea, my friend." Hardwick clapped a hand on Alex's shoulder, all merriment gone. "Do not let the chit linger too long along the shore. The tides here are treacherous. Especially if she's caught unaware."

Alex could feel his color heightening, the neck opening of his collar growing tight. "It would simplify my task if the waves did carry her away."

"And which task might that be?" Jollity once more tinged Hardwick's words. "Keeping her from your precious bed . . . or getting her into it?"

In the split second it took Alex to think of a scathing reply, his friend vanished. Where a moment before, Hardwick's firm grasp had warmed his shoulder, he now felt only the chill caress of a brisk sea wind.

But Hardwick's taunts echoed in his mind as he glared at the jagged rocks far below, watched the long, white-topped rollers crashing against them. He shuddered, rammed a hand through his wind-tangled hair.

Was it his imagination, or Hardwick's warning, or did the seaweed-strewn band of rocks along the cliff base appear much narrower than moments before?

And why didn't the MacDougall temptress come back up? Did she not know how dangerous it was down there once the tide came in? Where had she gone anyway? Even her dog was whimpering now, pacing the battlements in agitation. Worse, the beast kept glancing his way. Piercing him with worried-looking, beseeching stares.

Pretending not to see him, Alex adjusted his plaid against the tearing wind and scanned the tiny strip of shoreline, but caught no sight of the lass.

She'd disappeared as soundly as Hardwick.

Alex swore, then heaved a great sigh.

What was it to him if she'd vanished?

It would serve her right and solve his own problems if she'd indeed been swept out to sea.

Met that watery grave he'd been envisioning for her.

So why did the possibility not please him? And why did the ever-increasing roar of the waves make him want to charge down the steep stone steps and rescue her?

Why did he even care?

Because he was the biggest fool in all the Highlands, he answered himself as he bounded down the steps, taking them two at a time.

Mara stood a few paces inside the sea cave and decided she'd never seen so much wet, black rock. Or slime. Green slime, some of it shimmering eerily in shallow puddles of water, but the most of it covering the cavern walls. She blew out a low whistle and looked round, her eyes wide. The cave had to be the creepiest place she'd ever seen.

Dank and cold, it reached deep into the cliff, a dark and shadowy world filled with smells of the sea. Stinky smells, for unlike the brisk tang she usually associated with the ocean, Ravenscraig's sea dungeon reeked of rotting seaweed and dead fish.

Wrinkling her nose, she shuddered and hoped it really was only dead fish giving off such a stench. After all, a scary-looking array of rusted brackets and chains hung from the cavern's green-glistening walls.

Thankfully, countless barnacles grew on the nasty remnants of medieval torture, each tiny crustacean a welcome reassurance that it'd been centuries since her ancestors had used the sea cave for its original purpose.

Nor did it look like anyone had been here in years.

She frowned and nudged at a rusted chain, half buried in the wet sand.

She'd been so sure hottie Scottie had used the MacDougall chamber of horrors as a hiding place. She shivered again, rubbed her arms against the cold. He was the one person she wouldn't mind seeing dangling from an iron wall bracket or, better yet, wasting away in the cave's pit dungeon.

A medieval oubliette.

A little thrill of excitement shot down her spine. She knew oubliettes. Sometimes called bottle dungeons because of their shape, they were impossible to escape.

Gooseflesh rose on her arms and her breath caught. She couldn't believe she was standing so close to such a thing. And without the lights and safeguarding ropes that marked such dungeons in touristy castles.

This was her castle.

Her clan's dungeon.

Maybe even one of the great Robert Bruce's men had perished down there. The possibility existed. Any student of Scottish history knew the MacDougalls had been among the Bruce's most embittered enemies.

She took a deep breath. "One of the Bruce's own men," she whispered, her imagination running wild, the notion electrifying her.

Spurring her into action.

Heart pounding, she inched closer. The evil-looking crevice stretched across the cavern floor, beckoned irresistibly. She peered over the edge but saw only blackness. Scrunching her eyes, she wished she'd brought a flashlight. But she rejected the idea at once. It was surely better not to see what the darkness kept hidden.

She *did* wish she'd worn other shoes.

The tide was coming in. Already, icy seawater swirled around her ankles and spumes of stinging spray blew against her face, each new dousing making her eyes burn. "Blast," she muttered, blinking furiously.

She began backing away from the oubliette, cringing at the sucking noise her feet made in the streaming sand.

She'd no doubt ruin her shoes, but she wasn't about to remove them. She frowned again and swiped a clump of damp hair off her face. Somehow she'd lost her hairclip. No way would she add to her misery by sloshing barefoot through mounds of stinking seaweed and who knew what.

Not that her soggy loafers offered much protection. She glared at them just as a cold wave slapped the back of her knees. Her feet slid on something and she slipped. "Oooh," she cried, flailing her arms as the world tipped sideways and her bottom slammed into the slimy gunk.

The splash sent more saltwater into her eyes, and a second, more powerful wave crashed into her back, propelling her forward, straight toward the crack in the cave floor.

A gaping crevice that suddenly looked much wider than it had before.

"Oh, nooo!" She struggled against the racing tide, clawing the sand and clutching at slippery fronds of seaweed. "Somebody help me! *Please!*"

But no one came.

Only the tide with its frigid, pounding waves, each one sweeping her closer to the sea dungeon. "Oh, nooo," she wailed again, feeling the sand shifting beneath her, offering no hold at all.

Her heart stopped, horror making it impossible to breathe. The pit dungeon loomed right in front of her!

She closed her eyes, unable to bear watching the world disappear, but just before she could slide over the edge, someone grabbed her, hoisting her into the air. The brute force of her rescuer's grip caused her collar to cut into her throat, choking her even as relief made her giddy, setting stars spinning in her head.

She gasped, fighting for air, and the man loosened his hold. For one terrifying moment, she dangled over the sea pit, its yawning blackness staring up at her until her rescuer hurled her across his broad and well-muscled shoulder.

Sputtering, she hung upside down, her lungs burning and her breasts bouncing against the man's plaid-draped back as he strode out of the cave. At least that's what she hoped he was doing. Her eyes stung too badly to know for sure.

And the blood rushing into her head was making her dizzy.

She drew a shuddery breath. "Th-thank you. So much. But you can put me down now."

Ignoring her, the man only grunted. Then promptly tightened his hold on her. She tried to break free, but his grip was like iron. He even splayed a hand over her buttocks, that grip grinding a certain part of her against his shoulder.

Her face flamed. This was not the time or place for *that* kind of stimulation.

"Hey, watch the hand, mister!" she protested, trying to squirm free. "Better yet, put me down."

She might have been talking to a wall. Instead of releasing her, he merely shifted her in his arms and continued on his way. Out of the sea cave and along the base of the cliff, his every purposeful step causing his fingers to press more intimately into her private parts.

He practically had his hand between her legs!

Unintentional or not, his fingers kept sliding over her. An intimate rubbing that was beginning to bother her. Especially when one of his fingers probed a particularly sensitive spot. Mara jerked, riptides of tingles streaking across her most tender flesh.

"Put-me-down," she seethed, blocking the sensations caused by his poking and rubbing fingers. *"Now."*

But when he kept walking—and rubbing—she knew what she had to do.

She hadn't grown up on Philly's meanest streets for nothing.

"I'm sorry—I know you saved my life," she said, even meaning it.

But enough was enough.

So she opened her mouth as wide as she could and sank her teeth into the lout's back.

"Owwwwwwww!" He froze and she twisted free, kicking him in the shin for good measure.

She stumbled away from him, keeping her hands fisted and raised, ready for attack. Not that she expected one. Not now, with the bastard hopping on one foot and clutching his leg.

Feeling just a tad guilty, she squinted at him, trying to clear her eyes to get a decent look. Burning eyes or no, she didn't miss the jauntily draped plaid or the bejeweled dagger thrust beneath his wide leather belt.

It was *him*!

The hottie Scottie.

And looking as if he'd stepped out of one of her father's favorite books on Highland clans.

"You!" She glared at him. "How dare you follow me around!"

He glowered back. "Alas, it was my folly to think you in peril," he wheezed, holding tight to his shin.

"Your folly?" Mara planted her hands on her hips. "You do have a strange way of expressing yourself. I'll give you that. Who are you, anyway?"

"Sir Alexander Douglas," he stammered, his sea green stare piercing her. "Knight of the Scottish realm."

Mara blinked. This was worse than she'd thought. Not because he professed to be a knight. Everyone knew knights were dubbed all the time.

Especially famous singers and film stars.

No, it was the way he'd made the claim that gave her the willies. Or even his old-fashionedy Highland garb.

He'd said it as if he meant he was a *real* knight.

A card-carrying medieval one of the shining armor, big sword, and war horse variety.

Mara gulped. "You're mad."

"Aye, that I am," he hissed, letting go of his leg. "In ways that can be very dangerous for you."

"Don't come any closer!" she warned when he began limping forward, his plaid flapping in the wind. "Leave me alone and no one will have to know I saw you." She inched toward the cliff steps. "Just go away."

"By the saints!" He stalked after her, his brow darkening. "Do you think I wish to be here?"

"I only know that you are—and that I don't like it!" she shot back, her pulse frantic.

Then, resorting to a trick she'd learned in Philly playgrounds, she scooped up a handful of sand and threw it in his face.

"Fires of Hades!" he roared, grinding his fists into his eyes. "Black-tailed she-bitch! Bloody MacDougall spawn!"

Mara didn't wait to hear more.

Spinning round, she raced up the steps as fast as her soggy-shoed feet would carry her. Never in her life would she have hung around and waited for him to calm himself.

Even so, once she gained the wall walk, she turned and peered over the edge of the parapet.

Her nemesis was nowhere to be seen.

He'd vanished again, most likely returning to the sea cave. Not that it mattered. She now knew how he'd gained entry into her room. If he tried such nonsense again, he'd be in for a surprise.

She'd bar the door to the battlements.

If only she could erase his image from her mind. The tingles he summoned with a single glance, a mere *rub* of a circling finger.

Crazed or not, he took her breath away.

And was the first man to ever make her . . . burn.

Too bad he didn't have all his marbles. Imagine a man thinking he was a knight.

The Sir Lancelot and King Arthur kind.

Mara blew out a breath. She'd never heard anything more ludicrous.

Delicious as the notion might be.

Chapter 5

The instant the flame-haired hellcat scrambled over the top of the cliff, Alex rematerialized on the sandy, rock-strewn shore. Seabirds screamed overhead, almost as if they were laughing at him. He rubbed his chin with the back of his hand. "So much for chivalry," he muttered, glaring at the wheeling birds.

He knew better than to look anywhere else.

Especially at the cliffside path leading up to the parapets.

If he did, he'd still see her. Her breasts bouncing and her shapely hips wig-wagging as she'd hurried up the perilous stone steps. Saints, even the tumbling spill of her bright, coppery hair remained emblazoned across his mind. How each curling strand had gleamed and shimmered in the morning sun, a silky cascade just begging for a man's touch.

"Hell's bells and damnation!" He willed away the image, stared out across the water to the jagged line of the Inner Hebrides, the great hills of Mull, serried and blue on the horizon.

You are mad, she'd accused him.

And for certes he was.

But in ways she'd never begin to guess.

He breathed deeply, filled his lungs with the bracing sea air. "Split me, if she hasn't hexed me," he groused, squinting in the slanting sunlight. He raked a hand through his hair, set his jaw against his ill temper. Truth was, he knew exactly what ailed him. He'd been too long without a woman.

Centuries too long.

But he wasn't about to let a MacDougall female's ripe curves and swinging tresses goad him into foolishness.

His back hurt where she'd sunk her teeth into him, his shin throbbed, and his eyes burned like fire. Those were the things that mattered. Not how his tarse had filled and lengthened when he'd felt her full breasts pressing against him as he'd carried her from the sea cave.

Saints, he still couldn't believe the viciousness of her attack.

But his savaged body told the tale.

The vixen had done more damage to him than the boldest knight would dare.

Marveling at her cheek, he kept his gaze fixed on the isle-dotted sea, the rise of the sparkling swells. In another time, his heart would have leapt at such beauty. He'd even been known to compose verse about the glories of Scotland's magnificent Western Sea.

But this morn, he could think of naught but her.

The wench was obsessing him no matter how swiftly he tallied up her faults. How could he have thought such a she-demon needed rescuing?

And that wasn't the worst of it.

She'd mocked him.

He'd seen the disbelief on her face when he'd told her his name, revealed his knightly status. His scowl deepening, he scooped up a piece of driftwood and hurled it into the surf. Alone the name Douglas should have impressed her. Hardly a greater, more noble race of men had e'er strode across the heather.

Leastways in *his* day.

Yet she'd gaped at him as if he'd declared the moon was about to fall from the heavens.

He blew out a hot breath, curled his fingers around his belt. Truth was, he'd ne'er told a falsehood in all his overlong life.

Not even to a MacDougall.

A Douglas had too much honor to lie. And neither did they make war on women. To be sure, he knew of knights who took occasional ease from an unwilling lassie, and even some who'd raise a hand to their own lady wife.

But not him.

The mere thought made his gut clench and his blood run cold. Such villainy simply ne'er crossed his mind. Not once in all the years he'd been cursed to guard his bed.

Frightening MacDougalls had always been enough.

Until now.

Like it or not, *this* MacDougall required more effective means of persuasion.

Not that he would make good his threat to skewer her with his sword.

But that did not mean he couldn't ponder the possibilities. Occupying his mind with such pleasing wickedness kept him from dwelling on the more base instincts the wretched female roused in him.

Of course, there was one tactic he hadn't yet tried on her.

The brilliance of it elated him.

Feeling better already, he stretched his arms over his head and flexed his fingers. Soon he would go to her. For the sake of his dignity, he would repeat *exactly* who he was *and* his reason for being here.

If she still didn't have the good grace to believe him and relinquish his bed, he would simply tell her that he was no longer of this world.

State in the king's good English that he was a ghost.

For the first time that day, a smile tugged at the corners of his mouth. He could just see those amber eyes of hers widening in fear when she realized she stood face-to-face with a spirit. Indeed, imagining her reaction made him hard.

So he rocked back on his heels and closed his eyes, recalling the last MacDougall female he'd chased from his bed. A wrinkled old hag, she'd been, with flattened, withered breasts dangling near to her knees.

He shuddered at the memory. His rigid shaft

shrank and softened at once. He reached down and adjusted the lay of his now-relaxed male-piece, all lecherous thoughts gone from his mind.

Even so, Mara MacDougall would be wise not to vex him.

If she once more treated him to a teasing glimpse of her nakedness, he would not be responsible for his actions.

There were only so many things a man should have to endure.

Viewing a tempting morsel like the current MacDougall in all her flaming, bare-bottomed glory and not having a piece of her was not one of them.

Alex tossed another bit of driftwood into the sea and smiled. Something told him his days of playing the monk were coming to an end.

He just hoped the anticipation didn't kill him.

"A maniac?"

Murdoch's tufted gray brows shot upward so fast, Mara thought they might fly off. "Havers, lass. There might be a few chancers hereabouts, they come up from the South, the most of 'em. But a full-crazed *Highlander*?"

Mara nodded. "If his butter-soft burr wasn't Highland, then I speak with a Texas twang."

Murdoch scratched his chin.

He'd been pacing in front of the library's tall, mullioned windows, his kilt swishing just above his knobby knees, but now he stopped, stood staring at her.

"A Highlander," he repeated, sounding doubtful.

"We can be a cross-grained lot when riled, I'll admit. Stubborn as the day is long. But mad?"

"Mad as a hatter." Mara folded her arms, sure of it.

Murdoch only shook his head, reached to flip on a wall sconce. "Just dinna fash yourself," he said, stepping away from the soft, golden light. "I'll ring Malcolm's mum's croft and have him and a few of the groundskeepers scour the gardens and woods."

"He won't be there." Mara flicked a glance at the high ceiling and tried to bite back her agitation.

Murdoch didn't believe her.

"The man was down at the shore," she reminded him, her face heating as she remembered the lout's slip-sliding fingers. The way he'd *rubbed* her.

She straightened her spine, willed her discomfiture not to show. "I last saw him where the cliff steps end on the strand."

Murdoch shrugged. "That may be, but he willna be there now, will he?"

Bent with age but bristling with authority, he eyed her from beneath a particularly nasty-looking stag's head, the most moth-eaten such trophy to grace the library's book-lined walls. Every one of the bodiless abominations seemed to be watching her, their glass-eyed stares warning her not to dispute the old man's opinion.

"See you, lassie; any Highlander with a whit of sense wouldn't linger on that wee shingly bit o' shore with such a storm a-coming down," he declared, proving his wisdom.

Mara had to agree.

Behind him, beyond the vast, shadow-hung library, the day had turned dreich, sunless, and gray. Bursts of gusting rain pelted the window's mullioned panes, and wet, howling winds rattled the shutters. Somewhere, a loose one banged against a wall, and if the low, drifting mists were any indication, the sun wouldn't be showing itself again that day.

"Never you worry." Murdoch stepped closer to the windows, looked out at the streaming rain. "If the blighter is still out there, he'll be found."

"I hope so," Mara said, unable to keep the doubt from her voice. "The man is dangerous."

Shamelessly seductive.

A hot little rush shot through her and she swallowed, wished his image would stop haunting her. His deep, husky burr and the wicked things its smoothness did to her knees.

And other unmentionable places.

Mercy, a girl could climax just listening to him!

She frowned. Whether the brawny Highlander was ripped straight from her most secret fantasies or not, he was also amazingly rude. And quite possibly deranged.

No, quite likely deranged.

Her nerves tightening, she took a seat in a window nook, careful not to disturb Scottie and Dottie, Ravenscraig's Jack Russell terrier pair. The little dogs favored the cushioned coziness of the alcove's twin facing benches and were snuggled together, having made a nest of old plaids and tasseled pillows.

Smart doggies. The library *was* chilly, and growing icier by the moment.

So cold, she took a plaid from the opposite bench and draped it across her knees. Far below, the white-capped Firth of Lorne tossed and churned, the wintry look of the leaden waves making her shiver. Freezing as she was, she may as well have been bobbing about in the firth rather than sitting here, tucked into a woolen plaid and with a well-doing log fire crackling in the large, green-marbled hearth.

She bit her lip, puzzled.

The cheery flames didn't spend a shred of warmth.

But they *looked* nice.

Like the ghastly stags' heads and the many gilt-framed portraits of tartan-draped MacDougalls, the open fire gave the room a delicious feel of previous centuries.

Almost as if she'd stepped into a time warp.

To Mara, even a pretend glimpse at the faded elegance of such long-ago days was worth a few shivers. So she drew her feet up beneath her and forced a smile for the kilted steward.

"Just please tell Malcolm and the others to be careful," she warned. "The man thinks he's a medieval knight."

To her dismay, Murdoch hooted. "Are you sure he wasn't telling you a tall tale?"

"No." She shook her head. "He was serious. At least I think he believes it."

"Well, then!" Murdoch looked down, flicked a bit of lint off his kilt. "Malcolm can just tell the laddie we aren't in need of knightly services."

"You don't believe me."

"Och, lassie, I dinna doubt you." He glanced aside,

watched old Ben amble in and plop down on the hearth rug. "I'm just after thinking the lad found you fetching and meant to impress you."

He looked back at her. "Like as not, he's in Oban this very minute, nursing a broken heart o'er a fine dram." A mischievous smile lit the steward's eyes. "It's a rare Heilander what don't have a wee bit of the romantic in him."

Mara pressed her lips together. *Her* Highlander was pure walking sex. Not a Gaelic poet. A sensual predator. Virile and way too physical, he was a breathtakingly beautiful man filled with arrogance and dark urges she'd best not think about.

And his purpose was definitely not to impress her.

At least not favorably.

Her heart skittering, she pulled a pillow onto her lap. Penetrating cold was creeping up through the seat cushions, chilling her. She shivered again, clutched the pillow for warmth.

"The man is not a romantic," she said. "He wanted to frighten me."

"Humph!" Murdoch snorted. "Forget the scunner. If he's found, he'll be sorted. Why—"

"Sir! Prudentia needs you in the kitchens!" came a breathless voice behind them.

Murdoch swung round. "Och, she does, now?"

Ailsa, or maybe Agnes, nodded, her bright curls bobbing. "O-o-oh, sir, you must come. She's in a right dither."

The steward jammed his hands on his hips. "What's she railing about this time?"

Ailsa-Agnes moistened her lips. "She burned the stovies. And the lamb-pot."

"Then she's accomplished a wonder!" Murdoch started for the door, kilt swinging. "It's next to impossible to burn something on an Aga! The bleeding cookers run on a thermostat. There's not even a dial or knob to turn up the heat. How the devil did she—"

"That isn't what set her off." Ailsa-Agnes hastened after him. "It was the new ghost. She said—"

"The new *what*?" Murdoch froze on the threshold. "Dinna tell me she's going on about some bogey tale again?"

"She is, sir." The girl flushed, wrung her hands. "She says the ghost whispered in her ear just as the potatoes and the lamb burned to crisps."

"And what did the ghost say?"

Ailsa-Agnes's flush deepened. "Th-that he'd see the arse of every last MacDougall scorched just as black. And on the hottest hob of hell."

"What rot!" Murdoch exploded, shooting out the door.

The girl hovered on the threshold, threw Mara an apologetic look. "Will you be needing anything, miss?"

Mara shook her head.

What she needed was a stiff Bloody Mary. Or two. This couldn't be happening. The cook's ghost sounded like her Highlander. Enough so to make her skin tingle and her heart drop to her toes.

So she waited until Ailsa-Agnes took off after the

steward, then glanced around to make sure *he* wasn't lurking in the shadows. Satisfied, she pushed to her feet and exchanged the window nook for a seat at a dark oak table in the middle of the library.

A table cluttered with her laptop, reams of files and books, Lady Warfield's private records, and stacks of correspondence with clan and genealogical societies. A plate of parmesan oatcakes and a long-cold cup of the requisite tea.

Her work.

And sustenance.

She reached for an oatcake, feeling better already. Plunging into work was an excellent panacea. Especially against oversexed Highlanders and sly-eyed cooks who imagined encounters with ghosts.

What better way to bust such stress-bringers than to busy herself with her plans for One Cairn Village, a project she secretly thought of as Brigadoon Revisited.

Her very own tartan-ribboned ticket to fulfilling the most difficult stipulation of Lady Warfield's bequest.

The one that required her to reunite the clan and assure that its members looked favorably upon Lady Warfield's memory.

Mara puffed a strand of hair off her face and allowed herself a moment of silent satisfaction. She glanced at an untidy pile of envelopes, the most of them bearing foreign stamps, then looked across the room to Ben.

Unlike Scottie and Dottie, the aged collie didn't seem bothered by the room's cold. He still sprawled where he'd plopped down earlier, snug and content in front of the hearth fire.

"Your lady will be well remembered," Mara promised him, not at all surprised when he thumped his tail on the hearth rug as if he'd understood.

It was a promise she meant to keep, too.

And not just for her own selfish reasons.

Ravenscraig was growing on her, she wouldn't deny. But so were its people. The mystery piper no one would admit to. The twin maids with their bright curls and blushes. The tiny white-haired Innes, who persisted in asking Mara after Lord Basil's health. Gordie, the one-armed gardener, who'd even given her a sprig of lucky white heather.

Even Murdoch.

No, especially the cantankerous old man, she admitted, a hot thickness tightening her throat.

Unthinkable if Ravenscraig were overtaken by strangers from the National Trust of Scotland and the bandy-legged steward suddenly found himself displaced.

But that wasn't going to happen.

She wouldn't let it.

Cash donations for the MacDougall memorial cairn were already pouring in from all around the world. Some clansmen were even sending stones. Beautiful stones from every corner of Scotland and as far away as Cape Breton and beyond.

Her pulse slowing at last, she turned on her laptop and flexed her fingers. The memorial cairn was taking care of itself.

One Cairn Village was the project needing her best organizational skills.

Named in honor of the cairn she meant to see erected at its heart, One Cairn Village was also a nod to her genealogy-obsessed father, Hugh, and the plaid-hung house of her childhood: One Cairn Avenue.

A picture postcard of a Highland village of old, One Cairn Village would consist of a ring of white-washed cottages, each one boasting a bright blue painted door with a window on either side. The most idyllic spot would be chosen, a special place thick with gorse and heather and views of both the sea and the surrounding hills.

A haven.

A cozy retreat to attract MacDougalls and other Scottish Diaspora, with each cottage hiding a tiny craft or workshop that would offer everything from Innes's handmade candles and soaps to Celtic jewelry, woolen goods, heather honey, and pottery.

Gaelic and piping lessons could be given, and one cottage, the largest, would house a state-of-the-art research center for those eager to trace their own Scottish roots.

MacDougalls willing to stay and work at One Cairn Village would be made welcome. Other visitors could stay in smaller, equally quaint holiday cottages or the Victorian-style lodge she hoped to build near the village.

An ambitious plan, but doable.

If MacDougalls aching for a piece of the Auld Homeland took the bait and came.

Determined that they would, she opened one of

Lady Warfield's old-fashioned ledgers and ran a finger down the rows of carefully penned names and addresses.

Each one represented a member of Mara's extended family. Far-flung clan members who just might thrill to the thought of contributing a trade or talent to One Cairn Village.

Or at least wish to visit.

She'd scanned only a few pages when the spidery handwriting began to blur.

She couldn't concentrate.

"Not true," she grumbled, helping herself to another oatcake.

She was concentrating beautifully.

But on how good the hottie Scottie would be in bed, damn his gorgeous Highland hide!

Damn her for being attracted to him.

Frowning, she rubbed her hands together and blew on her palms. The temperature seemed to have dipped twenty degrees in the last two minutes.

Even Scottie and Dottie must've had enough of the frigid room, because Dottie suddenly gave a sharp little yelp and leapt off the window seat. Quick as lightning, she streaked out of the library, Scottie racing close on her heels.

Most likely *he'd* fled as swiftly, might even be halfway back to London by now. After the way she'd attacked him on the strand, she couldn't blame him.

What kind of a man would hang around after the woman he'd rescued from certain death thanked him by springing on him like a banshee?

Heavens, had she really *bitten* him?

Feeling shame about that part of it, she took a deep, unsteady breath. She'd sure blown it this time.

Not that she should care.

He had poked a finger against her clit, after all.

And a *circling* finger to boot!

She closed her eyes, stifled a groan.

Why did she always have such bad luck with men? Where was the knight in shining armor she'd been waiting for all her life?

And why couldn't she think about anything but Alexander Whatever-His-Name-Really-Was?

A man who thinks he's Sir Galahad.

That was a major problem.

Harboring secret fantasies about dashing knights was one thing. A modern-day man who claimed to *be* one was something else altogether.

That's where her Philly street smarts made her draw the line. She knew too much about loonies to allow herself to fall for one.

No matter how tempted she might be to go along with his little game, even for a short while. Knights no longer roamed the countryside, ravishing fortunate maidens. Those days were sadly over.

The chances of being swept off one's feet by a strapping, irresistibly sexy knight were about as likely as the odds of running into one of the many ghosts said to haunt the British Isles.

She bit back a hoot.

Her last tour had taken her to nearly every supposedly haunted manor house and pub in southwestern England, and she hadn't seen a single spirit.

Except the kind served in pint glasses!

Ghosts just didn't exist.

And neither did medieval knights . . . much as she might wish otherwise.

Truth was, she could use a few knightly kisses. Wild, searing kisses. Deep, open-mouthed zingers, full of breath and tangling tongues. And *intimate* kisses. Especially those. She'd only fantasized about such pleasure. Each time she did, a delicious tingly heat rippled across her sex. What bliss to have a knight slake such a blaze.

A Scottish knight whose husky-rich burr flowed through her like molten gold, warming and melting her. Just *remembering* his voice made her dizzy with need.

She just didn't want to be manhandled.

Or deceived.

It'd be far too easy to lose her heart to a man who was the living, breathing stuff of her dreams.

Too bad in hottie Scottie's case, he was also a roaming nightmare.

She sighed. Her head ached and the dull throbbing at her temples was making her eyes hurt. Trying to ignore the discomfort, she reached for the ledger and stared at the faded writing until the squiggles and loops ran together.

"Blast!" she snapped, shoving aside the book.

She needed to get her mind on something else.

Such as figuring out why castles never seemed to have central heating. The chill in the library went right to the bone. A penetrating cold the participants on her last tour would have called otherworldly.

Having none of that, she shot to her feet and strode to the nearest wall of books, made herself examine the impressive leather-bound volumes. *The Age of Chivalry, Knights in Medieval Society, The History of the Tournament.*

She groaned.

The throbbing at her temples worsened.

Such titles were not what she needed to see. Even so, she somehow found *The Age of Chivalry* in her hands, its heavy, gold-leafed pages opening as if by magic to a color plate depicting a crusading knight from the thirteenth century.

He knelt on one knee, his hands raised in silent supplication. Crosses adorned his flowing surcoat and a wicked-looking sword hung from a belt slung low around his hips.

She stared at the crusader, her heart thumping. Her mouth went dry. The queerest tingles started racing up and down her spine. Not because of the beauty of the oh-so-romantic knight, his chivalry and valor caught forever in the pages of a book.

O-o-oh, no. That wasn't it at all.

Nor was it the sudden cold breeze blowing past her cheek. A chill wind that swirled round her, raising gooseflesh and letting her know something was in the library with her.

No, *someone.*

And she knew exactly who.

Her breathing stopped, the very world seeming to hold its breath.

It was useless denying it.

She spun around. "You!" she cried, the high-pitched voice impossibly hers.

He smiled. "Oh, aye, that is who I am."

Mara swallowed, not about to argue with a nutcase. The book fell from her fingers. She hardly noticed, just stared at him, wondering how such a strapping man could move so silently.

And possess such grace and yet thrum with so much incredible masculinity. Sheesh, every tall, broad-shouldered inch of him took her breath, and his slow, lazy smile sent a dangerous excitement coursing through her.

She frowned, narrowed her eyes at him. "How did you get in here?"

"Many are the ways," he said, the smile tilting. He stepped closer, his sea green eyes filling with silky menace. "Lady, you would be astounded by the wealth of my . . . *abilities*."

Mara clamped her lips and said nothing.

He laughed and whistled the tune to "Highland Laddie."

"You!" Her eyes flew wide. "You were the piper!"

He placed his hands on his hips, looking pleased with himself. "Did I not say my talents would astound you?"

She backed up, bumped into the wall of books. "Some might say I am more astounded by your audacity."

"Ahhh, but your wit pleases me, Mara," he said, smiling at her in a way that banished the cold. "Or rather, it would did you not carry such a blighted name."

The cold returned. "Men are searching for you." Mara stood as tall as she could, took care to pull in her stomach. "Even now, as we speak."

"And do you think they'll be finding me? Or will you be calling out for them?" He leaned close, brushed a velvety-smooth kiss across her lips. "Somehow, I dinna think you will be," he murmured against her ear.

Mara went still.

Of course she wouldn't be crying out. She couldn't speak at all.

He towered over her, his eyes darkening as he reached to touch her cheek. Watching her, he slid his fingers along her jaw, down the side of her neck. The intimacy of his caress undid her, made her heart beat wildly and her nipples tighten. Any moment, her knees were going to buckle.

She knew it, could feel it coming.

Her total capitulation.

And there didn't seem to be a thing she could do about it.

She swallowed. "Who are you?"

But he'd stepped back, his dark gaze no longer on her but on the fallen book at their feet. Somehow, it had landed still opened to the beautiful crusading knight. Her Highlander was staring at the page, a ghost of a smile playing across his lips.

"I have told you who I am, but you did not believe me," he said then, a harsh note in his voice. Sure enough, when he looked back at her, the smile was gone. "So I have come to give you a chance to redeem yourself. My honor demands it."

Mara blinked, the sensual spell he'd been weaving round her instantly broken. "Just what is that supposed to mean?" she demanded, jamming her hands on her hips. "Why am I supposed to *redeem* myself? You're the rude one, not me. And you're trespassing, too. I could have you arrested."

Unfazed, he bent to pick up the book, closing it with care. "Lady, were I not so wroth with you, you would amuse me," he said, arrogance streaming off him. "You are besotted with a painted knight and peruse books on chivalry, yet you know nothing of chivalrous behavior. A knight's honor."

Mara's cheeks flamed. "I know you're a first-class loony. And I'm not besotted!"

He arched a brow, still looking completely unimpressed. "Aye, you know nothing," he repeated, setting down the book. "If you did, you'd be wary of the words you choose."

Mara's heart took an uneasy little dip. Something about his tone and the hardness of his expression frightened her.

She drew a deep breath. "Then why don't you tell me what it is I'm supposed to know?" she challenged, forcing a bravura she didn't feel. "Just spare me the knight bit, will you? I'm not in the mood for jokes."

His face darkened. "I told you once that I do not jest, lady."

"So now I'm a *lady*? And twice already." She jutted her chin at him. "Thank heaven for small miracles. I was getting tired of being a wench."

" 'Tis a foul tongue you have, Mara MacDougall."

"All the better to give you a piece of my mind," she shot back. Angling her head, she waited for his rebuttal.

But it didn't come.

Instead, he folded his arms and stared at her. Carefully checked anger rolled off him in waves and an uncomfortable silence stretched between them. Her knees began to tremble, and the pounding of her blood in her ears was becoming deafening.

"Don't stare at me like that," she said, unable to bear his silent, burning gaze. "Say something."

"My name is Sir Alexander Douglas," he obliged, speaking in a low voice as controlled as it was smooth. "I am indeed a knight of the Scottish realm and it was my king, the good Robert Bruce, who granted me the holding of Ravenscraig Castle. On my journey here, to claim Isobel MacDougall as my promised bride, I was ambushed and killed by her cousin Colin and his men. Since then it has been my sworn duty to keep their benighted issue from my bed."

He took another step closer, capturing her chin so she couldn't look away. "The bed was to have been my bride gift to the bitch. And it was she who plotted my murder."

Mara jerked away from him, reeling backward until she collided with the table. She stared at him, too stunned to breathe. "Let me get this straight," she said, struggling to keep her voice steady. "Are you telling me you're *dead*?"

"I am neither dead nor alive," he said, as calm as day. "That, my lady, is the pain of it."

"Then what are you?"

He cocked a brow. "You truly cannot guess?"

Mara shook her head. "I'm not sure I want to know. I—"

A great clap of thunder swallowed her words, an ear-splitting *boom* that shook the windows and floor and knocked out the power, plunging the library into inky darkness.

Mara gasped, her hands flying to her chest. She half expected him to pounce on her then and there, but when the lights flickered and came back on, he'd moved and now stood before the door.

"How did you get over there so quickly?" She pushed away from the table, bolder now that the long length of the room separated them. "No one can move that fast."

"Say you?" A corner of his mouth lifted in bemusement. "Did you not know ghosts have but to wish and can be anywhere they desire?"

"There's no such thing as ghosts," Mara insisted, freezing again.

"A pity you do not believe me," he said, looking anything but remorseful. "I shall now have to convince you otherwise."

Don't bother, she tried to say, but the words jammed in her throat.

Hottie Scottie was making her a gallant bow, backing out through the doorway. "Until we meet again, my lady," his voice floated back to her.

And then all was silent.

She was alone once more.

She stood frozen, gaping at the empty threshold,

the gloom beyond. Chills swept up and down her spine, and if her heart beat any faster, she feared she'd have some kind of seizure.

Sir Alexander Douglas, he'd called himself.

A romantic-sounding name.

A knight's name.

And one of the great Bruce's own sworn men.

Of course. How could it be otherwise?

Just like some nuts who believed in reincarnation, claimed to be Caesar or Cleopatra.

She bit back a hysterical laugh and glanced at the book on chivalry. He certainly looked the part. She'd give him that. If she were going to conjure up her own knight in shining armor, he would definitely be it.

Her breath still unsteady, she snatched up the book and clutched it to her heart. Much as she hated to admit it, if she tried really hard, she could go along with him pretending to be a knight.

Even tolerate his rudeness.

For a man as yummy as Hottie Scottie, there wasn't much she wouldn't do.

But she drew the line at him claiming to be a ghost.

She, Mara McDougall, late of South Philly, and, more recently, mistress of Ravenscraig Castle in Highland Scotland, wanted nothing to do with ghosts, real or imagined.

Not scary ones.

Not friendly ones.

And most assuredly not irresistibly sexy ones.

Chapter 6

Much later, Mara pushed away from the table and stretched, cricks and cramps plaguing her every move. She winced and rolled her shoulders, rubbed the back of her neck with stiff and aching fingers. Throbbing silence pulsed around her, the library's slightest stirs and whispers defeated by the stillness of the hour.

Even the crackle and hiss of the log fire had ceased around midnight, but a damp wind yet sighed past the windows. Scudding gray clouds, too, their drifting passage turning the night into a world of silver and shadows.

She shivered, swiveled round to peer into the room's deepest and emptiest corners. The ones behind her. There, where more than dust motes might shimmer in the quiet.

A quiet unnatural enough to make her bite her lip, narrow her eyes to better probe the darkness.

Her father had sworn that Scotland held magic. Dancing fairies and water kelpies, powers not of this world. All of that was there, he'd insist, alive and waiting, in the blue of hill, sea, and sky.

Don't doubt the very warp and weft of your heritage. The familiar words filled her heart, so real she could almost feel him behind her, his age-spotted hands resting on her shoulders. *There isn't an inch of the Highlands not steeped in legend. Wonders can happen there—if only you open your heart.*

And she could almost believe it.

Or, at least, she was beginning to admit there was . . . something.

A beguiling magic spun of mist, heather, and romance.

The lure of ancient stones and Gaelic myth, captivating and seductive, ever-present in the blood, and set free to flame out of control whenever ancestral memories were stirred. Especially if you dared set foot on Scottish soil. Then there could be no going back, no denial of the call of home.

Or so Hugh McDougall claimed.

Not about to refute him at this uncanny hour, Mara sat up straighter, squared her shoulders against any possible forms of *unwelcome* Highland enchantments. Then she steeled herself to scan the library one more time.

"I know you're here," she blurted, shoving back her hair.

Indeed, she was so sure of it, her breath caught and her skin tingled.

She could *feel* him. Every hunky six-foot-four Highland inch of him.

But not there where silvery spills of moonlight poured through the tall, mullioned windows. Nor anywhere near the cluttered, well-lit table where she'd been working since lunchtime.

He was there all the same. Hovering in the shadows, stony faced and disapproving, his arrogance and irritation filling the darkness as he . . . spied on her.

She frowned, imagined she heard a low masculine chuckle.

"Show yourself," she demanded, rubbing the gooseflesh from her arms, ignoring the prickles on her nape.

But glare round as she might, nothing knightly glowered back at her.

Nor anything more Highlandy than the faded tartans hanging on the wall.

Certainly not hard green eyes, proud and challenging, their amazing depths as brooding as an angry sea one moment, alight with secret bemusement the next.

Even the bone-chilling cold seemed to have receded.

What remained was the mess she'd made.

That, and her growling stomach. Grimacing, she pressed a hand against her tummy, glad that no one but her and old Ben could hear its rumblings.

But she'd devoured the last of the parmesan oatcakes hours ago and she'd simply forgotten dinner.

It still waited for her on a cloth-covered rolling cart, untouched and cold beneath a gleaming silver dome.

Whatever it had been, she'd ignored it. And she didn't want it now. Exhaustion weighed heavier than hunger, but she didn't regret a single moment of her efforts.

Every ache and pain had been worth the toil. The chaos of emptied bookshelves and scattered documents. Even skipping her dinner and straining her eyes until the backs of her eyelids felt like sandpaper.

She'd found what she'd been looking for: verification of the existence of a certain medieval knight.

Sir Alexander Douglas truly had existed.

A lesser kinsman to the powerful Douglases of the south, he'd been bastard born to a Macdonald woman of Moidart in the West Highlands, growing up in the shadow of that clan's remote Castle Tioram, until he'd gone to spend his later youth in the service of his father's illustrious family.

Ravenscraig's books on medieval Scotland described him as a young man of energy, initiative, and charm, claiming that Clan Douglas welcomed him enthusiastically despite his lowly origins. By all accounts, he rose swiftly to knighthood, eventually joining his better-known cousin, the Good Sir James, in his fierce support of Robert Bruce.

Soon thereafter, the well-loved bastard from an area of the Highlands so wild it was known as *Garbh chriochan,* or the Rough Bounds, carved himself a place in history by becoming one of the hero king's most trusted men.

So valued, the books revealed, that King Robert

had indeed granted him Ravenscraig Castle. Along with the hand of Isobel MacDougall.

An honor bestowed on the knight in the distant year of 1307.

Mara drew a deep breath, resisted the urge to open the books and reread the entries. Not that there was a need. She already knew every line.

Each one fit Hottie Scottie's story.

Until the part about Sir Alexander Douglas journeying to claim the MacDougall holding. The arranged marriage to the beauteous Ravenscraig heiress.

Lady Isobel MacDougall.

Mara's ancestress.

With her, the golden-voiced Highlander's tale veered from the truth.

"I'm sorry," she whispered, the two words slipping past her lips before she'd even realized she regretted her findings.

Irrefutable revelations.

And damning.

Sir Alexander Douglas had been a rat.

A draught of cold air swept past her on the admittance, but she scarce noticed. Her head ached and her eyes burned with what could only be fatigue. An increasing weariness that blurred the jumble of books piled beside her laptop. She blinked and touched one of the older volumes, caressed the smooth, embossed leather of its cover.

When she curled her fingers around the book's spine, the silence around her thickened. A shattering quiet, broken only by the soughing wind, the splatter of rain against the window glass. Glancing that way, she caught a distant flicker of lightning, heard the muted rumble of faraway thunder.

An odd sense of urgency seized her, the eerie feeling of being watched from behind. This time she wasn't about to turn around.

Instead, she released an agitated sigh. "How was I to know what the books would say?" she grumbled, half convinced he'd hear her. "Is that why you're so angry? Because history's maligned you?"

A condemnation he'd apparently deserved.

The *real* Sir Alexander, she amended, fixing her gaze on a wide band of moonlight slanting across the carpet. A scoundrel of the first water, the lout had been anything but ambushed and killed by Colin MacDougall.

The historical facts brought a very different tale to light.

And it wasn't a heroic one.

Chroniclers of his day claimed that Sir Alexander stole the MacDougalls' most prized possession, a precious ruby-studded brooch they'd gleaned from Robert Bruce's own cloak.

A sacred reliquary, known as the Bloodstone of Dalriada, seized by chance during a struggle at Dalrigh.

More damning still, every book she'd found on the era painted Sir Alexander as not having a chivalrous bone in his body.

Fully without scruple, he'd left Lady Isobel at the altar. Not only absconding with Clan MacDougall's priceless heirloom, but shaming their most revered daughter.

Mara leaned back in her chair, listened to the increased hammering of the rain. The squally wind. She laced her fingers together and cracked her knuckles. No wonder the wretch vanished from history after such a coup.

Like as not, he'd used riches gained from the sale of the MacDougall heirloom to finance a comfortable life far from Scotland's shores.

The rogue!

And what an appropriate historical personage for Hottie Scottie to choose as his knightly alias—a blackguard bent on frightening her away from Ravenscraig.

A con artist who preyed on rich women and thought he could win her over with such an incredulous claim.

Mara shuddered, stroked Ben's ears when he stretched to his feet and shuffled over to her. He let out a contented old-dog groan and dropped his head on her knee, gazed at her with canine devotion. Unthinkable if ever *he* should turn such moon eyes on her.

Or any female.

With his stunning good looks and a burr that would melt a woman at twenty paces, he very well could've left a string of murdered heiresses from Land's End to John O'Groats!

Mara bristled.

She wasn't sure how he meant to go about deceiving *her*, but his plan wouldn't work.

She might be inexperienced at being an heiress, but One Cairn Avenue had been good for something. She knew how to take care of herself.

No matter how hard he might try to convince her he was the ghost of a medieval knight.

At least he wasn't claiming to be Robert Bruce himself, or, Mara's second favorite, the devilishly dashing Alexander Stewart, the infamous Wolf of Badenoch.

Though she suspected he had both men's way with the opposite sex!

"But we aren't that gullible, are we, sweet boy?" She leaned down to kiss Ben's scruffy head. Indeed, if she weren't so tired, she would have laughed out loud.

The schemer couldn't have chosen a worse method to use on her.

A ghost!

Wouldn't he be surprised to learn that she knew exactly what kind of two-faced character he'd chosen for his assumed identity?

That little tidbit should put an end to his harassment.

Once he knew she was on to him, he'd surely vanish as quickly as his long-dead namesake had done centuries ago.

Only this Alexander Douglas would leave empty-handed.

She glanced at the windows again, watched the moon appear between fast-moving clouds. Almost full, it cast a wide band of silver across the inky waters of the firth before it disappeared again.

If only *he'd* stay vanished.

Better yet, if she'd stop letting him obsess her.

But it was too late, for he'd already kissed her. However briefly.

She could still feel his lips hushing across hers, the intimate warmth of his breath on her cheek. Remembered too well the jolt of sensual heat that one fleeting kiss had sent streaking through her.

An incredibly delicious heat, fluid and molten, shocking in its intensity.

She took a deep, shaky breath. Clearly her exhaustion and the lateness of the hour were getting to her. The man didn't deserve her, or any woman, rhapsodizing about his kiss.

Especially one that had been too swift for her to even get a taste of his tongue.

Damn!

Her heart skittered and her pulse leapt. Why did she have to think of that?

Blocking her mind before any further such nonsense could pop into it, she stood, pressed a hand to the small of her aching back.

It was high time she sought her bed.

"My bed," she emphasized as she started toward the door, old Ben plodding after her.

The silence and shadows trailed after her, too.

A palpable presence, closing in on her swiftly, giving her the willies.

As did the sound of stealthy footsteps approaching the library.

She froze, slid her fingers around Ben's collar.

Dragging him with her, she hurried across the

room, plastering herself against the wall beside the door at the same moment someone eased it open.

She willed Ben not to bark, hoped she didn't make a sound either. But her jaw dropped and she almost gasped when Prudentia glided past her hiding place.

Garbed in a flowing silken gown of a dusky rose color, the heavyset cook held her arms extended before her and clutched something that looked like metal clothes hangers in her pudgy hands. Fully in her own world, she began moving about the library with the rolling gait of a drunken sailor.

Mara stared at her, her eyes widening by the moment.

Humming softly, Prudentia made ever-smaller circles around the room, coming close enough on one sweep for Mara to recognize that the metal rods she held weren't clothes hangers at all.

They were dowsing rods.

Mara's heart began to pound, her cheeks flaming.

Dowsing rods belonged in the same category as ghosts and other such bunk that went bump in the night.

Things she wanted nothing to do with.

Still, she watched with morbid fascination. Repelled and intrigued at the same time. Until the woman stopped in the *exact* spot where Alexander Douglas had been standing when she'd first seen him that afternoon.

To her horror, the metal rods in the cook's hands went berserk, clacking loudly against each other as she moved in and out of the area where he'd stood.

"Speak to me!" Prudentia urged in an excited whisper. "Come to—"

"Stop that this instant!" Mara cried, rushing forward.

Ben barked.

The cook spun round. Her large bosom heaved and quivered and a peculiar gleam lit her beady brown eyes. The dowsing rods stopped clacking and pointed straight at Mara.

"Just what do you think you're doing?" A muscle twitched in Mara's jaw. "Those are dowsing rods!"

Prudentia composed herself instantly, drawing herself into an almost regal posture. "So they are, aye."

"Get rid of them." Mara took a step closer. "I won't have such things beneath my roof."

The cook eyed her with a look that could only be called superior. "There is a very distressed spirit present and you'd be wise to show a bit of compassion. Such entities need our understanding."

"Our?"

Prudentia nodded. "Those of us still on the earth plane."

"I think you're the one who will be in need of understanding when I inform Murdoch about this."

Some of the woman's haughtiness slipped away. "I'm only trying to help," she said, slipping the dowsing rods into her pocket. "The new presence is very upset. I don't think he likes you."

"I don't care if he hates me. There is no such thing as a ghost, Mrs. MacIntyre. Not here, not anywhere."

"O-o-oh!" Prudentia winced, pressed fingers to her

temples. "You shouldn't have said that. He says you've insulted him."

"I think it's time you went to your quarters." Mara placed a hand on the woman's elbow and steered her to the door. "If this doesn't happen again, I won't tell Murdoch."

Prudentia's mouth tightened.

"That auld pest would also do better to mind his tongue when spirits are present," she said, sweeping out the door.

Mara watched her sail down the dimly lit corridor, then let out a long breath the instant she disappeared around a curve at the far end of the passageway.

Strange or not, the woman *had* sensed something.

And the implication chilled Mara's blood.

Only a fool wouldn't recognize the coincidence that the dowsing rods had gone crazy in the exact spot where Hottie Scottie had accosted her.

Kissed her.

She shuddered. She didn't believe in coincidences.

But she did believe in fate. And hers was beginning to trouble her.

A chill went down her spine at the direction her thoughts were taking, so she squared her shoulders and turned back to the library.

She didn't step inside.

Tomorrow was soon enough to tidy the mess she'd made.

Even if she believed in destiny, she was also prudent. And the shadows in the corners looked darker than before. Closer, too. Long black fingers stretching across the carpet and pointing at her, just like Prudentia's dowsing rods.

And that wasn't all.

Moonlight played over a high wingback chair near one of the corners, and she could almost imagine a figure standing there. A masculine form, indistinct in the shifting light, but well enough defined to reveal height and broad shoulders.

And, impossibly, what could have been the dull gleam of mail.

Mara's heart thumped. She swallowed hard and blinked, and the illusion was gone.

"It won't work," she said, closing the door. "I am not afraid."

Especially not of a man-shaped moonbeam.

Even so, she took the winding steps to her bedchamber two at a time.

Alex materialized next to the wingback chair, all but choking on his indignation. He glowered at the closed library door where she'd stood framed on its threshold, every well-made inch of her limned by moonlight and the glow of the table lamp.

Fetching, she'd been.

A woman of spirit, all curves and ripe temptation, her coppery-bright hair tumbling round her shoulders and those lusciously full breasts straining at him. The hint of fine, chill-tightened nipples. Her large amber eyes flashing wide when she'd looked his way, seen him watching her from beside the chair.

And that's what annoyed him.

She'd seen him but refused to admit it.

Too bad she hadn't gone looking for him when she'd heard him play "Highland Laddie." Had she seen him then, she would've been presented with an eyeful too bold to deny. He'd piped in full Highland regalia, was hoping to catch her peeking at him from behind a curtain, planned to conjure a stiff wind just to show her what a true Highlander wore beneath his kilt!

But the wicked little spitfire hadn't seized the opportunity, and just as well.

His naked man-parts would surely have betrayed him had she goggled him.

"The lass is a plague," he growled, striding to the table where she'd worked, spent hours digging up every lie that had e'er been told about him. "Aye, the worst sort of plague."

But her scent lingered in the room, its bewitching, exotic notes making him crazy. And hard. Until he recalled the shuttered look that had come down upon her face when he'd revealed the truth.

Something he'd done for no other MacDougall.

Yet she still hadn't believed him.

"Lucifer's bollocks!" he swore, turning to the windows. He stared out at the storm-tossed firth, its dark waters gleaming like burnished pewter. Cold looking as the vixen's soul. Nothing he'd said had convinced her.

Once more, he'd failed.

Even pinning her nightclothes to the bed with his best dirk hadn't aided him in his quest to be rid of her.

Now he also wanted to be *in* her. Not just once, but again and again. Long, fluid strokes, slow and deep, then ever faster until . . . he groaned, rammed a furious hand through his hair.

Lusting after a MacDougall not only infuriated him; the very notion jellied his knees.

Ne'er would he have thought himself so . . . spineless.

Soon, he'd be little better than Hardwick.

"Nay, it shall not come to that," he vowed, dropping to his knees before the window seat. With a dark scowl and a single swipe of his arm, he knocked the tasseled pillows to the floor.

Then he leaned forward and rested his head against his folded arms.

Not that he expected the saints to listen to his prayers. Not now, in this maligned existence.

Colin MacDougall, that black-hearted whoreson, had made him into a *creature*.

A ghost.

A travesty of flesh-and-blood manhood whose pleas for guidance would likely be ignored by the Dark One himself, much less the good saints who followed the Holy Rood.

Even so, he muttered them.

After a time, he rose. Whether it pleased him or nay, he had work to do.

Mara MacDougall left him no choice.

It was time to give her irrefutable proof.

High above the library, in one of Ravenscraig's highest towers, Mara leaned against the closed and bolted door of the Thistle Room and heaved a great sigh. Silvery moonlight spilled across the floor and vaporous mists slid past the windows. Nothing stirred or stared back at her from the shadows, but a gullible sort could easily imagine the spirit of the past brooding all over the place.

Inside the bedchamber and in the wispy gray mist cloaking the battlements.

Mist she'd just ignore.

"Angry ghosts and dowsing rods," she panted, her heart tripping crazily.

Soon she wouldn't be hearing early-morning renditions of "Highland Laddie," piped by hunky Scotsmen, but the theme to *The Twilight Zone*.

Almost hearing it now, she pressed a hand to her breast, struggled to catch her breath. And her wits.

Her usual calm.

But she'd just careened through a maze of corridors and flown up three steep sets of stairs, one of which had been a dreadfully dark turnpike stair without a banister and with stone steps so narrow they must have been hewn for some *very* small people.

That one had also been much too medieval for her taste.

Better said, her present taste.

Until recently, she'd swooned over anything even vaguely reminiscent of her favorite period. But now, since a certain someone's arrival in her life, she much preferred things of a more modern era.

Safe things.

Normal things.

Such as people who neither claimed to be ghosts nor went in search of them.

She swiped a curl off her brow and tried not to hear the castle creaking and groaning around her. Night noises most likely caused by ancient water pipes, the wind, or the scuttling of insomniac mice.

Or perhaps . . . *him.*

Alexander of the roving fingers and fleeting kisses. He'd proven how quickly he could move. In more ways than one, she remembered, her every sense snapping to attention. He'd already breached the Thistle Room's tapestry-hung walls once.

That was before she'd known about the door to the battlements.

Now she knew better.

She also knew that almost all Scottish castles had secret passages. Many of them led to and from bedchambers. Hottie Scottie could've taken advantage of such a passage and might already be hiding in the room.

But a careful glance around the antique-filled bedchamber said otherwise.

All the same, she checked the door bolt and the locks on each one of the windows, even shoving a heavy upholstered chair against the door to the ramparts.

Feeling safe at last, she dropped onto her bed with a weary sigh. Someone had lit a fire for her, and the smoky-sweet scent of peat lulled her into a cozy mood.

The Thistle Room felt *good.*

Toasty warm, smelling of Scotland, and welcoming.

Smiling for the first time in hours, she kicked off her shoes, letting them drop where they fell. Within seconds, her stretch pants and turtleneck followed. She wiggled her toes, released a contented sigh. She loved sleeping in nothing but skin and dreams.

Being naked was her guilty pleasure.

Well, at the moment, almost naked.

She still had on her black lace bra and matching panties. She'd keep them on for a while, wouldn't get completely bare bottomed until she was absolutely certain she wouldn't be disturbed.

Not that anyone could get inside, but someone could knock on the door. At the rate she was going, poor dotty Innes might stop by to offer her advice for her wedding night with Lord Basil.

If the sweet old lady didn't faint from the shock of seeing Mara in her little-bits-of-black-nothing undies!

Hottie Scottie would surely have an entirely different reaction.

The kind that would make her heart pound, and slide right into her. Hot, hard, and deep. Slow and sinuous in-and-out glides, then fast and furious plunderings until she grew frantic and clutched him to her, screaming her need and losing herself in the glory of their pleasure.

The wild, uninhibited kind of sex that only happened in the pages of the steamiest romance novels.

And *wasn't* going to happen with a man who thought he was a ghost!

Even if his silky-deep Highland burr did make her wet.

She huffed in agitation, flipped onto her stomach. Maybe she should break down and buy herself a vibrator. Getting all hot and achy over the musical lilt of a crazy man's voice was about as low as a girl could sink.

Even a girl whose last boyfriend had been quicker than the lightning flashing outside her windows.

Her mood darkening, she wriggled across the covers toward the little radio and CD player on her nightstand and punched a button. At once, the stirring theme from *Phantom of the Opera* filled the room.

"I don't think so," she quipped, jabbing buttons until she found Tchaikovsky's *Pathetique.* Satisfied, she rolled onto her back and stretched.

That was more like it.

While she adored *Phantom,* and made a point of seeing the musical every time she was in London, its soundtrack wasn't what she needed just now.

She'd had enough phantoms recently. *Pathetique* suited her mood better.

Much better.

Closing her eyes, she let the music wash over her. And, as always, Tchaikovsky transported her. Straight into a romantic world filled with her most secret dreams.

A place brimming with bold, dark-eyed knights who flashed melt-your-knees smiles and lived their deepest passions. Brave and daring heroes who feared nothing and loved so fiercely they'd face down the devil for the woman of their heart.

Men who would give their last breath for honor.

Or their lady.

Mara sighed. She could swoon for such a man. For now, she'd just listen to Tchaikovsky and dream.

Fantasize about the dashing knight she'd always hoped would come galloping down Cairn Avenue to rescue and ravish her. He'd never appeared, but she'd held on to the dream. And such hauntingly beautiful music helped her conjure his image.

Only, for some reason, his brown eyes had mysteriously turned green.

Sea green.

And they were staring at her.

She sat bolt upright, her own eyes flying wide.

He stood at the foot of her bed.

In full knightly regalia.

Mara's blood froze. "Ohmigod!"

He leaned against the bedpost and folded his arms. "My lady, I sorely doubt there is one."

Her heart galloping, Mara shot a glance at the door.

It was securely bolted.

And the big upholstered chair still blocked the door to the battlements.

She swallowed. "Y-you can't be in here," she rasped, clutching a pillow to her breast. "I'm dreaming. If I shut my eyes and open them, you'll be gone."

"You know that isn't true, Mara."

"Then what are you doing here?"

"You should know," he said, a tinge of reproach in his voice. "I came to prove my word."

She blinked. "Your word?"

"What I told you today was naught but the truth, yet you doubt me." Beneath his helm's raised visor, his eyes narrowed dangerously. "I do not lie."

"I'm not calling you a liar." Her fingers dug into the pillow. "But what you claim is impossible."

He whipped out his sword, let the hiss of steel answer her.

Mara gulped, inched closer to the headboard. "Look, buster, I don't know what your game is, but that thing looks too real for me to argue with you."

"Make no mistake," he said, his eyes glinting like emeralds. "The blade is real and I do not play games. Shall I prove the sharpness of its steel?"

He advanced on her with slow steps and Mara shrieked. His sword gleamed as if lit from within, and even rheumy-eyed Murdoch would be able to see that its edges were razor sharp.

It was definitely not a reproduction or stage prop.

And when he lunged at her, she knew she would die.

Instead, she felt only a lightning-quick current of air at her ear. Before she could even blink, he'd sheathed the thing and returned to the foot of the bed.

A lock of her hair dangled from his gauntleted hand.

He flashed a devilish grin. "Proof enough, wench?"

Mara stared at him, the grin irking her more than the *wench*.

She lifted her chin. "That only proves that you

rented an authentic costume,'' she tossed at him. ''And that you're quick on your feet.''

His grin vanished. ''You vex me beyond endurance. Begone from my bed, woman, and now, or I shall slice off more than a lock of your hair.''

Mara flushed, not missing where his gaze rested. Too late, she realized she was scrunching the pillow so tightly, it'd slipped beneath her breasts.

And that one of her nipples had popped above the lacy edge of her bra.

She bristled, pride keeping her from covering herself. ''So you're lecherous as well as rude.''

His face darkened. ''A leprous infidel whore would stir me more than a female of MacDougall blood. But know this: Had I desired you,'' he vowed, wiggling the lock of hair at her, ''I could have taken you faster than my blade claimed its trophy.''

''Oh!'' Heat shot onto Mara's cheeks. ''Get out of here! This instant!''

''As you wish.'' He made her a low bow, then headed toward the wall next to the fireplace.

''Hey, tin man,'' she called after him, ''the door is the other way.''

He kept going.

But after a few feet, he stopped and glanced round at her. ''I do not need the door.''

He gave her one more bow, a curt one this time.

Then he strode right through the wall.

Chapter 7

Early the next morning, Mara hurried along a narrow footpath through a grove of ancient yews. Worn wooden signposts placed at regular intervals promised that she was heading toward Ravenscraig's stables, but her doubts increased with every twist and dip of the winding path.

Little more than a deer track, it cut through the thick-growing trees, each new turn giving her brief glimpses of the firth and the outline of the Inner Hebrides, endless isles stretched like hazy blue pearls along the horizon.

Mara's heart swelled, the beauty of her new home stealing her breath.

Better yet, the cold waters winking back at her looked as smooth as slate. Dark and undisturbed. And none of the mist wraiths curling across the rippled surface could be called *man-shaped.*

Grateful for that small miracle, she shook her head, chiding herself for even considering the possibility.

It was a fine misty morning. Nothing more.

Somewhere nearby, she could even hear the pleasing rush of a fast-flowing burn. She could smell its sweet cold water, sensed that its track paralleled the path.

As did the uncomfortable sensation of being watched.

She frowned, unable to deny it.

She'd only miscalculated the direction. Hottie Scottie wasn't out over the Firth of Lorne, floating about in drifting curtains of sea mist. He was here, much closer. Angry, dangerous, and maddeningly masculine, his presence eddied all through the grove.

Taunting and teasing until her pulse ran wild and goose bumps rose on every inch of her.

She blew out a breath, swiped at her hair. *"Bunk and rot,"* she muttered, repeating Murdoch's assessment of the unholy as if the three words were a mantra.

"Utter bilge," she added for good measure, borrowing that one from a soured shrew who'd lived at the corner of Cairn Avenue.

Not even topping five feet, the tiny woman with her sharp tongue and fierce stare packed a blistering quip for everything under the heavens.

But well-aimed barbs or not, Mara's ghostly Highlander seemed unimpressed.

Certainly not intimidated.

Far from it, the powerful essence of him kept swirling around her. Tantalizing and proud, his awareness of her shivered across her every nerve ending, penetrating her shields and barriers. Forcing her to believe.

To question when he'd become *her* ghostly Highlander.

Not wanting to know, she slid a glance into the trees, preparing for the worst. Judging by his past antics, he might well be leaning against a yew trunk, arms folded, and glaring at her.

Invisibly, of course.

Since last night she knew he could be anywhere.

Do anything. Even seduce her.

See right through her clothes.

"Dear God, I'm losing it," she breathed, skirting a spongy-looking patch of moss. "I'm being stalked by a *ghost*."

A damned sexy one.

She groaned, clamping her lower lip between her teeth as she quickened her pace. So long as she only sensed him and didn't hear him striding after her or spy a sudden flash of weaving steel arcing through the mists, she'd be fine.

She hoped.

Determined to prove it, she inhaled deeply of the tangy air. Fresh Highland air thick with the woodsy scent of damp earth and ferns. Rich, pungent smells that would've delighted her were this an ordinary morning.

But it wasn't, and tearing through an eerie-looking yew grove didn't help.

Especially knowing that the trees lived over a thousand years.

Her mouth went dry at the thought. Large as the Ravenscraig yews were, they'd surely been around in tin man's day, may even have witnessed his treachery. Stood by as he thundered along this very path in the dark of night, the famed Bloodstone of Dalriada tucked securely in a pouch at his belt.

Tin man, indeed.

Apparently so!

She shuddered, drew her jacket tighter against a cold wind knifing past her.

With the wind, the grove seemed to creep in on her, growing darker and more impenetrable-looking with every step she took. Even the firth slipped from view, its sudden absence leaving her hemmed in by the yews' low-spreading branches and her own ill ease.

Equally disconcerting, some of the larger trees appeared hollow, their empty interiors crowded with blackness. Dark shadows demanding exploration.

But not now.

"No-o-o, thanks," she declined, hurrying on.

Thomas the Rhymer came to mind. The great thirteenth-century mystic supposedly slept in just such a hollowed yew, awaiting his rebirth in a similar grove somewhere in the vicinity of Inverness.

If such a hidey-hole was good enough for him, a sword-swinging, MacDougall-hating ghost surely wouldn't hesitate to use a hollowed tree for his own shady purposes.

And it wouldn't be sleeping.

No, he'd be spying on her.

Plotting his next move or maybe even laughing at her.

Certain she wouldn't appreciate his humor, Mara glanced round, scanning the ancient twisted trees and wishing her imagination wasn't quite so rich.

Where were the stables?

Half running, half stumbling, she tripped over a root, her arms flailing. As she righted herself, she grumbled, "The devil was in that," borrowing another of the Cairn Avenue shrew's choice quips.

If only she had a thimble of that besom's vinegar. Instead, she pressed a hand to her hip, breathing hard. Cold winds whipped around her, icy gusts that tossed her hair and tore at her clothes. Almost like unseen hands trying to strip her until she stood naked and shivering on the peaty path.

But the notion steeled her and she straightened her back. "You don't scare me," she vowed, lifting her chin as the wind slackened. "And you'll never see me naked!"

Ahhh, but I already have, a rich Scottish burr echoed behind her. *And closely enough to know your flaming MacDougall tresses are not tinted.*

Mara's eyes flew wide. "You bastard!" she cried, whirling around.

But nothing greeted her except the empty grove and a lingering trace of his voice, silky deep and disturbing.

He'd seen her naked.

And in a much more intimate way than that one quick look at her exposed nipple. He'd somehow seen her between her legs and, heaven help her, knowing he had sent a coil of heat spiraling through her.

Tingly heat, shamelessly delicious.

For one crazy-mad moment, she imagined his hard, manly body pressed to hers. Skin to naked skin. His breath soft and warm on her flesh. Knightly kisses igniting her senses, his hands exploring her curves, rousing her in ways she'd never dreamed a woman could be stirred.

She'd never desired a man so feverishly—or felt more foolish for wanting one.

Sir Alexander Douglas wasn't *real.*

He was everything she didn't believe in. And he hated MacDougalls.

No matter that, technically, she was a *Mc*Dougall.

Either way, getting all hot and bothered just because he was six feet four and gorgeous and had a voice that weakened her knees was unhealthy.

And wanting to kiss him until she grew dizzy, drowning in the taste of him, was against all reason.

Downright dangerous.

A fact she couldn't ignore since last night.

She'd spent hours tossing and turning, terrified he'd reappear. Her heart had pounded so rapidly, she'd feared she'd have a heart attack.

Her knees *still* shook. And not because he was so incredibly sexy she sometimes forgot to breathe when he towered over her, pinning her with those stormy sea green eyes and making the rest of the world melt away as if only he existed.

She puffed a strand of hair off her face, felt her palms damping. How she'd managed to dress this morning and descend so many stairs without landing in a heap at the bottom was beyond comprehension.

He'd shocked her that greatly.

And he was still unnerving her. Lurking somewhere, staring at her with such piercing intensity, her toe collided with a boulder blocking the path.

"Owwww!" She grabbed her foot, glaring at the rock—a lichen-blotched chunk of granite that seemed to glower right back at her.

But wasn't anywhere near the path she'd been following.

She blinked and looked around. The offending rock rose from a patch of rough deer grass at the edge of a bracken slope and a broad stretch of grazing pasture.

The footpath through the yew grove was nowhere in sight, the wretched trees now well behind her. Somehow she'd broken free of their clutches. Nothing more ominous crowded her now than a tangle of juniper, gorse, and broom.

And the eyes staring holes into her weren't *his*, but a horse's.

A magnificent brute gorging himself on grass a few paces from where she stood. All sleek lines and muscle with a glossy black coat, the beast eyed her with unblinking interest.

Several other horses, similarly impressive, watched her from a distance. But it was the nearby stable block that made her heart leap and banished the horrors of the yew grove.

"Holy guacamole," she breathed, her jaw dropping.

Awe sweeping her, she picked her way across the tussocky grass, her excitement mounting the closer she came to the ancient building and its cluster of byres.

Low slung, stone built, and with a gray slate roof, Ravenscraig's stables stood heavy with the weight of years. Centuries of wind, rain, and long cold winters had taken a toll, softening edges and darkening stone, but therein lay their enchantment.

Anything but scribbled dates and jotted memories, the stables lived and breathed history.

Each rough-hewn stone hummed with age, but also enough bustle to keep thoughts of *him* at bay.

Wishing she could forget him completely, she approached the stable, her arrival not seeming to disturb the broody hens scratching and pecking in the dirt near a drystone wall, or the handful of sheep and shaggy, red-coated Highland cows foraging near the byres.

Everything seemed normal . . . except for the humming stones.

Mara's nape prickled. Wild possibilities whirled inside her. Romantic as it was to imagine old stones vibrating with age, actually hearing that humming was something else entirely.

But then she recognized the sound for what it was: soft, repetitive *thuds* and the murmur of male voices.

Highland voices, and coming from behind the stables.

A mystery quickly solved when Scottie and Dottie shot out of nowhere, their stubby legs pumping and their brown and white bodies splotched with blackish goo.

"How many times am I a-telling you wee buggers not to play in the dung heap—" Malcolm the Red skidded to a halt behind them, his flushed face turning an even brighter red.

"Miss Mara!" He stared at her, eyes widening and chest heaving, a reeking manure shovel clutched in his hand.

Scottie and Dottie dashed forward, sniffing at her heels until the young Highlander gave a sharp whistle.

"Those two are in fine fettle." He shook his head as the little dogs ran off toward the broody hens. "But what sees you out and about so early? Murdoch didn't say you'd be coming down here."

"He didn't know," Mara said, shivering as a stray wind riffled her hair. "No one does."

Think you? A rich burr much deeper than Malcolm's purred at her ear.

Mara gasped, but Malcolm didn't seem to have heard. "Ach, well, I wish we had known." He slid a glance at another young man just stepping out from behind one of the byres. "We would've put off the dung loading."

"Dung loading?" Mara looked from one young man to the other, not missing the black flecks on their thigh boots. "You mean mucking out the stables?"

"Aye, but more than that," Malcolm told her. "Iain and I were just loading dung for the National Farmers' Union." He paused, his freckled face lighting.

"And for you. Every shovel will help raise funds for One Cairn Village."

Mara blinked. "They pay you for . . . manure?"

Malcolm grinned. "Not the NFU, but the folk they send the manure," he explained, shoving a lock of bright red hair off his brow. "See you, there are some who believe manure can be converted into electricity. It's the methane gas that's a by-product of the dung. Folks in the know claim that with the right heat exchangers, the dung will provide a new and inexhaustible source of energy."

"The people researching the possibilities pay well for each lorry of manure we deliver," Iain put in, joining them. He flashed Mara a confident smile. "Whether anything comes of it or nay, Murdoch says we've already tallied up enough revenue to lay the foundations for your project."

Mara's heart clenched. "I've never heard of such a thing, but it sounds . . . promising. Truly, I don't know what to say," she said, meaning it.

What she did know, she wasn't about to reveal—that if such a harebrained scheme existed and was real, maybe the claims of a medieval Scottish ghost who'd already proved his knightly prowess weren't so far-fetched either.

But the possibility made her head ache, so she flashed her best smile and ignored trouble. "Malcolm, you asked why I'm here," she said, summoning all her courage. "I thought I'd go riding. And I'd like a lively mount. Not some docile bag of bones."

"Och, nay, lass, you canna be doing that," Malcolm argued, looking appalled. "Murdoch would hang us by our toes."

Iain cleared his throat. "See you, we couldn't give you a gentle mount even if you wanted one," he said. "Ravenscraig's horses are right spirited. Even the mares are high-strung. These stables have been the pride of the MacDougalls for centuries. We've the finest Anglo-Normans you'll find anywhere."

"Anglo-Normans?" Mara's belly tightened. "That sounds rather archaic."

Malcolm attempted a smile. "Och, he means their roots are in a breed of Norman horse that was once prized as a medieval war horse," he explained. "They were rare in these parts, but one of your ancestors, Colin MacDougall, is said to have brought the first one here in the early fourteenth century. Legend claims he wrested the beast from another knight in battle."

Mara swallowed, the queasiness in her belly spinning into a cold hard knot. "Murdoch said something about a seal colony," she blurted, changing the subject. "I'd like to ride to see it."

Malcolm's brows shot upward. "Och, nay; that's even worse. You canna go there," he said, his burr thickening. " 'Tis way too far and the cliffs are dangerous. Besides, what if the heidbanger is still about?"

"Heidbanger?" Mara decided then and there to purchase a Scottish dictionary. "What in the world is that?"

"A crazy person," Iain translated. "The kind you wouldn't want to meet in a place as remote as the seal colony. Begging your pardon, miss, but all Oban knows there was such a loon badgering you last night, and that he got away."

Mara shot a glance at Malcolm, but he only shrugged.

"Word spreads quickly." He shook his head as if making light of it. "But dinna you worry. Whoe'er he was, he's no here now. We searched all night and didna find a trace of him."

Mara smiled. She had them now. "Then there's no reason I shouldn't ride out, is there?"

Iain looked down and shuffled his dung-splattered feet.

Malcolm's brow crinkled. "Are you sure you won't reconsider?"

"No." Mara held her ground. "I'm in the mood for a good ride and I want a feisty mount." When neither of them budged, she added, "You needn't worry that I'm inexperienced. I've ridden before."

She just hoped they wouldn't guess that had been on a rented pony ambling up and down Cairn Avenue on her fifth birthday.

"By the Rood, Alex, how long are you going to let the lass suffer?" Hardwin de Studley stood near the edge of the sea cliff, his great cloak flapping in the wind. "You've filled my ears with blether about your honor for an eternity, yet you do nothing to aid a helpless maiden."

"Leave be, I warn you," Alex pressed him, his gaze on the blue-crested waves of the firth. "Your arrows are sailing past their mark."

Hardwick sighed. "Any fool can see she can't handle a horse."

Alex glanced up from the isle-strewn waters and looked at his friend. "You see a wench in need in every female that walks. And we both know the kind of help you aspire to offer them," he said, trying to ignore the other's protruding *affliction*.

An impediment the woman-chasing lout's wind-whipped cloak couldn't begin to hide.

Alex winced, some of his own irritation flagging.

"Yon flamed-haired she-devil is anything but helpless. Ne'er have I encountered a bolder wench," he declared, folding his arms. "She has herself to blame. She's the one who told those two sniveling striplings to saddle a sassy mount."

Hardwick hooted. "Hah! I should've known," he crowed, his dark eyes flashing. "You're jealous!"

"Whelps, both of them," Alex denied.

"Och, to be sure," Hardwick agreed, clearly enjoying himself. "The strapping one with the bright red hair stands as tall as you. And the other wasn't exactly a reed in the wind."

"Women have addled your wits."

"Nay, they sharpen them." Hardwick angled his head, gave Alex a probing look. "Those two whelps, as you call them, are why you've let the lass sit there for nigh onto an hour while her mare fills her belly with clover."

"You no longer know me if you think I care aught about wet-behind-the-ears stable boys ogling a MacDougall." Alex blew out a breath, hoped the heat in his face didn't mean he was flushing. "It matters not a whit to me how many green lads she lets fawn over her. And even less how long she requires to master the skills of riding."

And he wasn't going to look her way again.

Saints, she could be a Saracen whore the way she sat her steed, her shapely legs spread in brazen invitation and her generous breasts jiggling each time her fool horse deigned to move.

Ignoring her, Alex narrowed his eyes on her mount. "I'm far more interested in the mare," he said, studying the beast's lines. "Do you not see the resemblance to Pagan?"

"What if I do?" Hardwick shrugged. "The deed you seek to avenge is long ago and best forgotten. What does it matter if the MacDougalls made well with Pagan's seed?"

He paused to adjust the hang of his cloak. " 'Tis *my* seed alone that interests me when such a tempting vessel is near."

"You are worse than a rutting stag."

Hardwick grinned. "I but speak the truth, my friend."

Alex snorted.

His friend arched a mocking bow. "Look upon the lass and tell me she does not stir you. Or has spleen withered your manhood?"

A muscle jerked in Alex's jaw. "I should call you out for that," he said with a withering glare. "Be glad I am a well-tempered man."

"What folly—neither of us would win." Hardwick laughed. "We'd succeed only in maiming ourselves. Think what a loss it would be to the fairer sex were I to lose a certain part of my anatomy."

Grabbing Alex's arm, he gave him a conspiratorial wink. "Would you want that on your conscience? For truth, if you weren't so fettered by duty, you'd put your *lance* to good use as well," he vowed. "Yon sweetmeat is ripe for the plucking."

Alex jerked free. "She is ripe for more than that," he returned, careful to keep his tone from revealing his true meaning.

Instead he turned back to the sea, all the ways he'd sample her ripeness running through his mind. Making him hard. And in a worse way than Hardwin de Studley could ever dream to experience, permanent arousal or no.

Hardwick desired all women.

Alex burned for only one.

A truth he did not want to admit. Not to Hardwick, not to himself, and certainly not to *her*.

Especially after visiting the site of her planned One Cairn Village earlier that morning and seeing the work progressing there. Trees being cleared and foundations laid, the ever-growing pile of stones for her memorial cairn.

An abomination he'd learned was to carry a bronze plaque glorifying his archenemies. Colin MacDougall and his scheming mistress, the ill-famed Lady Isobel of evil memory.

Checking himself with an effort, he clenched his fists and stepped closer to the cliff edge. "Bloody MacDougall bastards," he breathed, staring down at the swells breaking on the rocks until his eyes burned and his need diminished.

There was only so much a man could endure.

His heart hammering, he set his jaw so fiercely, he wondered his teeth didn't crack. Gall rose in his throat, so hot and thick he nearly choked.

"Did you know she is immortalizing two of the worst jackals in all her benighted clan's history?" he ground out, keeping his stare on the rocks. "I have seen the design for the memorial tablet, heard the workmen speak the names in wonder and awe."

He drew a sharp breath, kicked a pebble over the cliff edge. "Ignorant fools."

"Ahhh, yes," Hardwick crooned as if he hadn't heard a word, "show me your back so I do not see your desire. Gaze out to sea and pretend you haven't met your match. Tell me you are not aflame to possess the wench."

Alex clamped his lips together. There was nothing he could say.

His friend knew him too well.

"Your silence speaks loudly," the knave said, proving it. "I shall leave you now. Our old friend, Bran of Barra, has invited me for feasting. You'll be spared my presence for a while, at least."

"Saints be praised," Alex breathed, still not looking at him. "I'm weary of your clattering tongue."

Hardwick stepped in front of him, blocking his view. "You could join me," he suggested, catching Alex's arm. "The old Islesman's table is always heavily laden and his wine flows freely. Not to mention the women . . ."

"Bran of Barra's hall is a breeding ground for the pox," Alex said, jerking free. "I'd rather be gelded than touch one of the whores he procures for his guests."

"Gelded?" Hardwick rocked back on his heels and laughed. "Why bother? You haven't dipped your wick in centuries. Unless you've been lying to me."

Alex turned back to the sea. "Matters of greater importance have occupied me. I—"

"I know, your accursed bed," Hardwick cut him off. "But for the sake of old times, do me the favor of looking after the lass after I go. If you listen to your heart, you'll make haste to aid her."

Alex made a noncommittal grunt. He wasn't aware that he had a heart.

Not since a long-ago day he chose to forget.

"Perhaps you'll stop being so stubborn once I'm gone," Hardwick suggested, stepping away from him. "One parting word before I go: If you do not assist her, sooner or later, one of those *whelps* will."

Then Hardwick was gone.

This time none of the usual laughter lingered behind.

Only a hint of friendly recrimination and Alex's own maddening desire.

Scowling, he rammed a hand through his hair. The lass could perch on her unmoving steed until the sun froze. He was not going to turn around. Not that there was any need.

Her image was already emblazoned on his soul.

Such as it was.

And that only made matters worse.

Were he a flesh-and-blood man, perhaps she would

be the female to mend the wounds inflicted on him by her ancestors. And certain other pressing matters he suspected she could heal. He'd surely seen enough of her to know she was made for passion.

His passion.

Since he'd seen her in his bed, clad in naught but two tiny bits of black lace, he'd suffered a raging need so fierce it consumed him.

More annoying still, her affection for the cross-grained auld seneschal bothered him. Not in the way he resented the two overgrown stable lads, but because the knobby-kneed steward minded him of his own da.

A great champion in his day, but bent and muddle minded in later years, he'd welcomed Alex with open arms and always treated him with the same love he'd shown his legitimate sons.

At times even more.

His fool eyes burning again, Alex let out a deep breath and stared at the sea. "She's a MacDougall," he growled, his mood darkening.

She'd likely stab him in his sleep with his own dirk if ever he did risk bedding her.

Pacing now, he unfastened a hip flask from his belt and tossed down a healthy swig. Fiery *uisge-beatha.* Fine Highland spirits guaranteed to banish painful memories and any dangerous softenings toward Mara MacDougall.

Whether she seemed fond of grizzled old men or not.

Enough wickedness could be told about her dastardly blood to keep the most prolific bards occupied for eternity.

Even so, he quaffed one more generous gulp of *uisge-beatha,* then swung round.

Just as he'd suspected, she still sat astride the balky mare. Her hands clenched the reins in a white-knuckled grip that showed her just as stubborn as the horse she couldn't control, and frustration or anger flamed red in her cheeks.

Of especial interest, the early morning chill had done wondrous things to the tips of her breasts.

Alex swallowed. Damn but the lass had luscious nipples!

How he wished *he'd* caused them to peak in such a provocative manner. Better yet, he'd love to rip away the clingy black top she wore and bury his face in the fullness of her creamy breasts, drink in the bewitching scent of the smooth and silky skin he'd feasted his eyes on but hadn't yet touched.

A lacking he meant to remedy.

The corners of his mouth twitched with the beginnings of a wicked smile and he started forward. He couldn't stand by and let her struggle with Pagan's descendent all morning.

Liking the idea better by the moment, he summoned the energy to materialize.

After all, helping her was the only thing he could do. As a knight of the Scottish realm, he was honor bound to rescue damsels in distress.

It had nothing to do with the prospect of the tall, broad-built stable lackeys coming to her aid if he did not.

Nothing to do with it at all.

Chapter 8

Mara gripped the reins and let her breath out slowly. She also straightened her back and did her best to look unafraid. Cool, calm, and collected. Totally in charge. But feigning an attitude of dignity proved difficult with arctic chills sliding up and down her spine. Especially when some of them swept round and teased across her nipples.

Almost *plucking* on them.

No, caressing them.

And in delicious, luxuriant ways that made her tremble. A deliberate and concentrated pleasuring that could easily dampen her.

Instead, she summoned her fiercest Cairn Avenue bravura. She lifted her chin to the wind, defying its claim as she strove to ignore the titillating sensations. Pretend the shockingly cold air swirling so intimately against her was no different from the brisk sea wind blowing in from the cliffs.

But it was, and when her wretched mare quit chomping grass and began to prance and quiver, she accepted what she'd known all along.

She was no longer alone.

A glance to the side confirmed it.

He was striding toward her! And coming from the edge of the cliffs—an area that had been empty just moments before.

Mara stared at him, Cairn Avenue forgotten. Her senses went wild and her knees turned to water. A sizzling excitement began pulsing through her, the living air seeming to crackle and burn. On he came, the intensity of his stare making her heart pound and her blood quicken.

No way had she been so occupied with trying to get her mount to move that she wouldn't have noticed him walk past her.

She almost laughed out loud at that impossibility. Ghostie or no, Hottie Scottie was too delectable to have been missed.

O-o-oh, yes, she'd have noticed.

But she hadn't. And that spelled trouble.

It meant he'd appeared out of thin air.

"Not possible," she breathed, then swallowed hard at the foolishness of her denial. "You're not there," she added all the same. "I'm just having a bad dream."

"Och, nay, lass, I am the *stuff* of your dreams," he purred, coming closer. "You shouldn't wear your soul in your eyes if you didna want me to know."

Mara went still, all too aware of the predatory aura about him, his purposeful stride. Her chest tightened until she could hardly breathe, and when she opened her mouth to argue, the words jammed in her throat.

"You know very well that I'm here, don't you, Mara, lass?" His mouth curved with just the trace of a smile. "For truth, you should be glad I am. Did you not ken that the boulders hereabouts are far more dangerous than that wee clump of granite you stubbed your toe against in the yew grove?"

Mara gasped.

The little smile playing across his lips turned devilish.

"Och, aye," he went on, waving a hand at the innocent-looking boulders dotting the cliff top, "where'er you see two or more boulders clustered together, there's often deep holes in between. Or bottomless fissures hidden by the bonnie patches o' heather I've seen you admiring. Even worse—"

"I am not some greenhorn who's never seen a hill or wood," Mara bristled, not about to admit she'd never indeed stood on such a wild, windswept cliff.

"Even worse, adders teem in the heather," he continued as if she hadn't spoken. "And they love summer, enjoy slithering onto large, flat rocks and basking in the sun. Or spooking the horses of unskilled riders."

He paused, letting his gaze dip ever so briefly to her tightened nipples. "Dinna get me started on how often the mists come up from the sea or slide down the braes, how swiftly they can thicken."

Mara looked at him, wanting to frown but not quite able.

His silky-smooth burr did that to her.

And something else.

Maybe the way his sea green eyes darkened when he spoke of the dangers of hill and moor. The slight furrow that touched his brow. As if he truly cared if she'd happened across such a calamity.

Crazier still, she found herself believing he did.

After hearing all the hazards he'd rattled off, she was rather glad he'd appeared.

She wasn't about to admit it, but were he real, she'd even be thrilled. She pushed that thought from her mind. Too many misgivings tempered her appreciation. It wasn't every day a girl held a conversation with a man she might or might not be imagining.

At least this time he wasn't decked out like the tin man.

Now he looked halfway modern, had on the same reddish brown outfit he'd worn when she'd first seen him in Dimbleby's Antique and Curio Shoppe.

Medieval hose and tunic, she recognized now. But a sinfully revealing getup that suited his powerful build and glorified his broad shoulders and long, manly legs. His well-muscled calves. Mara gulped, *that* part of her reacting again.

She'd always had a thing for sexy calves on a man.

The jeweled dagger he'd used to skewer her nightgown was tucked jauntily beneath a wide leather belt slung low around his hips, and he made the mistake of allowing himself an amused smile when he saw her recognize it.

"There was nothing funny about that." She leveled a hard stare at him. "And for a knight, certainly nothing honorable."

His full-of-himself smile vanished. "Och, lass, did you not ken Highlanders have an irrepressible sense of mischief?"

"I haven't known that many Highlanders," Mara admitted, glancing aside. "I might be of Scottish descent, but I'm from Philadelphia. I was raised at One Cairn Avenue. A place as far away from Highland Scotland as the moon."

He tilted his head, clucked his tongue sadly. "O-o-oh, lassie," he said with a touch of smugness, "if you haven't known a Highlander, I'm afraid I must tell you, you haven't lived."

Mara's breath caught at the implication, something sharp and hot pinching her heart because the first man to ever tease and tempt her so deliciously had to be not only the most gorgeous, but also one she couldn't have.

Ever.

Not unless she wanted to risk joining him in whatever realm he dwelt in when he wasn't following her around. Something she did *not* want to do.

Whether he was sex breathing or not.

"Ah, well," he said then, something in his tone making her think he was teasing again. "I'd thought to rescue you. For the second time, I might add. But if you prefer to gaze out at the firth, I shall leave."

Mara swiveled back around. "You're a . . . a ghost."

"Aye, that I am," he agreed, making it worse by winking at her.

A wink that deepened his dimples and brought back her tingles.

He gave a short laugh, clearly misreading the stricken look she knew must be all over her.

"Och, come, it isna so bad as that," he crooned, his burr thickening, its rich deepness melting her.

He stepped closer. "Or are you afraid I've come to escort you to the netherworld?" he asked, locking gazes with her until she shivered. "If so, then cast aside your doubts, for I've no idea where such a place is and have no wish to go looking. My only desire is to guard my bed."

She blinked. "Then what are you doing here?"

Lusting after you and telling lies.

The silent truth hurled at her, Alex bit back a snort. "I told you," he said, his voice more harsh than he would have wished; "I thought to come to your aid. Or would you be stranded here until darkness?"

She angled her head, and the slanting sun reflected in her hair, making the fiery strands shimmer like molten flame. The light fell across her face, too, revealing the sparkle in her amber eyes, showing him the doubt still lingering there.

The fear she couldn't quite disguise.

And with good reason, for he'd told a falsehood.

His goals had changed. Now his only desire was getting her *in* his bed. Preferably naked. That, and wishing he were still flesh and bone, wondering why he felt absolutely no urge to frighten her.

Only to calm and soothe her, then claim her for his own.

The saints knew he was already hard for her. Again. This time simply from standing so near to her and breathing in her scent.

And, he admitted, because of her puckered nipples.

He clenched his fists, tried not to notice. But they were so beautifully hardened. And they strained so sweetly against her top, he couldn't help but burn to feel them beneath his fingers, ache to know how they would taste when he licked and suckled them.

Grazed them with his teeth, then dragged one deep into his mouth, sucking hard and steady as he slid a hand into the damp curls between her thighs, let his fingers explore and excite her.

Alex groaned, turned away from her. He shoved a hand through his hair, fury churning inside him.

He had to have her.

She consumed him like a fever, and soon he wouldn't even be able to breathe if he couldn't clutch her to him, sink himself into the tightness of her sleek, female heat.

Already he was on the brink of madness, the depth of his need for her stunning him. More frightening still, it wasn't just her lush curves and sultry kiss-me-all-over eyes, but the way those eyes could light a room when she smiled. How her laughter warmed even the coldest corners of his dark and lonely world.

The wonder that spread across her face when she lost herself in romantic musings about his *real* world.

The long-ago one that no longer existed except in

tumbled stones, rusted relics, and leather-bound chronicles filled with lies.

Alex shuddered, hid his misery behind a cough.

Most mortals he'd encountered no longer appreciated the world that had been his. That Mara MacDougall seemed to care, even in an overly fanciful way, stirred him with a fierceness he couldn't control.

Not anymore.

Truth was, he needed her.

If he still possessed even a shred of valor, he'd vanish and never show himself to her again. Or at least continue with his original plan and frighten her away.

But the lass desired him. He could scent the arousal on her.

He had but to glance at her nipples or the sweet curve of her lower lip and the stimulating musk of her need streamed off her, an erotic tide to flood his senses.

And addle his wits.

Make him the kind of self-serving blackguard he'd always despised—a knave with naught but drink, women, and pillaging on his mind. Alex scowled, smoothed a hand over his mouth. Soon he'd be no better than Bran of Barra, the overlord of letch, and all his rutting friends.

"Are you sure you can help me?" The lass was watching him, doubt clouding her eyes. "I mean . . . er . . . can you even touch real things?"

"You wonder?" A muscle jerked in his jaw, but when he spoke, his words were smooth and measured. "Did my sword hand not claim a lock of your hair? Did you not kick your foot into my shin after I carried you from the sea cave?"

"I'd forgotten," Mara admitted, heat stealing onto her cheeks.

It was hard to think when just looking at him made her so . . . orgasmic. In fact, she'd almost swear the wind was playing with her nipples again, especially when his gaze flicked oh-so-casually across her breasts.

She smoothed back her hair, hoped mind reading wasn't one of his supernatural powers. "Then you'll help me get back to the stables?"

He held up a hand as if swearing to his honesty. "Wherever you wish to go."

Mara considered.

Not that she had much choice.

Already, her mare had lost interest in their exchange and was once more chomping grass. Poky as the beast was, it could well be midnight before she managed to get off the cliffs if she declined Hottie Scottie's assistance.

Still, it wouldn't do to give in too easily. "How do I know you can ride?"

He gave her a slow, sexy smile. "I can."

Mara patted the mare's neck. "She doesn't want to do anything but stop and eat," she said, his smile making her all hot and achy. "What makes you think she'll cooperate for you?"

"For a lass who makes moon eyes at painted knights, I'd think you'd know the answer to that."

Mara flushed. Of course she knew about medieval knights. This one just had an annoying knack of robbing all coherent thought from her mind.

But she knew about knights. Oh, yes.

What she didn't know, she fantasized about. Such chivalric heroes handled their mounts with legendary expertise.

Supposedly they were equally skilled with women.

Heat snaked through her at the thought. Deep, pulsing sexual heat that pooled low in her belly, then slowly spread through her entire body until her most female places screamed in anticipation.

She bit her lip, so aroused she didn't dare breathe lest he guess how much he excited her. She actually hurt inside, feared she'd soon cry out if he didn't kiss her. Or, better yet, slip his hand between her legs again. This time rubbing her until she shattered into a gazillion little pieces.

She shifted on the saddle, need trembling through her. Never had she known such persistent throbbing. Tingly pulsations so hot and exquisite she could hardly stand it.

And just from the way he was looking at her.

How could an *apparition* make her feel this way? Why couldn't he be the garden-variety ghost? Wispy and all whitish gray? At the very least a little bit transparent?

Why did he have to look so real?

So melt-her-bones sexy?

And why was she allowing herself to fall for him?

"As a certain ill-fated friend often tells me, your

silence speaks tomes," he purred, his voice rich and smooth. "So you are aware of a knight's various . . . skills?"

Mara gulped, knew he meant more than mastering horses. She sat tall, every square inch of Cairn Avenue daring her to be bold. "I suppose this is your chance to prove yourself," she challenged him. "Show me what you can do."

His smile turned wicked. "As you wish."

Mara narrowed her eyes. "No funny business."

"I'll not jest you, lass," he agreed, coming closer. "You have my word."

Unfortunately, jesting wasn't what she'd had in mind.

But she wasn't about to argue with him. Not with the mare already tossing her head and prancing at his approach.

Especially so long as she sat on the animal's back.

But when Hottie Scottie fixed the mare with his sea green stare, she stopped sidling and stood perfectly still as he began crooning words that sounded like Gaelic into the horse's ear.

He rubbed her muzzle, too, smoothing gentle hands along her neck and shoulders. Large well-formed hands that looked all too real and that he moved with confident self-assurance, each soothing stroke proving his skill.

He glanced at Mara then, his gaze just a touch arrogant. "Will you trust me to see you back to the stables now, Mara MacDougall?"

"No," Mara blurted before caution changed her

mind. "Not quite yet. I wanted to see the seal colony."

"Then I shall take you there," he agreed, vaulting up behind her. "I'll make certain you enjoy . . . the ride."

Mara's breath caught at how quickly he seized the reins, spurred the mare into a smooth canter. "Just relax," he urged, holding her fast against him.

He laughed then, tightening his arm around her as he brought down his free hand in a loud, open-palmed *thwack* on their mount's rump.

And then they were flying. First thundering across the boulder-strewn grass and splashing through sparkling burnlets, then sailing over ever-rising slopes and past steep, rocky-sided gorges.

Ever onward they pounded, the wind in their faces, until Mara laughed, too. Giddy with excitement, she held fast to his encircling arm, certain her heart would burst at any moment.

From the wild joy of the ride, and especially the rousing warmth of his thighs rubbing so intimately against hers.

The triumph that filled her when he held her even tighter and cried out, "See what you have done to me! Made me forget you're a bloody MacDougall!"

And she had.

He was wholly and irrevocably under her spell.

Totally ensorcelled.

She'd cursed him as thoroughly as had her villainous ancestors with their dastardly brooch. For no other reason could he imagine why he'd send a horse plunging up one of the most precarious cliffs in all these benighted lands—just so a MacDougall could peer down at a welter of stinking, barking seals and their offspring.

But he'd done that and more.

And enjoyed every exhilarating moment.

Alex frowned at his weakness, then frowned some more because she couldn't see his dark mien.

Not sprawled on her belly on the grass.

Worse, she'd positioned herself between his obligingly spread legs—to keep from slipping over the cliff edge, she'd said as she'd stretched out beneath him.

A siren's trick, Alex was sure.

Not that he'd really minded.

Far from it, he'd gladly opened his legs for her, even enjoyed watching as she'd wriggled her luscious body into the best position to view the seal colony at the bottom of the steep drop-off.

Besotted fool that he was, he'd especially liked how she'd gripped his ankles as she'd inched forward to better look over the edge. A dangerous edge that instantly reminded him of his curse, his bounden duty to guard his bed and keep it free of such as her.

His brows snapped together and he glared up at the heavens. By the holy saints, had he lost his mind? Gone soft as a doddering graybeard?

Apparently he had.

Why else would he stand there like three kinds of a dimwitted fool while her glorious form stretched so invitingly beneath him? Why didn't he take advantage and get rid of her when he had the chance?

One flick of his foot would send her tumbling into the sea. He could be instantly relieved of her.

If the fates were kind, he might not even be plagued by another MacDougall for a century or two.

Peace would be his.

So why didn't he do it?

Before he could decide, she gave a little gasp of wonder. He looked down just in time to see her raise her hips and scoot closer to the edge. Another siren's ploy designed to make her deliciously rounded bottom wriggle and sway.

Wriggle and sway . . . *tantalizingly.*

Alex choked back a groan. His manhood sprang rock hard.

Worse, she was so close to the drop-off. Literally hanging over it, craning her neck and so absorbed in watching the cavorting seals she'd never know what happened were he to send her plunging down to meet them.

But he couldn't.

Not when her excited *oohs* and *aahs* were giving him such pleasure. He couldn't remember the last time he'd seen someone so filled with awe and delight.

Well, maybe the day she'd stepped into Dimbleby's and fallen in love with his bed.

Alex harrumphed. Every muscle in his body tensed, and frustration welled inside him, making his head pound.

Truth was, rather than having done with her, he was much more concerned with what it would be like if she fell in love with him.

Even more damning, he suspected he already knew how it would feel to love her.

Blessedly, her grip on his ankles brought more acceptable thoughts to his mind. Indeed, each time her fingers clutched tighter or even just moved, another rush of hot blood went racing straight to his loins.

What would he do if she held his *man-part* in such a grip?

Already his breathing had turned ragged and his heart hammered so fiercely, he wondered she didn't hear it. He'd also hardened to fullest stretch, every inch of him throbbing so painfully he feared he'd soon shame himself.

A very real possibility if she dared wriggle her delectable hindquarters even one more time.

Instead, she glanced up over her shoulder. "O-o-oh, do you see the little ones?" she cooed, the wonder in her voice spearing his heart.

But then her eyes widened and she blinked, spikes of hot awareness shooting all through her. "Aren't they cute?" she managed, amazed her tongue had formed anything even halfway coherent.

She should have known better than to look up.

Especially when she was lying between Hottie Scottie's widespread legs!

She gulped, unable to tear her gaze from the indecently endowed piece of manhood displayed so blatantly above her.

Thank God he wasn't wearing a kilt!

She'd have climaxed on the spot. As it was, those ballet tights he wore showed everything. And left no doubt as to what was on his mind.

And he wasn't just hard. His shaft was . . . twitching.

"You're—" she snapped her mouth shut, unable to blurt the obvious.

He already knew anyway.

Unless ghosts couldn't feel their own hard-ons?

Her cheeks flaming at the possibility, she ducked through his legs and scrambled to her feet. Dusting the dirt off her knees, she tried not to look at the bold ridge of his arousal.

"We'll ride back now," he said, the strain in his voice answering her unasked question.

"Yes, well, . . . ah . . . I guess we should," Mara stammered. She shook back her hair, knew she must be crimson. "Thanks for bringing me up here."

He raised an eyebrow. "I'm glad you enjoyed the view."

He said nothing else. Just looked at her with the most disconcerting stare, then turned and strode for the mare, leaving her to gape after him.

And she did. Mercy, she was sure her heart had stopped beating. *He knew.* She'd near swooned at the sight of his gorgeous sex, and he was taunting her.

Scalding embarrassment squeezed her chest. Maybe he really could read her mind?

Even knew her last boyfriend hadn't only been faster than a jackrabbit, but also barely larger than her thumb? Or that Lance the Lightning Bolt had never even bothered to touch a hand to her, much less rub her clit?

Hottie Scottie had done both. And now he was smirking at her.

Well, she'd just turn the tables on him.

Pull a Cairn Avenue shrew.

"Oh, yes, I did enjoy the view," she called, hurrying after him. "But I've seen larger."

He stopped in his tracks. "Indeed?"

She smiled. "Yes, of course."

He gave her one swift, scorching stare, then resumed walking.

"Larger seal colonies, that is," she huffed so soon as he was out of earshot.

She glared after him, finding the ease with which he swung up on the mare's back exceedingly annoying. He looked more at ease on a horse than any rodeo cowboy she'd ever seen on television. Wasn't there anything he couldn't do?

Sir Alexander Douglas oozed good looks, had more sex appeal in his little finger than most Hollywood stars in their entire bodies, and had a way with horses that was nothing less than magical.

He played a mean "Highland Laddie" on the pipes and could walk through walls.

What more could a girl want?

Mara sighed. Angry or not, her heart leapt as she watched him guide the mare through several steps that looked like they'd been choreographed by London's Royal Ballet.

He really was too perfect.

But there was one thing he wasn't: a flesh-and-blood man.

He was a spook. A shade.

The ghost of a medieval Scottish knight.

Mara took a deep breath and tried to fix an unimpressed look on her face. She failed miserably. Like it or not, if she'd still harbored any doubts about him, she couldn't anymore. Not after seeing him with the mare.

He was indeed what he claimed to be.

And she was falling for him.

It was written all over her.

And Alex was torn between shouting in triumph and roaring in outrage. Also a bit ashamed that he'd put on such a performance for her, but she'd pushed him too far with her doubts. Especially her fool comment about his man-parts.

He'd seen enough naked men to know how he measured against most. More than favorably!

"That was incredible," she said suddenly, the glow in her eyes making up for the ridiculous slur.

Alex started. How had she come so close without him noticing? The answer came as quickly as the rapid thundering of his heart.

She'd been able to sneak up on him because he'd been too busy mooning over her to notice.

It wouldn't happen again. He'd be on his guard from now on.

And he'd stop paying heed to such things as the way her puckered nipples drove him to such distraction. Or how the sea wind played with her hair, sending its fresh, flowery scent to tease his senses.

He especially wouldn't acknowledge the way her black breeches clung to her shapely legs. He squared his shoulders, ground his teeth against the lust surging through him. But, saints, garbed as she was, even a simpleton needed but one look to visualize the triangle of bronze curls between her thighs.

A beckoning treasure hidden by only a thin stretch of black cloth, and a temptation powerful enough to bring the strongest man to his knees.

Alex locked his jaw, drew a tight breath.

She had to be the devil's own to entice a man so boldly. In his day, her witchy ways would have landed her upside down in a pot of boiling tar.

After every man within rutting distance had had his way with her.

Quickly, before the ache in his own loins drove him to join their ranks, he leaned sideways and scooped her into the air, plunking her down in front of him.

"Oh!" she gasped, squirming like a basket of freshly caught eels.

"Be still," Alex warned. "Unless you wish to learn of a knight's *other* talents? Dinna test me, for I'm already burning to enlighten you."

The wiggling ceased.

Unfortunately, the throbbing at his groin didn't.

Scowling, he dug in his spurs and sent the mare into a wild canter. Then, his heels still digging, a bold, racing gallop. A folly he recognized at once. A grave tactical error that slammed the witch-woman's body hard against his own and caused her wild mane of flame-colored hair to fly about his face, near blinding him.

And that wasn't the worst of it.

Nay, the greatest torment was the exotic scent of

dusky rose and jasmine clinging to those flying tresses. Where her scent had only teased him before, now the tossing strands of her hair whipped against his cheeks and slid across his lips. Each stinging, silken glide deluged him with her fragrance.

Intoxicating him.

Leaving him no choice but to jerk hard on the reins. So hard the mare reared up in protest, her forelegs pawing the air. The instant her flailing hooves plunged back to earth, Alex swung down, sweeping his witch-woman with him in one swift, furious motion.

"Another knightly feat," he flashed, pulling her into his arms. "But not near so satisfying as this!"

He seized her face with both hands and slanted his mouth over hers, kissing her long, hard, and deep. A devouring kiss meant to scorch her to her toes. His own blood flaming, he slid his hands down over her breasts and closed his fingers on her nipples, toying and teasing until she moaned a response. The wench fantasized about knights and he aimed to please her.

But she stole his thunder by pressing hotly against him, clutching fast and rubbing against his groin. She opened her mouth beneath his and their kisses turned savage. Wanton joinings of tongues, sighs and breath, and so heady, so potent, his knees nearly buckled.

Never had a lass pressed into him with such abandon, clinging so tight and trembling with sweet, reckless need. He groaned, pulling her even closer as the cliffs began to spin and the racing clouds became a whirling white blur against the tilting blue of sea and sky.

He groaned, certain he'd never known such stunning bliss. Awed by his need, he slowed his toyings with her nipples, now simply flicking his thumbs back and fore over the thrusting peaks, circling the tightly ruched rounds of her aureoles. He gloried in the feel of her, half feared he might die from the pleasure—if only he could!

"Kiss me deeper, let me feel your tongue," she begged then, breathing the plea into his mouth, her need and the shivery words nearly unmanning him.

"Lass, lass," he moaned, thrusting his tongue deeper indeed, sweeping it against hers. Again and again, each velvety glide undoing him, making his blood run hot and thick.

Her blood was on fire, each touch of his fingers to her breasts stealing her control, every rapturous swirl of his tongue against hers catapulting her to shattering levels of passion she never would have believed existed.

"O-o-oh," she cried, indescribable need screaming inside her.

But when the rhythmic rocking of her hips grew frenzied and her hands stole beneath his tunic, her nails scoring the bare flesh of his back, Alex knew he could take no more.

Somewhere through the shimmering haze of passion, warning bells rang louder each time her tongue twirled hotly around his. The tighter she clung to him, the more each soulful sigh she breathed against his lips tolled his coming doom.

He'd lost control.

He, the seducer, was being seduced.

The minx's kiss more potent than the headiest Norman wine. He was intoxicated beyond redemption. Slaking his thirst for her body would never be enough. He wanted her heart and her soul as well. All of her. Her laughter and smiles. Even her sadness and heartaches. Every one of her mortal years.

Nothing else would satisfy him.

And the saints knew, he could never satisfy her. Not in the way she deserved.

"Enough," he gasped, breaking the kiss.

Revulsion swept him. But not because he'd kissed a MacDougall—because of what he was.

A ghost.

A creature. An abomination of nature.

Heaven only knew what quirk of nature allowed him to manifest as a solid man. He choked back a bark of bitter laughter. At the moment, he was a very solid man indeed!

And a despicable one.

The lass was melted against him, clinging and grasping, her hips still rocking against him in blatant invitation, her hitched breath begging him to continue what he'd so rudely interrupted.

"Sons of Hades," he swore, thrusting her from him. Although it ripped his soul, there was nothing he could offer her.

Nothing to commend himself to any flesh-and-blood woman.

Even the spawn of the bloody MacDougall bastards who'd cursed him deserved better than falling in love with a ghost. Phantom or no, he still possessed enough honor to cringe at damning any woman to such a fate.

His head clearing, he knew what he must do.

Gripping her arms, he looked deep into her eyes, steeling himself against the hurt he was about to inflict. "See here, wench, I willna be charmed," he lied, his voice as cold as he could make it. "I'll admit you tempted me, but the ruse is over. I've seen through your wickedness."

"Wh-what?" She blinked, her kiss-bruised lips forming a little O of surprise. "I don't understand. You kissed me! And it was . . . it was beautiful . . ."

She let the words trail off, clapped a hand to her cheek, all color draining from her face. But she recovered quickly, her amber eyes snapping with fury.

Her rapid, agitated breathing made her breasts rise in a way that nearly undid Alex's resolve, but the anger coursing through her and her searing glare pleased him. Outrage would keep her from hurting, maybe even send her into the arms of a *real* man.

One who could give her more than heated kisses and a few wind-felt pluckings to her nipples.

Alex scowled, this time not needing to feign his displeasure.

"You're a witch-woman," he provoked her, the heart he hadn't known he possessed imploding inside him. "Be glad I won't arrange to have you stoned. Or worse!"

She stared at him, her cheeks a livid red again. So much pain filled her eyes, he could hardly bear looking at her. "You bastard!" she raged, her anguish lancing him. "I didn't pull you off that horse!"

Her entire body shaking, she jabbed her fingers into his chest, emphasizing each word with a sharp poke. "You could've killed us, jerking that beast to a halt like that. Then you dragged me down and kissed me. *Plundered* my mouth and nearly broke my ribs squeezing me so tight. You! Not the other way around!"

Alex shuttered his face, simply stared at her. If he dared open his mouth, he'd recant every word. Drop to his knees and explain, begging her to forgive him and let them savor whatever bliss the heavens might grant them.

But he held his tongue. His damnable honor not letting him speak.

She backed away from him, swiped her hand over her mouth. "I can't believe I let you touch me. You're not even real. A figment of my imagination!"

The words sliced Alex, wounding him in a way no arcing broadsword could ever harm him. The truth of her accusations damned him with an intensity that was nigh onto unbearable.

But he'd had to goad her, had to make her loathe him.

Only so would she find peace.

As for himself . . . it scarce mattered.

He had eternity to lick his wounds. She had but this one mortal life.

He had sacred vows to keep. He'd been a fool to think he could outrun a curse that had held him in its vise for so many centuries. And a greater fool not to realize how cruel his error of judgment would prove to her.

Seeing no other option, he moved with lightning speed, sweeping her into his arms and heaving her onto the mare's back before she could think to protest. "Stay put," he ordered, releasing her only long enough to swing up behind her. "And be still this time. Don't squirm."

And she didn't.

She sat before him as stiffly as a piece of wood, which was fine with him. And much better for her.

But as they pounded across the last stretch of open headlands, there where her damnable One Cairn Village would soon stand, she finally raised her voice.

"What are you going to do when we get back to the stables?" she demanded. "Someone might see you."

"No one sees me unless I wish it. And you have the tongue of a bell clapper. Be still," Alex snapped, hoping the insult would quiet her. Make her revile him enough not to care what he did when they reached the stables.

Above all, he wanted to vanish.

First they had to put her infernal project behind them, and the site curdled his blood. Shuddering, he brought his open palm down on the mare's flank and spurred across the naked, upturned earth, tried not to see the telltale signs of her dream.

His nightmare. A ringing slap in his face.

Just riding across the ground set his hair on end.

"I asked you a question, tin man," she badgered,

the quiver in her voice belying her strong words. "What will you do when we get back?"

"Sons of Lucifer," Alex swore, urging the mare to greater speed as they sailed past the pile of stones for her memorial cairn. "I shall do what I have always done."

"And what's that?" she had the gall to ask.

"Guard my bloody bed."

"You mean my bed."

"Nay, it is mine," he snarled, doing his best to ignore the way her bottom pressed against his still-roused manhood.

He grimaced. Her bed, she'd said.

His bed, he'd insisted, and his heart had split on the lie.

The bed was neither his or hers.

It was theirs.

And he was the world's greatest fool for admitting it.

Chapter 9

Several evenings later, Mara stood in her bedchamber admiring the changes she'd made. Not alterations so much as additions. Carefully selected items, strategically placed to ensure she need never again enter the room only to be seized by a strong awareness of unwanted company.

In particular, the six foot four, annoyingly seductive kind.

But also the room's uncanny chill and the assorted creaks, groans, and thuds in the night she was certain Hottie Scottie conjured just to unsettle her. For three nights he'd plagued her with such trickery, at times causing bangs loud enough to shatter the windowpanes, then letting the lights flicker on and off.

Waking her in the small hours by the sound of the door opening and closing—although it had been securely bolted!

"Such pranks are history, tin man," she breathed,

pacing the room, feeling more confident with each stride. "You've been outfoxed."

She glanced at Ben, sleeping snug and content in the glow of the hearth fire. Oddly, the old dog hadn't seemed to mind the knightly shenanigans.

But she'd had enough.

Especially since The Kiss that never should have happened. She shivered and rubbed her arms. At least she hadn't actually *seen* him again.

Good riddance.

For all she cared, he could spend his time in the sea cave, bodysurfing incoming waves. Or better yet, howling away the hours in the gloomy unlit dungeon of some other gullible's Highland castle.

Hers had just become out-of-bounds.

If Ben missed him, she'd play him some old videos of *Casper the Friendly Ghost*.

There were only so many insults a girl should tolerate, and she'd reached the end of her patience. Hottie Scottie, tin man, or whatever guise he chose would be in for a rude surprise if he dared to make a repeat appearance.

"No more trotting beside someone who isn't there," she huffed to Ben's sleeping form. "No more sniffing ripples in the air or wagging your tail at nothing."

And no more shivery sighs or heated glances for her.

Not that she cared, phony as every one of his smoldering, make-her-burn looks had been.

Hottie Scottie, indeed.

She frowned, nudged a piece of lint on the carpet.

The ogly eyed bastard had burned her all right. Even swept her to the edge of a tremendous, earthshaking climax only to plunge her into a shocking, icy void just when she'd started to shatter. And that without even undressing her.

But it wouldn't happen again. Now she was prepared, had taken measures.

And from what she'd been told, they were good. Highly effective and able to repel even the hardiest specter.

Hoping that was so, she went to the heavy oak dressing table and picked up a finely tapered candle. She sniffed it appreciatively. Handmade by Innes and delicately scented with lavender, it was a charmed candle.

An antighost candle.

Or so the dotty old woman claimed, proudly informing her that Ravenscraig's resident spook expert, Prudentia, had said spirit-cleansing blessings over Innes's latest batch of special lavender candles. Her heather soaps, too, not that Mara wished to go to such extremes. She didn't need Hottie Scottie appearing in the shower with her, should Prudentia have erred with her spell castings.

Nor did she really trust in the cook's self-proclaimed powers. No mumbled mumbo jumbo could turn ordinary housewares into apparition deterrents.

But she was willing to try anything.

Even if employing such dubious methods incited Murdoch's considerable wrath.

Although, much to his credit, with the exception

of a few *harrumphs* and narrow-eyed glares at the cook and Innes, the bandy-legged steward had grudgingly allowed that Mara could do as she pleased in the Thistle Room.

And she did please.

So long as the mere thought of Hottie Scottie still set her heart to pounding, she had little choice.

Furious or not, she was suffused with tingling excitement at just the memory of his fingers toying with her nipples. Remembering his tongue swirling against hers, an agony beyond bearing. So she set down Innes's purple-hued antighost candle, took a deep breath, and went straight to the tall windows across the room.

Great looping swaths of MacDougall tartan had hung there since yesterday, and the sight filled her with satisfaction.

Immense satisfaction.

As much as the ghostly Highlander loathed her clan, the new window dressings should annoy him enough to keep him from seeking her chamber.

If not, she had other antiapparition booby-traps in place.

Countermeasures she doubted even he could parry.

A nervous laugh rising in her throat, she pulled back a panel of the heavy plaiding and peeked outside. Blessedly, her special window treatments were still there: Braided clusters of large, pungent garlic bulbs lay in wait against the outer glass, as did fine bunches of freshly cut red-berried rowan branches.

Mara smiled. Better doubly secure than unprepared.

Equally reassuring, the wall walk looked empty, the whole of the battlements quite still. No mailed knights or hot-eyed Highlanders patrolled the flagged stones. Or, an even more daunting image, no Hottie Scottie leaned arrogantly against a merlon, arms crossed and glaring at her.

Mara released the breath she'd been holding and turned back to the room. She hoped she hadn't forgotten anything.

But Innes's antighost candles were already lit for the night, and their golden flames reflected nicely in the row of little mirrors she'd placed along the marble mantelpiece. Even the freestanding mirror wore its own red-ribboned cluster of rowan. A wooden crucifix adorned each wall, one even winking at her from the back of the bedchamber door.

She'd also placed small silver bowls of sacred well water on every available surface. This, Prudentia had insisted, was an incredibly powerful impediment to nocturnal visitors of the supernatural variety.

Mara sniffed, unable to squelch her doubts. The improbability of the water's magic made a muscle beneath her eye twitch. Whether the water was sacred or not, she made a mental note to thank the twin housemaids, Agnes and Ailsa, for making the trek into the hills to the ancient Celtic well.

Then, before she had time to feel even more foolish, she picked up the nearest bowl and began flicking the icy droplets about the room, taking especial care to trickle a broad protective circle around her bed.

"Almost done," she promised Ben, dribbling a circle around him, too.

Just for good measure. Not that she thought Hottie Scottie would harm an innocent old dog.

Truth was, he seemed rather fond of Ben. Even of Scottie and Dottie, although those two only growled at him or nipped at his ankles—when they didn't avoid him altogether.

Mara sighed. Sir Alexander Douglas had clearly been a dog lover, a quality she usually credited highly. And one the kiss-her-senseless Highlander seemed to have retained into ghostdom.

But at the moment she didn't want to think anything nice about him.

Doing so left her feeling oddly bereft.

So she turned away from the sleeping dog and set down the empty silver bowl. She'd done all she could, and there wasn't any point in letting her heart fill with what-ifs and might-have-beens.

Especially when *he* was so insufferable.

She brushed off her hands, wished she could forget him as easily. Instead, her heart skittered and her mouth had gone way too dry.

But at least she was here and not cowering in some inn in Oban, afraid to enjoy her inheritance.

She was also enough of a MacDougall not to let a ghost ruin her pleasure in sleeping naked. Well, *almost* naked, she decided, beginning to strip. She'd keep on her sexy black teddy. Though Highland nights never really darkened in summer, with so much thick MacDougall plaiding at the windows, the room was cast in heavy shadow.

Dim except for the glow of the fire and Innes's candles.

But she wasn't of a mood to flip on any lights. If tin man *was* lurking somewhere, glaring invisible daggers at her, he could just strain his ghostly eyes.

In fact, maybe she'd encourage him by putting on a little show.

Feeling deliciously wicked, she flopped onto the bed. "My bed," she challenged the silence.

Then, rolling onto her side, she began a set of leg lifts, raising and lowering her leg with deliberate slowness. He'd already revealed that he couldn't resist peeking between them, so she'd just oblige him.

Hopefully he'd run so hard, he'd get blue balls.

Her naughty little black teddy should be worth that, at least.

An utterly decadent bit of sheer lace and froth, the thing had cost her a mint. But she'd been unable to resist it from the moment she'd seen it displayed in a Covent Garden lingerie boutique. She'd bought it on plastic, intending to save the teddy for a night of sizzling seduction and hot, heart-pounding sex.

Wild, pull-out-all-the-stoppers, really-let-herself-go sex.

The kind romance writers tried to make innocent readers believe really existed.

"Har, har, har," she scoffed, flipping onto her back and folding her arms behind her head. Who'd she been kidding? The only men she ever met were anything but seduction worthy.

So far they'd all been nerds or nutcases. Or carried so much baggage they'd give an airline worker a double hernia.

The only gallant ones to notice her sported four legs and wet noses.

And more recently, she attracted ghosts.

Or rather, a ghost.

So she set her face in a scowl she hoped was fierce enough to ward off a whole battalion of such buggers and lifted her leg again, this time poking at her bed's new dressings.

So soon as her naked toes touched the bright tartan curtaining, a jolt of icy tremors shot through her. MacDougall plaid on the windows was one thing, but outfitting her magnificent four-poster in clan colors was something else altogether.

No longer feeling quite so bold, she withdrew her foot and slipped beneath the covers. They, too, were of fine MacDougall tartan, but pulling them up to her chin felt good.

Half expecting to hear his deep, Scottish voice ranting at her, she ignored the prickles on her nape and tried not to look at any of the grand old portraits on the bedchamber walls. If she dared, she suspected it wouldn't be one of her bearded, plaid-draped ancestors frowning at her, but him.

Just before he'd step down out of the heavy gilt frame and proceed to rend every bit of MacDougall tartan in the room. She didn't doubt he could do it, either.

Anyone who walked through walls and vanished off the backs of horses in broad daylight could likely do anything.

Sure of it, she burrowed deeper into the covers. If

she lived to be a hundred, she'd never forget how he'd simply disappeared when they'd reached the stables.

O-o-oh, yes, the man had quite an impressive repertoire.

And nothing he might yet do should surprise her.

What bothered her were his slurs against her ancestors. Not that she'd ever much thought about them. Certainly not like her father with his foible for genealogy.

Sheesh, he'd sometimes talked so animatedly about ancestors like Colin MacDougall and the Lady Isobel that Mara had almost expected them to march up Cairn Avenue and ring the doorbell, announcing themselves to dinner.

Hugh McDougall was obsessed with roots.

Much to Mara's surprise, since arriving at Ravenscraig, she found herself caring, too. Not in her father's crazed, glaze-eyed fashion, but enough to be perturbed each time Hottie Scottie sought to blacken their name.

The MacDougalls were a fine Highland clan. Ancient and proud. If they'd viewed Robert Bruce as their mortal enemy, they'd had their reasons.

Now that she could no longer doubt tin man's claim to be a ghost, she had to assume he'd known them. A possibility that left only one conclusion.

He was a blackguard who twisted the truth to suit his own purposes.

History books didn't lie.

But scoundrels did, and he was obviously a dastard of the first water.

Dangerous, intriguing, and way too sexy.

Mara bit her lip. Pulsing, insistent heat began beating inside her. Whirls of tantalizing sensation coiling low in her belly and spreading all through her, clear to her red-painted toenails.

She sighed. There could be no denying it. Just as she loved sleeping naked, so, too, did her heart flip for bad boys.

It was just a shame that this one had to be a ghost.

That pushed the envelope a tad too far.

But before she could thrust him from her mind, a blast of chill air swept into the room, billowing the plaid drapings and guttering every one of Innes's lavender-scented candles. Within seconds, the temperature plunged from cold but endurable to freezing. "O-o-oh, no," Mara breathed, her eyes widening as the hearth fire leapt and hissed.

Peats did not shoot up tall, multicolored flames—peats glowed softly. Gently. Even she knew that.

But then they *were* smoldering gently again and all was still.

Just as it had been.

Mara swallowed, wondered whether she'd fallen asleep without knowing it and maybe just wakened from a nightmare.

Several of the little silver bowls of sacred water were now strewn across the floor, their contents seeping into the thick Turkish carpet—proof enough that the tempest had been real.

At least as real as the ghostly Highlander who'd sent it.

She breathed deep. It *had* to be him. Since he'd let

the wind do his dirty work, maybe her precautions were working. At least enough to keep him from manifesting.

Exactly what she'd hoped to achieve. Much as a tiny part of her would miss him.

Being ravished by an honest-to-goodness medieval knight might be straight out of her fantasies, but she'd rather he'd come to her as a time traveler than an apparition. Ghosts just weren't on her agenda. Hot or not, he'd have to be banished.

It was time for Prudentia's secret weapon.

Her heart thundering, she scrambled off the bed and retrieved a bundle of dried sage from behind the row of mirrors on the mantelpiece.

"Away with you," she vowed, speaking the words the cook had taught her. Then she touched a match to the herbs. They caught flame at once, sending a plume of acrid fumes straight into her face, burning her eyes.

"Begone!" she warned, her tone sending Ben under the bed. Mara frowned after him, swiped a hand across her streaming eyes. "See what troubles you cause, Sir Alex! Scaring a poor aging dog. Go back to Dimbleby's and haunt some other stick of furniture! Leave Ben and me alone."

She began choking, but kept moving around the room, waving the burning sage as she went. Soon, noxious smoke thickened the air. A reeking cloud so dense she wouldn't be able to see the bastard if he manifested right in front of her.

"Damn," she gasped, her throat on fire.

Ben whimpered beneath the bed.

"Okay, I'll stop," she reassured him, shaking the sage to extinguish its burning tip. Her efforts only caused even thicker smoke and sent a rain of ashes to the floor.

"Double damn!" she cried, jumping when some of them landed on her foot.

Desperate, she grabbed a vase of pink delphiniums, tossing the flowers onto the bed and plunging the burning sage into the water. Prudentia's ghost-proofing weapon extraordinaire went out with a last puff of smoke and a fizzle.

Then all was quiet.

Except for the roar of Mara's blood in her ears and peals of rich, male laughter coming from outside the windows.

His laughter.

She'd know it anywhere.

Even among a thousand laughing mirth-filled men. And the implication made her heart stop.

No, her heart was racing. Pounding with giddy relief that she hadn't banished him.

Worse, mirth started building in her own chest, and only her aching throat kept her from laughing with him. *Alex,* she'd called him, the realization hitting her like a fist in the gut. And that, too, was reason to laugh.

But for very pathetic reasons.

Reasons underscored by the sudden silence from the wall walk.

Hottie Scottie was gone.

And much as she'd like to, she couldn't go chasing after him.

"Oh, Ben, what am I going to do?" she whispered, watching the dog shuffle back to his place on the hearth rug.

Knowing there was nothing she *could* do, she sank onto the now-damp bed and looked around at the shambles of her ghost-busting efforts. The yards of tartan everywhere made the room look like a fabric warehouse run by Scotophiles. Enough candles, crosses, and rowan were scattered about to fill an ancient Celtic church.

Not to mention the mirrors and other touches.

Groaning, she pulled a few crushed delphiniums from beneath her and pitched them to the floor. Not one to wallow in self-pity, she tried to look on the bright side.

At least no one could see her. Heaven help her if they could.

They'd think she'd gone stark raving mad.

But then maybe she had.

Why else would she have let herself fall in love with a ghost?

It was the tartan that vexed him.

And he was still reeling from the shock. Alex shuddered, only half aware of the thick gray mist curling around him. In his mind he still saw the Thistle Room. How he'd stood on the parapet wall walk, unable to do aught but gape.

One look into the plaid-draped room, and he'd forgotten every shred of remorse he'd felt for bedeviling the lass these last few days. Something he'd done for her own good, hoping she'd finally break and leave Ravenscraig.

Resume her work with her Exclusive Excursions and journey to some far-flung corner of the world where she'd forget him.

Especially that they'd kissed.

Or how close he'd come to taking her right there on the sun-warmed grass above the seal colony. He groaned, the memory squeezing his heart. Shaming him. He was a lust-blinded fool, worse by far than Hardwick, for he'd allowed the wench to sneak past his defenses.

Guidsakes—even now he was hard for her. Hot, throbbing, and almost splitting with need.

He blew out a furious breath, rammed a hand through his hair. "Hell's fire and botheration," he seethed, knowing himself lost.

And most damning of all, his burning desire to bury himself inside her was only half of what pained him.

The far greater agony was remembering their wild ride across the cliffs. How sweet and right she'd felt in his arms, nestled so intimately between his thighs. How her gasps of delight and laughter had warmed him, for that short space in time, even making him feel real again.

Those feelings, too, were reasons he'd tried so hard to make her nights miserable.

So she'd leave before her attachment to him strengthened. And before she could realize how desperately he wanted and needed her. Guess how just hearing her call him Alex had nearly brought him to his knees.

Before he caused her the kind of anguish he was now suffering.

Instead she'd stayed, armoring herself with her work and making it her business to lure the saints only knew how many MacDougalls to Ravenscraig, coaxing promises from each one that they'd participate in One Cairn Village.

Or at least be present for the great unveiling of her MacDougall memorial cairn.

A foul and benighted undertaking that filled him with bile. God's blood, he couldn't even walk across the building site without his guts turning inside out. But a dream that lit her eyes almost as much as they'd shone that bright blue day on the cliffs.

Only then, *he'd* put that sparkle there. Until their time together had soured, of course.

Scowling, he clamped his hands around his sword belt, tried to cool his seething temper.

Why couldn't she have been reasonable? Lost her nerve and fled in terror as every other MacDougall bed stealer down the centuries had done?

Instead she pursued her plans with all the zeal and determination he never would have credited a lass of her sorry race.

When she wasn't busying herself turning Ravenscraig into a haven for displaced, Highland-hungry MacDougalls, she'd dragged so many lengths of the wretched clan's tartan into her bedchamber, he doubted he'd be able to wipe the sight from his memory for another hundred years.

Mayhap even longer.

"Devil's minx," he swore, frowning into the chill mist and wondering if he'd ever be warm again. "Fiend take the MacDougalls! *All* of them."

Especially her, with all her lush curves and dips, her silky-smooth skin and hair of flame. The bits of black lace she'd donned just to rouse him.

And she had.

"Och, aye," he admitted, clenching his fingers on his belt. He grimaced at the sharp ache in his loins, the viselike tightness in his chest.

The lass could count herself fortunate he'd retreated to this between-the-realms place rather than remain on her wall walk.

He wouldn't have been able to control himself much longer had he stayed.

How dare she outfit his bed in MacDougall tartan? Sakes, the insult was so great, she might as well have slapped him in the face.

It wasn't just that she'd turned his bed into a MacDougall shrine. The brazen wench had festooned her entire bedchamber in the abominable colors.

"She's daft, too," he muttered, stalking through a particularly dense patch of fog. "Daft and dimwitted."

Why else would she have filled the room with those other ridiculous trappings?

"Clusters of garlic and rowan on the windows!" He kicked at a swirl of mist, took some satisfaction in the way it eddied and rippled—almost as if fleeing his wrath.

He hooted a dark laugh and strode on. "Mirrors

and silver bowls on the mantelpiece. Crosses on the walls."

Did she think he was a vampire?

A warlock?

If so, she needed her head washed. He was naught but a lost soul. A good and honorable man in his day, trapped in time and place through no fault of his own. Sometimes he wandered about in this mysterious gray place and other times he roamed the earth world of the current present day.

That last whenever his bed happened to fall into the bloodstained hands of a MacDougall.

He could also visit other long-ago centuries if he chose to do so. Only his own time was lost to him.

But a fiend, he was not.

Simply a misbegotten result of MacDougall treachery and their charmed brooch.

The devil-damned Bloodstone of Dalriada.

A brooch he *hadn't* stolen. He'd barely closed his fingers around the bloody thing before Colin and his henchmen had loosed their arrows into him.

"Bloody MacDougall bastards," he snarled, and the swirling mists darkened, turning from milky gray to angriest black, the very air crackling with his anger.

"Spawns of Satan," he swore, girding himself against the onslaught.

But it was too late.

Already jagged bolts of lightning streaked past him and thunder boomed, each ear-splitting clap shaking the cushiony fog at his feet and surrounding him with the sharp stench of sulfur.

A warning.

An unmistakable reminder of the foolhardiness of his wrath.

Fury still coursed through him, but he grit his teeth and forced himself to clear his mind. "Damnation," he breathed, pressing his fingers against his temples until the darkness lightened and the thunder was no more.

He lowered his hands, cursing himself for his folly. How could he have forgotten that particular annoyance of this gray resting-place for the damned?

This land of shadows filled with mist but also quiet. Blessed peace, leastways for those who didn't overstep themselves as he just had and likely as he still was, for he couldn't stop frowning.

And he hadn't come here to scowl.

He'd only hoped to find solitude. Soothing calm to wrap round his ragged edges, make him forget. Trouble was, he couldn't forget, and the hotter his anger blazed, the more he risked another such thunderous visitation.

Only next time the lightning bolts wouldn't merely shoot past him.

They'd skewer him, leaving him with scorched, itchy scars that sometimes needed a half-century to heal.

That, he knew from sad experience.

Just as he knew he was not returning to *her* bedchamber.

He would go where he should have gone days ago. Then, when Hardwick suggested it. But better late than not at all.

His amorous friend would no doubt still be there, enjoying days of revel and feasting. Even if he weren't, Bran of Barra would welcome him.

And without thunder and lightning bolts. The offensive reek of sulfur.

Far from it, every need and wish a man could have was met on the Isle of Barra—and so often as desired.

There were reasons Hardwick spent so much time there.

And now Alex would visit Bran MacNeil as well. His decision made, he smiled. Even the hot throbbing in his loins no longer troubled him. Soon he would slake that fire, make himself whole again.

As whole as a ghost could be, he amended, his excitement mounting.

Eager to be on his way, he folded his arms across his chest and concentrated on garbing himself suitably for a visit to the wild isleman's notorious keep. As if by a wizard's hand, his finest Highland raiments replaced the simple hose and tunic he favored. Satisfied, he carefully adjusted the voluminous great plaid and gleaming mail he wore beneath, then went great-strided to where the billowy gray mists appeared less dense.

A slow smile curving his lips, he whipped out his sword with a flourish and brandished it in a windmilling motion, slicing at the shifting curtains of fog until he'd cleared a gap large enough to peer through.

Sheathing his blade, he waited as the mists around the opening drew back even more and the formidable square keep and curtained walls of Bran MacNeil's isle-girt holding came into view.

Bran's banner flew from the highest tower, its bold colors whipping proudly in the wind. Not that Alex had expected the randy Hebridean chieftain to be elsewhere. Scores of galleys lay at anchor in the little bay that surrounded the formidable castle rock, their tall masts, slanting spars, and upthrusting prows piercing the sea mist and indicating that Hardwick was far from Bran's only guest.

Indeed, a closer look showed swarms of fierce-miened, plaid-wrapped islesmen moving about the bailey, each one a-glitter with flashy Celtic jewelry, a well-made, sultry-eyed woman of ease clinging to each arm. The bushy-bearded Hebrideans were also hung about with more steel than Alex had seen in centuries, but he knew, at Bran of Barra's, such displays were only for show.

Drink, women, and carousing were the reasons men flocked to Bran's keep.

As always, the hall door stood wide, the milling throng already jostling for entry. Many of the revelers were scantily clad women, each one procured for the pleasure of Bran's guests. Skirling female laughter and bawdy song filled the hall's smoky, torchlit depths, where visitors celebrated a raucous feast already well in progress.

A feast some might call an orgy.

Alex snorted. He'd say *many orgies.*

Debauchery at its finest.

And exactly what he needed. So he squelched any

remaining doubts about participating in such depravity, closed his eyes, and willed himself to manifest in Bran's bailey.

At once, the mists rushed him, the impact almost squeezing the breath from his lungs as the air contracted and spun around him. A whirling vortex spiraling him ever downward until the din of Bran's hall was no longer faint but a deafening cacophony.

Alex squeezed his eyes tighter, clenching his fists and concentrating.

Then he was there, solid ground beneath his feet, his ears immediately assailed by the lusty cries of several women deep in the throes of ecstasy.

"O-o-oh, aye," he breathed, smiling as his loins clenched in appreciation, his shaft swelling and lengthening even before he opened his eyes.

He wasted no time, striding right into the fray, his eyes peeled for a pleasing wench. Preferably half-naked, big-breasted and with fine plump thighs ready to spread wide.

A lusty bawd, well versed in every manner of lasciviousness.

Above all, skilled enough to wipe Mara MacDougall from his mind.

Once and for all time.

Chapter 10

A rank stench hit Alex full force the moment he materialized in the middle of Bran of Barra's bailey. Drying seaweed and dead fish, fresh and steaming animal dung, and the unmistakable ripeness of too many hairy, unwashed bodies—the smells assailed him from all sides, taking his breath and instantly deflating his reason for being there.

He stood frozen, trying not to inhale.

Saints alive, even his eyes stung.

He blinked and started toward the keep, taking great care where he stepped.

How could he have forgotten the foulness of the early fifteenth century? Or, were he honest, his own as well? A good hundred years before Bran's time, his world had reeked just as powerfully. Truth be told, some baileys in his day had smelled far worse than Bran's.

Besides, he hadn't come here to be kind to his nose!

His purpose was to tend certain other matters—as a sudden burst of high-pitched female laughter reminded him. Glancing round, he spied the source, a cluster of stout young serving wenches filling water jugs at the castle well.

One had an exceptionally comely bosom, its creamy fullness spilling from her low-cut bodice. Whether deliberate or not, the top crests of her nipples could be plainly seen. Better yet, the crinkly pink flesh puckered even more under his appreciative perusal.

"Lasses," he greeted them, glad he'd dressed in his finest Highland trappings.

"Sir," they purred in unison, their hot eyes and bold stares definitely affecting him.

"We have more in need of filling than these ewers," the large-bosomed lass cooed, eyeing him suggestively as she raised her jug in his direction. "Mayhap you'd care to be of service to us?"

Alex flashed her a grin, the bailey's stench no longer half so bothersome. "Perhaps later, sweetness. Just now I'm for speaking to your laird and a friend, Sir Hardwin de Studley."

"Bran's feasting in the hall," another of the wenches supplied, "and Hardwick's *in* . . . well, you'll see when you find him!"

"To be sure," Alex agreed, not missing her meaning.

Nor the pleasing heat her bold words sent spilling into his loins. Already, he was stirring again. Not with the raging granitelike hardness that had driven him here, but with a nice tingling heaviness that was making his shaft twitch in a most enjoyable manner.

He sighed deeply. Aye, most enjoyable.

There was much to be said for a semiaroused state. Prolonged pleasure led to the most satisfying releases. And a shaft only somewhat hardened and still swinging free between a man's legs could prove a delicious torment.

Especially if that man happened to be wearing a great plaid with naught but his saffron shirt and Highland pride beneath.

Savoring that bliss now, Alex let his gaze rest on the first maid's welling bosom. In particular, upon the pink crescents of her almost fully displayed nipples.

"Aye, Hardwick will be deeply into whate'er he's found to please him," he said, the suggestiveness of his own words making his shaft stiffen a bit more. "Mayhap after I've seen him, I'll come back to you? Perhaps help fill your . . . *ewer*?"

"Just ask for Maili if you canna find me," the lass purred, letting her gaze roam over him. "I am e'er in need of your kind of assistance."

Then, clearly wishing to heighten her appeal, she set down her water jug and lifted her hands to her unbound hair, the movement causing the hardened peaks of her nipples to pop into view. Large nipples, beautifully taut, and thrusting right at him, begging attention.

Alex groaned. His tarse swelled and stretched even more. "Lass, you take my breath away," he said, and took a step toward her, his wish to announce himself to Bran before he partook of the Islesman's *hospitality* fast losing consequence.

As he neared the maid, the sun slipped out of the clouds, its slanting light falling across her magnificent breasts, shining on her hair. A glorious mane vaguely the same color as Mara MacDougall's.

Curling tresses tumbling freely over her shoulders in a wild cascade of gleaming bronze, each bright strand suddenly seeming to glare accusingly at him.

Alex stopped short, his *need* receding again.

He stifled a frown. Nothing was going as he'd planned.

Clearly misinterpreting his hesitation, the lass began fumbling with the laces of her bodice, untying them until the material gaped wide and her large breasts sprang free. "Look well on what will be waiting for you," she called, plumping them. "And remember my name is Maili. Dinna you let Lord Bran offer you another!"

Then she smiled—a crooked, yellow-toothed smile.

Alex's own smile froze, the lingering heat in his groin chilling.

He swallowed, forcing himself to give the lass a friendly nod and a wink. Feeling guilty, he plucked a clutch of wild flowers out of the air, offering them to her with all the knightly aplomb he could muster.

"You would be any man's undoing," he said, knowing she'd understand the words in a way that would please her.

Then he turned away and strode off in the direction of the keep, hoping his revulsion didn't show on his face. Saints, he suspected he'd even seen lice crawling in her hair! How could he have thought, even for a moment, that the lass at the well resembled *her*?

His stomach turned upside down that he'd even considered the possibility. Frowning, he quickened his pace, skirting a huge pile of black-glistening winkle shells, empty and stinking, only to trip over a length of crumpled and twisted plaid.

MacDougall plaid, and with the lady herself draped across it!

"A God's name!" Alex's heart slammed against his ribs. He stared down at her, his eyes seeing her, his mind screaming that he couldn't be.

Unless she was dream walking—sleeping soundly in her bed and dreaming so deeply that the power of her slumbering thoughts allowed them to materialize.

Which meant she was dreaming of him.

He swallowed, his heart thundering so loudly, he could scarce hear himself think. Nor could he move. Not with her sprawled beneath him again.

Only this time she was nearly naked, wearing only that wee bit of see-through black lace. Even worse, she was lying on her back.

Lying on her back and staring up at him, her gaze riveted on that dangling part of him that the folds of his great plaid did nothing whatsoever to hide.

"Sweet lass, if you keep looking up at me that way, I willna be responsible for what I do," he warned, knowing she couldn't hear him.

But taunt him she could, dream-spun illusion or

no. She writhed on the plaid and made soft little mewling noises, her every sinuous move giving him brief, tantalizing glimpses of her charms. The rise and fall of her passion-flushed breasts, a quick flash of nipple. Then, saints help him, thanks to a lift of her hips, the dark triangle of her feminine curls, a maddening temptation almost too sweet to look upon.

He did, though, and his entire body tightened in fierce, urgent need. She shifted her legs, her body arcing, showing him even more. The narrow strip of black lace covering her hid nothing. Flimsy and sheer, it only revealed her darkest secrets and the dampness gathered there, let the rich musk of her arousal drift up to intoxicate him.

"Mara." He looked down at her, his heart falling wide on the sweetness of her name. His control shattered, the whole, hard length of him screaming for release. "I must have you—now, this moment," he vowed, almost exploding when she reached for him, curled her fingers around his hot, aching shaft and began stroking.

She closed her eyes in ecstasy, arching her back as the sweetest sigh escaped her lips. Her straining breasts flushed a deeper red and her fingers clenched tighter, gliding up and down, up and down, furiously milking him—and he could not feel a thing!

"No-o-o!" he roared, damning the veil of her dream that cheated him of her touch. "I-canna-bear-it," he hissed through his teeth, hot anguish sweeping him.

And then she was gone, leaving only a length of ragged and soiled tartan. MacNeil of Barra tartan, and quickly snatched up by a harried-looking laundress as she hastened past, a bundle of linens and plaids clutched to her breast.

"My pardon," she called over her shoulder as she scurried away, the mud-stained tartan trailing behind her.

Alex stared after her, too stunned to move. Gradually, his heart stopped racing and he dragged a shaky hand across his brow, not at all surprised to find it damp.

"Saints, Maria, and Joseph," he breathed, grateful that if he had to succumb to such a public display of rutting fever, it had happened in Bran of Barra's bailey, where nary a soul seemed to have noticed.

Or would have cared if they did.

Even so, he dragged a hand down over his face, heaved a ragged sigh. Ne'er had a wench so consumed him. Had she not been a dream figment, he would have fallen to his knees and taken her on the cold and muddied cobbles.

And more than once! No matter who might've looked on.

Only she mattered.

Having her.

She'd worked her witchy magic on him in other ways, too. He pinched the bridge of his nose, amazement making his head pound. Had he really thought of her as dreaming in *her* bed?

Not his, but hers?

Aye, he had. And he supposed that, come the night, the moon would now fall from the sky.

But he hadn't come this far not to escape her, and he would.

Even if it meant bedding every wench Bran had to offer.

To that end, he marched long-strided across the bailey, making for a tall stone building with a high sloping roof. Bran's keep. Within its stout walls nestled the Hebridean chieftain's far-famed hall-of-all-pleasures.

The sun glinted off the keep's narrow round-topped windows and Alex stepped faster, shouldering aside a few lurching drunkards as he crossed the drawbridge, then mounted the steep stone ramp to a door set high into the thickness of the wall.

Massive and iron studded, the door yawned wide, leaving entry into Bran's private realm unchallenged. Alex paused on the threshold, adjusting his plaid. Then he drew back his shoulders and stepped inside.

He gasped despite himself, ill prepared for the sight before him.

Seldom had he seen such a throng. And the din was deafening. Shouting, jostling men were everywhere, crowding the trestle tables and milling about the aisles. A full score of blowsy, bare-breasted women preened near the huge open hearth, some singing bawdy songs, others airing their skirts—much to the delight of their bearded, ale-swilling audience.

Laughter and lewd encouragement filled the air, and with the desired result!

A muscle twitched in Alex's jaw. And elsewhere. Such bold displays of naked female flesh were more than . . . entertaining. But just as when he'd made himself visible in the bailey, unsavory smells rushed him from all sides.

He steeled himself, tried not to rumple his nose. Offending his host was the last thing he wanted to do.

But the floor rushes were matted and soiled and obviously hadn't been changed in more centuries than he cared to guess. Worse, they squished beneath his feet, and the stench rising up with every step was almost powerful enough to knock him out.

His stomach began lurching, and the thick, smoky air near choked him. The fresh, clean air of his Mara's world flashed through his mind and he swallowed a curse, disguising it behind a cough. Already heads were swiveling, curious glances flying his way.

Not that he cared who gawked at him.

Nor did it matter if he did, for it was too late to leave.

He'd been seen.

His host was sitting in one of the window embrasures, a half-clad wanton on his knee. "Lo! Do my own eyes deceive me?" the Hebridean chieftain boomed, springing to his feet. "Is that yourself? Alex Douglas? Come to grace my hall?"

Narrowing bloodshot eyes, he snatched an ale from a passing reveler, drained it, and then tossed the empty tankard onto the floor rushes. "Lucifer's knees, it *is* you!" he bellowed, slapping his thigh. "On my soul—this is a right surprise!"

Then he was hurrying forward, all laughter and charm, his bushy-bearded face splitting in a grin. "Welcome, welcome!" he cried, grabbing Alex's shoulders, shaking him. "My house is yours. And anything in it that might catch your fancy!"

He released Alex, gave him a hearty cuff on the arm. "So many of my *fancies* as you desire."

"And one for you." Alex reached inside his plaid, produced a quickly fashioned shoulder belt of finest leather, magnificently tooled. "For your fine welcome."

Bran of Barra grinned. "Leave it to a Douglas to come bearing gifts worthy of a king," he said, unrolling the belt with obvious delight. "I say thank you!"

Alex opened his mouth, then shut it on another faked cough. He'd been about to deny his reason for being there, but before he could form the words, *her* face rose up out of nowhere, her amber eyes staring at him from the shadows.

Staring coldly. Angrily.

Heat shot around Alex's chest, clamping like a vise.

He swallowed, feeling like a wee laddie caught doing what he ought not. "You are as generous as I remember," he said to Bran, forcing the expected gallantry. "The splendor of your hospitality is staggering—"

"Heigho!" Bran cut him off, jammed meaty hands on his hips. "So you *have* come to join in our merry-making? Say it is so!" He rocked back on his heels, looking pleased. "Does this mean you've finally chased the last MacDougall from that accursed bed of yours?"

Alex flushed. He slid a glance in a certain direction, relief washing over him when he saw that his lady's image was gone.

"That bed and the MacDougalls still plague me,"

he admitted, opting for the truth—if not the whole of it. "Mightily of late. So I came to seek diversion, aye."

Bran cocked a bushy red brow. "The sort such as yon Hardwick favors?" he teased, jerking his head toward the hall's raised dais.

Alex took a deep breath, then looked down the hall, knowing what he'd see. And he wasn't disappointed.

Hardwick lay sprawled the length of a cushioned trestle bench meant for honored guests. A buxom wench with flowing hair the color of midnight sat astride him, the rhythmic rocking of her shapely hips leaving no doubts as to the type of diversion she was bestowing.

Alex's loins quickened at the sight, the whore's lusty cries sending heat all through him. His shaft swelled at once, its hard length tenting his plaid.

But it was *her* he needed.

Mara bloody MacDougall. Herself, with her hot temper and affection for old dogs and bandy-legged graybeards.

Not some Hebridean light-skirt whose face he'd forget before he pulled out of her.

Something inside Alex caught fire, a burning, ripping pain deep inside his chest. But he ignored it, focused only on the throbbing at his groin.

"No need to answer, my friend," Bran was saying. He threw an arm round Alex's shoulders. "It's plain to see you came for the same reason Hardwick fair lives here!"

Beaming, he propelled Alex deeper into the hall.

"I have just the wench for you—Galiana. She'll see to your wants and satisfy your every wish, even fetch you a fresh maid after you're done with her if you so desire."

Alex nodded, his throat suddenly as tight as his man-parts.

Now that the time to break his centuries-long abstinence was finally upon him, he couldn't shake the nagging fear that no other female but Mara would suit him.

Unthinkable if he ended up like Hardwick—sporting a ragingly hard lance yet unable to find release.

He pushed the thought aside, refused to consider it. He could thrust his sword wherever he chose, and he'd take great satisfaction in the task!

After he'd recovered from Galiana, he'd work his way through a whole score of Bran's *fancies,* savoring them all until every last drop of desire drained from his sated body.

Only then would he risk returning to Ravenscraig and facing Mara MacDougall. See her banished in earnest.

Before either of them tore an even greater hole in their hearts.

"Well?" Bran's deep voice rang out beside him. "Is she not all I promised?"

Alex started. He hadn't even realized they'd reached the dais.

But they had, and Bran stood grinning at him, his hand on the shoulder of a well-made woman draped in scarlet and gold. The Islesman lifted the woman's heavy flaxen braid, bringing it to his lips for a smacking kiss.

"Behold Galiana," he said, his barrel chest swelling. "She carries the blood of Norse kings, is unequalled in her skill. I would not offer her to just anyone."

Alex swallowed, unable to speak. The woman *was* desirable, and . . . challenging.

She breathed sensuality of the darkest, most elemental sort. She was generously made and bold of eye; just looking at her would send lust beating through any man. Already, Alex's mouth had gone dry and he could feel love juices gathering on the knob of his shaft.

But there was an old dog casting about in the rushes not far from where the beauty sat—an old dog that looked strikingly like Ben and that stopped its snuffling to fix Alex with an unblinking stare.

An unblinking, hostile stare.

"Well, my friend? Will she do?" Bran was eyeing him, one brow arcing. "If not, there's plenty more to choose from. Red ones, black ones, dusky wenches from afar. Even a maid or two, if you prefer them untried."

Alex shook his head, waved a dismissive hand. He'd seen enough to know the woman would suit. Best of all, her hair was white-blond and not burnished bronze. And her frank gaze was the clear blue of a spring sky, not the amber-gold of sun-warmed honey.

"Aye, she will serve me well," he said, knowing she would. Wishing the admission didn't make him feel like the world's greatest lout.

Doing his best to ignore the old dog's glare.

Instead, he kept his attention on the woman, let her bounty make him forget. The sensual curve of her lips sent a jolt of heat to his groin, and he could even see her nipples through the transparency of her gown, the dark vee of her nether curls. Her creamy white skin looked silky-smooth, her curves lush enough for a man to drown in.

"Lady Galiana—I welcome your company," he said, the words thick, but honest.

He needed her. Just not for the reasons she surely assumed.

She appeared pleased as she nodded, the slight flaring of her eyes revealing her consent, her eagerness to share pleasure with him.

"Then, so be it!" Bran announced, pulling the woman to her feet. He patted her ample bottom, gave her an affectionate shove forward. "Take my friend Alex to the finest chamber available and see to his comfort."

Then the big Islesman turned away, dropping his bulk into his laird's chair and yanking another beauty onto his lap, one hand already sliding inside the maid's low-cut bodice.

"Lord Bran knows how much a woman enjoys a man's touch," Lady Galiana commented, stepping close to rub her own full breasts against Alex as she slipped her hand through his arm. "I would know if everything I've heard about the *touch* of Douglas men bears truth?"

"Then show me to my chamber," Alex returned, "and I shall endeavor not to disappoint you."

"O-o-oh, I can already see that you will not," she purred, smoothing her hand across his groin as they exited the hall. She leaned into him, letting her fingers cup and measure his fullness, the thick, steely length of his need. "You are a man like no other."

Alex doubted that and almost told her so, but her skilled ministrations felt too good for him to care. Exaggerated praise or nay, so long as her fingers spun such magic, her cooed words mattered little.

The lass clearly knew her way with men and, already, her roving fingers were chasing Mara MacDougall from his mind.

Blinding him, too, for at the end of a dank-smelling and poorly lit corridor, just before the entrance to an even darker-looking stairwell, they collided with a solid object.

A tall, broad-shouldered object with raven black hair and a tented plaid to rival Alex's own.

"By the Rood!" Alex swore, blinking at Hardwick.

"Holy Saints!" Hardwick swore back, his eyes almost bugging from his head. "What are you doing here?"

"That should be obvious." Alex glared at him. "Or is your memory so short that you do not recall suggesting I pay Bran a visit? For the fine Hebridean air and other . . . delights?"

Hardwick frowned. "I but jested, as I thought you knew," he said, his gaze flicking to where Lady Galiana's fingers moved with deliberate slowness over Alex's thrusting arousal. "You have no reason to visit this haven of whores. The only female you need awaits you at Ravenscraig."

Alex stiffened. "I saw you earlier, you craven," he said, putting back his shoulders. "It would seem you don't mind dipping your own wick in Bran's offerings."

Hardwick's mouth twitched. "Perhaps because my heart is not given."

"And you think mine is?"

"Think?" Hardwick snorted. "I know it is. I have seen the way you look at her."

"She is a MacDougall."

"You love her."

Alex clenched his fists, something inside him twisting. "I am a ghost—if you've forgotten!"

Hardwick laughed. "She does not care."

Alex could feel the back of his neck flaming. "I love no woman, you fool."

" 'Tis you who are the fool," Hardwick shot back, sending another disapproving glance to Alex's crotch, where Lady Galiana continued her wily assault. "If you do not hie yourself back where you belong, I shall be tempted to challenge you to meet me in the lists."

This time Alex snorted. "Take yourself back to the hall and seek amusement where you will. I shall do the same—with or without your approval."

"I was but speaking as your friend," Hardwick said, sounding offended. "You are incapable of seeing into your heart."

"I have no need to do so."

Hardwick shook his head. "You err, my friend. No man's need is greater."

"I'd be tending those needs about now—had I not

had the misfortune of running into you," Alex snapped, but Hardwick was already gone.

And Lady Galiana was reaching for him, pulling him with her up the curving stairs.

Unfortunately, each upward step hammered Hardwick's words deeper into Alex's mind. The meddling bravo had achieved at least one of his goals.

He'd ruined Alex's evening.

As for his other intentions, he'd wasted his breath. Alex didn't need to search his heart. He already knew it.

Only too well.

He did love Mara MacDougall.

May the saints have mercy on him.

Tick, tick, tick.

Mara tossed in her bed, punched her pillow a few times, then pulled another one over her head. When had her alarm clock turned so ridiculously loud? *Tick, tick, tick.* It sounded more like Big Ben than a travel-sized number no bigger than the palm of her hand.

"O-o-oh, stop," she pleaded, rolling onto her stomach. She frowned into her pillow. Why didn't she just admit it? She knew exactly when the ticking had become so grating.

The moment Hottie Scottie had stepped into her dreams and loomed above her, resplendent in his great plaid, a huge Celtic brooch gleaming at his shoulder, his Highland *magnificence* dangling right above her!

She drew in a sharp breath, dug her fingers into the pillow. In truth, he hadn't dangled for long.

It had taken little more than her startled gasp for him to run full stretch. And even less for the sight to make her all hot and shivery. The sheer eroticism of watching him fill and lengthen had undone her, filled her with a desperate, streaming need she doubted would ever be quenched.

She was *still* damp.

Still aching.

On fire and tingling, just as she'd been when she'd reached for him, closing her fingers around his hardness, reveling in how hot, silky, and hard he felt as she stroked him, how she'd struggled to hear only his husky moans of pleasure—and not the incessant ticking of her travel alarm.

But the tiny clock had won, its annoying clatter overpowering her sexy Highlander's purred encouragement until she heard nothing else and even the hard, male length of him was suddenly no more than a thick fold of MacDougall plaid clutched tight in her hand.

A very thick fold.

Mara groaned, desire winding tight inside her, her frustration almost devouring.

"Damn," she cried, blinking back the stinging heat wetting her lashes.

They'd come so close!

She'd felt him in her hand, breathed in the rich muskiness of his clean male scent. One, two more strokes and she just knew he would have whipped aside his plaid and yanked her up against him, taking her with all the fierce, urgent passion she needed.

"No-o-o," she choked, places deep inside her hurting so badly she could hardly breathe. She bit back a sob, willed her body to stop burning for him, tried to ignore the maddening blaze enflaming her. The shattering of her heart.

Instead, the infernal ticking grew louder by the second, each metallic *click* making her crazy. Fisting her hands on the pillow, she lifted her head and glared at the offending timepiece.

Two-thirty in the morning.

She hadn't slept a wink.

Not that anyone could blame her. Sitting up, she crammed a few pillows behind her and surveyed the room, finding it worse than she'd feared. The night shadows didn't begin to hide the damage. The Thistle Room looked ransacked, demolished by a lunatic.

A lunatic named Mara McDougall.

She snorted, swiped a hand across her cheek. Who but a deranged person would listen to the advice of a crackpot like Prudentia and turn an exquisite tower room fit for a princess into something best described as a haven for aura readers and other such New Age fruitloops?

It was pathetic.

Her entire life was pathetic.

Most pathetic of all was her raging frustration in losing her dream. Mercy, even in imaginary form, Hottie Scottie throbbed with more sensual heat than any flesh-and-blood man she'd ever encountered.

And she wanted him.

Ghostie or no. She didn't care.

If she could just have his kisses, touch him without having him vanish, she'd die a happy woman. He didn't even have to really take her if he couldn't. Just sitting before a cozy fire with him, enjoying his smile and listening to his husky-deep voice would be enough.

If she could just have him.

But she doubted she could, and the unfairness of it gutted her.

All her life, every supposedly good thing had always come with a catch. Every bowl of soup, a fly in it. And everything she'd wanted always seemed to skip along ahead of her, just inches out of her grasp.

Especially love.

"Love," she scoffed, snatching a crushed delphinium from beside her pillow and throwing it toward the fireplace. It sailed in a promising arc but didn't make it past the end of the bed. Like so much in her life, it missed its mark, and landed with a damp splat against one of the bedposts before sliding down to settle in a wilted clump on the bed coverings.

No, a stinking clump.

Mara wrinkled her nose. No wonder she hadn't been able to sleep. The room smelled awful. Damp wool, dead flowers, old incense, and the pungent scent of burned sage contaminated the entire bedchamber.

American heiress dies of asphyxiation after inhaling antighost-charm fumes in Scottish castle.

Hah! Such a headline would set the tongues wagging. Back home and beyond. Puffing a curl off her brow, she imagined the repercussions.

The sniggers and scandal.

The Cairn Avenue shrew's beady eyes glinting

with I-knew-she'd-come-to-no-good satisfaction. Her father's sorrow and mortification. Kindly old Solicitor Combe overcome with guilt and remorse. Antighost fumes, indeed. Her lips twitched in an almost-smile.

Thank goodness.

If she could see humor in her plight, she hadn't completely lost it.

Feeling somewhat better, she slipped from the bed, swirled a plaid around her shoulders, and crossed the room. A swift yank was all she needed to pull aside the newly hung MacDougall drapes and allow silvery light to flood inside.

Moon glow alone wouldn't dispel the stench of her foolish attempts at exorcism.

She needed fresh air.

Lots of it.

And not just for her room. More than anything, she needed to clear her head.

"That, and banish Hottie Scottie and his Highland *magnificence* from my mind," she muttered, opening the door to the wall walk and stepping outside.

She went straight to the crenellated wall and leaned against one of the merlons, lacing her hands on the cold stone and staring out across the firth. The isle-strewn waters looked almost translucent in the clear silver light, and a pale half-moon glimmered in the pearl-hued sky.

She shivered and drew the plaid closer around her shoulders. She would not imagine a tall, splendidly built Highlander standing beside her, sharing the night's magic.

And it *was* a magical night.

She could feel it in her bones, in the way the soft air hummed with . . . romance.

Simmer dim, the Highland Scots called these nights of luminous half-light, and the beauty of it up close and shimmering all around her was almost more than she could bear.

Leastways tonight.

But she'd be damned if she'd flee the battlements as easily as she'd run from her bed. Not even if her bare feet froze to the icy stone flags of the wall walk.

What was a little cold when she might never again see the man she'd come to love so deeply?

If you could call a ghost a man.

Mara lifted her face to the wind. She would not bemoan her fate. Sir Alexander Douglas was more than enough man for her. All she needed. The only man who'd ever truly stolen her breath, filled her with impossible dreams, or made her heart weep with wanting him.

But he wasn't here now, and there wasn't much she could do about it, so she stared down at the dim, shining water, the odd green glow at the base of the cliffs.

Odd green glow?

She blinked, looked closer. The glow was definitely green and strange. And, worse, it was pulsing.

She opened her mouth to gasp, but nothing came out. Instead, she clutched a hand to her throat, her eyes widening as the faint glow grew into a whirling shaft of iridescent green light.

Radiant, otherworldly light moving slowly down

the shingled strand. And coming in her direction! Too stunned to move, she watched in fascination as the glowing column took the shape of a woman.

A beautiful woman, lit from within.

And as transparent as glass. Mara could see the curve of the shore right through her.

The woman was a ghost. And with the realization came a horrible suspicion.

Maybe Hottie Scottie had sent her?

Mara's heart stopped. She couldn't believe it. That she'd been standing out here, shivering in the cold, aching for him and wishing him back, only to have him send a see-through female friend to do what he hadn't been able to do—scare her away.

No, it couldn't be so.

She refused to believe that. Nor was she going anywhere.

Not tonight. And not in a year. Ravenscraig was hers now, and she had no intention of giving it up.

If the green beauty had other reasons for drifting along Ravenscraig's cliff strand in the middle of the night, perhaps to lay a claim to *her* Highlander, she'd be in for a surprise.

Mara wasn't about to share him.

Whoever the ghostie was, she wasn't giving Mara much of a chance to challenge her, for she'd already disappeared.

Vanishing almost before Mara was even sure she'd seen her. But she had. The trembling in her knees and the pounding of her heart proved it.

Whether the woman was gone now or not.

She'd been there.

"No kidding," Mara gasped, reaction making her mouth dry.

Holding fast to the merlon, she leaned out as far as she dared and stared down at the deserted strand. Nothing but moonlight shone on the water, and no iridescent female shape glided among the rocks.

Everything looked as it should.

And she felt silly.

She took a deep breath and pushed away from the wall, the lure of sleep suddenly overwhelming. As quickly as she could, she sought her bed, pulling the covers to her chin.

A green lady! Had she imagined the whole thing? Perhaps seen the Scottish version of swamp gas?

She didn't know and it didn't really matter.

All she cared about was making Hottie Scottie hers.

The sooner, the better.

Chapter 11

"Does this please you?" Lady Galiana shifted Alex's bare foot in her lap, drawing it closer against the vee of her thighs. "Is the oil warm enough?"

"O-o-oh, aye." Alex leaned his head against the rim of the cloth-lined bathing tub and gave her a slow smile, every inch of him tingling with pleasure. "I am well pleased."

"Say you?" The flaxen-haired beauty locked eyes with him, lifted a brow. "I have not even begun to please you," she purred, massaging more scented oil into his toes.

She held his gaze, pulling gently on each toe. "Good sir, if you think this is pleasing, wait until I massage . . . higher," she said, never breaking her rhythm, her caressing fingers working a sensual magic he'd never dreamed.

Alex swallowed, his world contracting to the wooden bathing tub, the curls of steam rising off the heated water, and the Nordic beauty's tantalizing movements.

Bran hadn't exaggerated her skill.

She was a true Valkyrie; her erotic mastery took his breath and each glide of her fingers across his skin made him feel as if a thousand sweet, soft lips were playing over his foot. All at once.

He shifted in the tub, anticipation spiking inside him. Delicious sensations streaked from his toes to his loins, hardening him. Most encouraging of all, his ache for *her* was receding. Not much, but enough to give him hope. And the little stabs of guilt Hardwick had hurled at him no longer sat quite so deep.

Flickering torchlight gilded the Norsewoman's bountiful curves and he watched her gladly, enjoying how her magnificent breasts rose and fell in time with her ministrations. "Sweet lass, you asked if the oil is warm enough," he said, catching one of her hands and placing a kiss in her palm. "Were it any warmer, I'd melt."

She smiled and dipped a hand in the steaming water, trailed dripping fingers down his chest. "Then perhaps we should move to the bed?" she suggested, her gaze following the path of her fingers as they slid lower.

"You are a well-favored man," she crooned, skimming her fingers over the thick curls at his groin. "It will be a rare pleasure to attend you."

"Soon, lass, soon," Alex breathed, her mention of the word *bed* unleashing another stinging bout of the guilt jabs.

Suppressing them, he closed his eyes, focused on

her hand moving over him. She was stroking him in the same way Mara had stroked him during her dream walk. Then, when she'd reached up beneath his plaid and closed her fingers around him.

But unlike Mara's dream fingers, he could feel Lady Galiana's.

Feel them and imagine they were Mara's.

Which was exactly what he shouldn't be doing.

He frowned, bit back a groan.

He deserved to take his ease. Especially when it had been so long since a woman had touched him intimately. Between the warm water swirling around him and the practiced magic of the Norsewoman's fingers, it was only natural that he'd hardened to bursting.

Glancing up at the raftered ceiling, he drew a sharp breath, closer to the brink than he'd been in centuries.

Then her fingers dipped even lower, playfully dancing over his tightened balls, kneading and caressing them. "You could intoxicate a woman," she breathed, taking his engorged length in another firm grip and stroking.

"Have mercy!" he hissed, almost bucking out of the water.

Damn his soul for being so needy. And damn Mara MacDougall for making him burn with such raging desire that one of Bran of Barra's light-skirts almost had him spilling his seed into the bathwater.

Shame himself like a beardless squire catching his first whiff of a woman.

And it was *her* fault he was so vulnerable. Had

she not enflamed him beyond all reason, he'd be the seducer here. Tireless and masterly, he'd have the Norse beauty and any other of Bran's *fancies* quivering with need and writhing beneath him, screaming their pleasure as he satisfied them one by one.

Perhaps even two at a time!

Once, in the days before Isobel MacDougall, he'd even managed three.

But now he could think only of *her*. And doing so had him about to spill before his aching shaft came even close to the flaxen-haired wench's honeypot.

A sweetness that suddenly held no interest whatsoever for him.

Even repulsed him.

Indeed, just the thought of sinking himself into any female except Mara MacDougall instantly dampened his desire, diminishing his need in a painfully visible manner.

A display even more embarrassing than had he lost control and loosed his seed too soon.

Alex scowled. His head began to pound. "Sakes alive," he ground out, clenching his hands on the rim of the bathing tub, humiliation flashing through him.

He grit his teeth and closed his eyes, unable to meet the Norsewoman's eyes. He knew she'd be troubled. Perplexed at best, mocking and scornful at worst.

And with good reason.

He was scornful with himself. Was Mara's hold over him so strong he couldn't even function with another woman? Even after centuries of monking?

A humbled glance downward through his lashes gave him his answer.

Och, aye, it was undeniably so.

No one but his flame-haired, amber-eyed minx of a MacDougall would do.

And he was stark raving mad.

Madly in love.

"Do I displease you?" the Norsewoman probed, her tone proving she already knew.

Alex sighed. "It isn't you," he said, opening his eyes and looking up at her.

To his amazement, she no longer appeared quite as beautiful as she had in the hall. Perhaps it was the torchlight, but her white-blond braid suddenly minded him more of sun-bleached straw than silken flax, the pale shade striking him as colorless compared to Mara's burnished copper tresses.

"If it isn't me, then what is it?" the Valkyrie demanded, her annoyance palpable. "Have I less charms than you are accustomed to? Or shall I display them more freely?"

Standing tall, she smoothed both hands over her full breasts, lifting and plumping them until the pale pink rims of her nipples appeared over the gold braid at the edge of her bodice. "Do you not like what you see?"

Alex hesitated. "You are lovely," he hedged, crossing his legs to hide his lack of appreciation. "Well made and . . . rousing. A proud woman," he added, trying to sink lower into the tub. "You would heat any man's blood."

"But not yours?" she countered, her cheeks beginning to redden.

"My heart is given," Alex spoke true, unable to pretend any longer. "And with my heart, my body as well."

Lady Galiana sniffed. "More than half the men who visit Bran's hall have wives or sweethearts elsewhere in the realm."

"I am . . . otherwise."

"Then prove it," she challenged, tugging down her bodice so that her bared breasts sprang into view.

Looking defiant, she plucked on her nipples, rubbing and pulling on them in ways so titillating, the sight should have made him as hard as granite.

Another man would've been stirred beyond the breaking point. She had enormous breasts, and their swollen tips begged attention. The kind of nipples a man could play with for hours, lapping and suckling at leisure, enjoying every moment.

And the Norse beauty's nipples were his for taking. Thrusting right at him, demanding his touch. Waiting. Urging him on.

The rest of her charms would be offered with equal generosity and abandonment.

Of that, he was sure.

But he didn't want her.

Nor did her huge breasts entice him. Not on closer inspection. Truth be told, they bore a strong resemblance to a milk cow's udders. And her oversized aureoles made her look worn, as if a thousand men had taken their turn suckling her.

Like as not, they had.

Even so, he couldn't look away. Nor could he speak. He'd trapped himself in a nightmare of his own making and couldn't seem to wake up.

Mortified, he hunched deeper in the wooden bathing tub and simply stared at her, wondering why he'd found her so desirable only moments before.

Now he could see the sallow tinge of her complexion, the deep lines running parallel to the lips she repeatedly pursed in at him in annoying invitation.

Why hadn't he noticed the telltale stains on her scarlet and gold gown? Obvious remnants from earlier encounters with other pleasure-seeking carousers? Truth be told, some of the soilings looked mightily fresh.

Alex swallowed, revulsion sending a shudder down his spine.

"Ahhhh, you do like what you see," she purred, clearly misinterpreting the shiver.

She stepped back a bit, her smile practiced seduction as she smoothed a hand down her abdomen, then slowly rubbed between her legs. "I knew you would prefer me to the MacDougall wench Hardwick mentioned."

"Mara—" Alex snapped his mouth shut, his eyes flying wide as his love's image flashed across the Norse harlot.

He blinked, his heart thundering in disbelief. But he couldn't deny it—Lady Galiana had company.

He could still see her standing there, plucking a ripe nipple with the fingers of one hand and stroking her most intimate parts with the other.

But he saw *her,* too.

Mara MacDougall.

His very own love, and she was prancing around her bedchamber wearing nothing but that tiny one-piece bit of clinging black lace.

That, and a MacDougall plaid hanging loosely about her shoulders.

He started to curse upon noting the plaid, then, much to his astonishment, discovered he didn't care.

Of much greater importance was that she was coming closer, a shadow image meshing with the Norsewoman, her sweet perfection superimposed atop Lady Galiana's hardened features.

Alex gripped the edge of the tub again, felt the room begin to spin. He tried to look away but couldn't. Beneath the fingers playing with the distended tips of Lady Galiana's enormous teats, he saw the creamy swells of Mara's breasts. When the Norsewoman suddenly yanked up her skirts, revealing a tangle of white-blond nether curls, he saw instead the lush, flame-colored triangle topping Mara's shapely thighs.

A temptation so powerful it took his breath. White-hot desire shot through him, its fierceness burning him. His loins tightened and his shaft filled with urgency, swelling and throbbing with his need to plunder those bronze curls.

"Saints of mercy!" he cried, desperation seizing him, a furious, shocking need to drag her against him and sink deep, deep inside her.

He had to have her.

Now.

Jumping to his feet, he sprang from the tub. "Mara!" he called to her, almost crashing into a standing candelabrum because the room was still spinning, whirling even faster now.

The speed made him dizzy and he hunched forward, bracing his hands on his legs, struggling to clear his pounding head.

"Lass," he tried again, straightening, searching for her in the blurring haze. "Where are you? Dinna leave me. *Please.*"

But only silence answered him.

Until somewhere in the swirling madness he heard a woman's sharp intake of breath, felt soft female hands grasping at his jutting arousal.

One hand, then two, and then four . . .

"O-o-oh," Lady Galiana's voice reached him. "You are so large. So long and thick, so hot."

Alex . . . a second voice pleaded, much fainter. *Her* voice, so beloved, but miles and centuries away, calling him fervently, luring him back to her.

Please . . . I need you. Want you.

Alex's heart began to thud and he clenched his fists, blinking as thick gray fog poured into the special love chamber. It swirled around him, making it difficult to see. The floor tilted, too, swaying and weaving until he lurched, struggled wildly for balance.

Still he heard the Norsewoman praising his endowments, felt her clutching at him through the mist, clinging to him in frenzied desire.

Then he caught another fleeting glimpse of his

Mara. *So good, so good,* he thought she said. Though he didn't understand why she sounded so breathless, almost as if she were calling out in passion.

Then Lady Galiana loomed in front of him again, her voice rising above Mara's, her hands grasping as she fell to her knees, pressed her face against his groin. "I will make you forget her. You will see. Come, let me . . ."

Don't stop, please, whatever you do, don't stop . . .

Mara's voice swelled with strength. Golden and sweet, its pureness filled his ears, warming him as the dark mists spun faster, speeding him through the black chasm of time.

My Highlander . . . sooo good . . . she cried, and the wonder in her voice lanced his heart.

Then her hands were all over him. Caressing and stroking even as the Norsewoman pulled on him, grasping wildly as she struggled to keep him from being swept away by the rushing winds.

"No-o-o . . ." the Valkyrie wailed, her voice fading.

And then he found himself alone, and there was only the familiar rush of the wind and whirling mist spiraling him through the darkness, carrying him back where he belonged.

Back to his bed.

And the woman he meant to make his.

No matter what it cost him.

"Alex!" Mara stared at him, her heart bounding. She pressed a hand to her breast, unable to trust her eyes. "My Highlander," she cried, certain she'd melt at his feet. "Are you really here?"

He stepped closer and smiled, his naked body silver gilded by moonlight. "Och, aye, lass, I am here," he confirmed, his sexy burr stealing her breath. "Just as you canna trap wind, so can nothing keep me away from you."

He looked wet. Tiny droplets of water sparkled on his shoulders and glittered in his chest hair, winking at her like a scattering of diamonds. Even as he reached for her, she knew she could only be dreaming.

The room was spinning around them, a shimmering, whirling mist blotting out everything but her bed and the two of them. Even the air pulsed in excitement, and she clung to him, clutching fast, unable to get enough.

She needed him close, skin to skin, sharing breath and sighs. Never letting go.

"Sweet minx," he breathed against her hair, the way he said the words letting her know he understood her need. "You are mine. Always and aye."

He caressed her back, his hands sliding everywhere, his touch leaving her breathless. Cascades of prickling desire spilled through her and she shivered, her need growing frantic. His kiss electrified her, each bold thrust of his tongue into her mouth sweeping her to such heights as she'd never believed existed.

"O-o-oh," she moaned, tingling warmth coiling inside her.

"Shush, lass, just feel." He tightened his arms around her, crushing her against him and deepening their kiss. A tempestuous melding of tongues and hot breath. So deliriously good, her entire body shook with such incredible pleasure she feared she might die of its intensity.

"I am yours, Mara." He drew back to look at her, his eyes ablaze with passion. "See what you have done to me. I canna breathe without you. I no longer even care about your name, though I'd rather give you mine."

"Yours?"

Her breath caught, but he'd seized her face in his hands and was kissing her again. This time rough, swift, and furiously.

"I must have you," he vowed, the words claiming her. "Forever. No matter what it takes to keep you. Remember that on the morrow."

"On the morrow?" She blinked, his tone frightening her.

But he only pressed his fingers against her lips. Worse, he pulled away and the loss of physical contact lamed her, set her reeling.

"No-o-o! Don't leave me!" She grabbed for him, afraid he'd vanish, but he only flashed another of his devastating smiles and shifted his position, slinging a leg over her hips to straddle her.

"I'm no going anywhere," he purred, looking down at her. "Not this night."

Mara blinked, another little tremor of ill ease rippling through her, but she chose to ignore it.

This was, after all, her dream.

So instead of fretting about what he might or might not have meant, she thrashed and twisted on the bed, kicking away the covers and arching her back, letting her hungry body beg him to ravish her.

And he did.

Unlike the last such dream, when he'd simply stood frozen above her, this time he acknowledged her. He'd already kissed her to the very edge of a climax again, and now he was looking deep into her eyes as he knelt above her, his powerful thighs rubbing sinuously against hers. She bit her lip, the feel of his naked skin brushing hers exciting and thrilling her.

"You are mine, Mara, and ne'er you forget it," he growled, his silky-smooth burr melting her, the hot carnality streaming off him, heating her blood. "I've waited too long for you and I willna let you go now that I have you."

I do not want you to let me go.

The admission almost split Mara's heart, but her throat was too thick for her to release the words. Instead, the sweetest golden warmth spooled through her, its possession both unsettling and incredibly dear.

A muscle in his jaw twitched, almost as if he'd heard. He eased her down against the covers, splaying a hand across her belly to hold her in place. "Be still and just lie there, Mara. Let me look at you, for I've a need."

"I have a need, too!" she cried, the throbbing between her legs a torment she couldn't bear much longer. "You're my dream and I want you. Now. Please!"

Before I wake up and lose you again.

She grabbed his hips, digging in her fingers and holding fast, drinking him in. She wanted to drown in the wonder of him, imprint his image on her soul and keep him there.

For the empty nights when she failed to dream.

When he was gone to her.

But she pushed all thought of the future from her mind and reached out to touch him, skimming her fingers along his shoulder and collarbone, then down over his sculpted chest muscles. She toyed with the smattering of hairs there, marveled at their beauty and softness. They glistened like spun gold and, to her, were infinitely more precious.

Just the feel of them beneath her fingers almost undid her. He felt so real. Her breath caught at the impossibility and her throat thickened in a painful way.

But she blinked back her cares and kept looking at him, glorying in every magnificent Highland inch of him.

Especially the *good* inches.

Those inches, too, were fully displayed, and such a chance might never come again, so she meant to enjoy it to the fullest. She'd outdone herself with this dream, or else all her conjuring stars were in place. Why else would he have waltzed into her sleep full naked?

So wet and shimmering. Gloriously bare.

She shivered, all her senses alive. He was so beautiful, it almost hurt to look at him. His hard, well-muscled body gleamed in the pale moonlight, and his hair was damp, as if he'd just stepped out of a shower.

He smelled good, too. Clean, fresh, and . . . manly. Deliciously sexy.

And so ragingly hard her breasts swelled with longing and her nipples puckered. Streaming anticipation flooded her and *that* part of her pulsed and tingled with such urgency, she would've screamed had her mouth not gone so dry.

His entire maleness hovered not a hand's breadth above her, its nearness and heat making her burn. Only a shiver of air and the lace of her teddy's crotch piece separated them.

She wanted him more than she'd ever desired another man.

Hot waves of pounding need raced through her, and if she weren't dreaming, she'd surely break apart from the force of her passion for him. The all-consuming hunger overwhelming her so powerfully that just breathing in the same air as he did nearly brought her to her knees.

But since she *was* dreaming, she'd ride her bliss.

After all, it was her dream.

"Okay, Hottie Scottie, two can play this game." She lifted her chin and slipped a hand between her legs to undo the tiny clasps of her teddy. "I know you enjoy looking—"

"Hottie Scottie?" He blinked, confusion flashing across his face. But only for a heartbeat, because the filmy material of her teddy's crotch fell away, freeing her to his view as boldly as he'd presented his wares to her.

He looked down at her. "O-o-oh, lass, I will show you hot," he purred, a slow smile curving his lips. "Shall I love you as only a Highlander can love a woman?"

Mara bit down on her lip. Her heart flipped and she couldn't speak. Deep inside her something wild and primordial was unraveling. Coming undone and letting her revel in the intimacy of being so exposed to him.

Thrilling excitement whipped through her, seizing her breath and making her part her thighs, baring herself even more. Her pulse roared in her ears and her heart hammered so fiercely, she wondered it didn't spring from her chest.

"Well, lass? Are you mine?" He kept his gaze on the triangle of her sex, reached down to cup her, rubbing slowly. "Will you burn for me?"

I am burning, she wanted to scream, but the words jammed in her throat. She was crazed with wanting him, could only nod and rock her hips. Quiver and tremble as her knees opened a bit more, giving him greater access.

"Och, aye, that's good," he said, sounding pleased. He tilted a smile at her, teased his fingers across her intimate curls. "Show me more, Mara. I would see all of you."

"And I would have all of you." She narrowed her eyes, looked pointedly at his arousal. "Inside me."

"In time, sweet." He touched a hand to her breast, palmed and tweaked her nipples. "I will lose my seed so soon as I enter you and I've waited too long for this pleasure not to prolong our enjoyment. You are beautiful and it pleases me to look at you."

His eyes darkened then and he drew back his shoulders, his gaze raking her intimacies. His expression turned feral, almost like a ravening wolf eyeing a plump rabbit he meant to devour.

And she wanted to be devoured.

Ached to be consumed by him.

"Touch me again. There, like you did before." She pushed her legs against his thighs, opening herself, hoping to seduce him with a more thorough view of her womanhood. "I will explode if you don't," she breathed, quite certain she would. "I need you."

"And you shall have me," he vowed, seizing her knees and pulling her legs up through his, urging them wide until her entire femininity was opened to him.

"O-o-oh, yes," she moaned, loving it. An exquisite, almost unbearable pulsing began beating through her, hot and lascivious. Scintillating beyond endurance.

She trembled, her craving for him shading her every sigh, melting her.

"See, lass, you like having me look at you." He touched her again, traced the very center of her. "Or will you deny what I can see writ all o'er you?"

"No, I won't deny it." And she couldn't.

There was something maddeningly tantalizing about being so fully opened to a man's lustful stare. Feeling *his* stare on her was a bliss so dazzling she could hardly breathe.

Never had she experienced anything so erotically rousing as his rapt perusal of her most intimate flesh. His gaze absorbed and burned her, sent little flickers of flame everywhere he looked. Irresistibly delicious flames that licked at her, flicking over her as light as air one minute, lapping leisurely and thoroughly the next.

"You must look at me, too, Mara." He circled his fingers around his hardness, bringing it closer to her heat. "Is this what you want?" he asked, rubbing the swollen tip over her dampness. "Can you feel me this time? Do you need me inside you? You must tell me. Say the words."

She reached for him, knocking away his hand and wrapping her own fingers around him. "Yes, of course I can feel you," she cried, her voice breaking. "You are granite hard, all hot and silky in my hand and I need you inside me. Deep, deep inside me. You know where."

She arched her hips off the bed, rocking frantically and trying to thrust him inside her, but he only smiled and closed strong fingers over hers.

"Not so fast," he warned, sliding his shaft up and down her softness, his steely grip on her hand making it impossible for her to sheathe him. "I am not yet done with looking at you."

He arched a brow. "Or are you not enjoying yourself? Is this not what you wanted? For me to pleasure you?"

I want you to be real. She stared at him, the silent words ripping her soul. *I want you to love me. Need me and want me as much as I need and love you.*

But instead of crying out her deepest wishes and perhaps shattering her dream, she turned her head to the side and nodded, letting her body beg him for release rather than risk having him see her heart's weeping in her eyes.

An orgasmic dream was better than not having him at all.

Lots better.

Any moment she'd explode into a thousand tiny pieces, flood herself with the streaming wetness of her climax. But she didn't care if her glory cries carried across every hill in Scotland. Pleasure-spending sex god or no, *this* Hottie Scottie was only a dream figment.

If ever her real ghostly Highlander returned to her, he needn't know she'd wantoned herself so brazenly.

Besides, if he saw her in the throes of a rollicking orgasm, he might take mercy on her and do more than toy with her clit and pluck at her nipples.

She knew he wanted her. His bucking shaft and tight balls proved his desire.

But he remained poised above her, keeping up his sensual rubbings and leaving her no choice but to thrash about and hope he'd soon put an end to her misery.

Not that she didn't feel good already.

Her Highlander knew what to do with a clitoris. And having him stare at her so intimately was positively decadent. No man had ever done such a thing, and she doubted she would've allowed it. But with Hottie Scottie, it felt right.

No, delicious.

A glorious, tantalizing bliss.

Her bliss. And so rousing to watch Alex's entire body strummed with the wonder of it. Never had he seen a woman wear her arousal so beautifully.

Peaking arousal, if the rich, earthy musk rising off her was any indication. He breathed deep, holding in the scent of her, letting its potency drench his senses. So soon as he released it, he slid one finger down the soft dampness of her cleft and slipped it inside her, finding her hot, sleek, and wet.

Tight, wet, and convulsing around his finger.

Alex groaned. She arched against him, the urgent thrusting of her hips telling him everything.

It was time; she could wait no longer.

And neither could he.

"Och, lass, I will have you now." He stretched out beside her and pulled her into his arms, kissing her hard. She kissed him back, clamping her legs around him and pressing close, her breath hitching, her every wild, open-mouthed kiss more frenzied than the one before.

"That's it, minx, show me you need me," he urged, cupping her bottom, kneading and squeezing the plump rounds, the feel of her smooth, naked skin in his hands making him crazy, setting him on fire.

"Yes!" she cried, grinding herself against him, showing no mercy. She rubbed her breasts into him, jammed a hand down between them to seize him and slide his aching shaft all over her slick wetness. "Oh, Alex, you feel sooo good."

"Not half so good as you," he purred, nearly spending when she tightened her fingers on him, not stroking as she'd done before but holding him in a firm, possessive grip and thrusting him inside her.

Not far, only an inch or two.

But enough to make all the stars in the heavens explode in his head. They crashed down around him, blinding him and making his world spin until he was sure he'd slide right off. He blinked hard, his entire body shaking with the power of her passion, the glory of her.

"Sweet lass," he got out, somehow rising up on his elbows to look at her. "Dinna move or I'll plunge full deep and this will end before we've started."

"I want it to end!" She clung to him, rocking her hips, her frenzied movements drawing him in another inch or so. "I've waited too long to have you."

"Nay, you err," Alex hissed, using all his strength to pull back until just the tip of him hovered inside her. " 'Tis I who have waited—an eternity. And I would savor you. Every precious moment with you."

He focused on her stormy, lust-glazed eyes, tried to ignore the frantic windings of her body, the wondrous, velvety heat pulsing so close, waiting to sheathe him.

"I want to love all of you," he breathed, palming her breasts, circling a moistened finger around one puckered crest, then lowering his head to lick and suckle the other, drawing it deep into his mouth.

He sucked hard, pulling strongly, the taste of her ripping away his restraint, his shaft sliding deeper with each hot draw on her nipple until he'd plunged full deep. He lost himself at once, cried out at the hot, sleek feel of her wetness.

He drew a sharp breath, her tight, satiny heat almost unmanning him. His world began to spin faster, each giddy whirl letting him sink deeper into her clinging, welcoming warmth.

But he remembered to reach down and rub that special place, kept a questing, circling finger there as he stroked deeper, each smooth in-and-out glide claiming another piece of him, making his world splinter around him.

"O-o-oh, Alex!" Her voice was breathless, a hitching cry somewhere in the madness, its sweetness wrapping round him, binding him to her as deeply as he rode her silken depths.

She arched her hips, turning wild, clutching at him and clawing his back, her writhings and cries undoing him, making it impossible to give her the slow, thorough loving he'd planned.

"Lass, I canna hold back—"

"Then don't! I can't either," she moaned, grabbing his face and pulling him down to her, smothering him with kisses.

"Harder, faster," she pleaded, panting the words into his mouth as she kissed him, her thrusting tongue matching the rhythm of their furious joining. "Don't stop," she screamed, going suddenly rigid, clenching hotly around him. "Please, God, don't stop!"

But it was too late.

The whirling stars were exploding all around and inside him and his seed gushed into her in a furious, hot rush. "Mara," he gasped, collapsing against her as he shuddered within her, every last drop of energy draining out of him. "Remember what I told you . . ."

I will do anything to have you.

The words shimmered in the air, hovering over the bed, silvery and true, but not near as bright as the glittering light of the splintered stars spinning around him. They whirled ever faster, their brilliance overpowering everything until he could see his words no more.

He couldn't see Mara either.

Or his bed.

Not even the room. Only the blinding light piercing him so viciously, each hot, stabbing thrust a lightning bolt lancing straight through him, breaking him apart until the crackling light finally receded and he was left battered and broken, drifting in the familiar gray mists he knew only too well.

He clenched his fists against the pain, refusing to acknowledge the searing heat, the scorch marks branding his naked flesh.

He'd been a fool.

But he'd meant what he vowed. He'd find a way to get back to her.

Do anything to have her.

Anything? Mara blinked, some still-coherent part of her catching his words. She lifted her hips, meeting his thrusts, her desire sharpening, turning fierce. But his words wouldn't let her go, and a tiny edge of doubt colored her pleasure.

What else could he possibly could do for her? Already she was burning with stunning need, his long, plundering strokes running deep, even touching her soul.

Branding her.

She cried out his name again, wrapped her legs even tighter around him, let him hurtle her toward the greatest orgasm of her life. He'd given her his heart, too. She'd seen the love blazing in his eyes when he'd first plunged into her.

A wonder she'd think about after her climax.

Just now, she couldn't concentrate beyond the throbbing, heart-pounding pleasure spreading all through her. Sensations so powerful she couldn't even feel *him* anymore. Only the hot pulsing surge of her orgasm as it swept over her, shattering her into a thousand tiny glittering pieces.

"Ohmigod," she cried, going rigid. Her entire body trembled and she clutched so fiercely to his shoulders that her fingers went right through him, her nails digging deep crescents into her palms.

But she scarce noticed.

She was floating now, the heated throbbing deep inside her sated. Satisfied, and slowing to a delicious lightly pulsing warmth that cushioned her so beautifully, even rocked her gently back to earth.

Back to the Thistle Room and her empty bed.

She frowned, aimed a glare at her alarm clock. Barely three a.m. and the blasted thing was beginning to sound infernally loud again.

Rolling onto her side, she hugged herself and blocked her ears to the ticking. She also plumped a pillow for her head, closed her eyes, and treated herself to reliving every incredible moment of her dream.

After all, it was hers to enjoy.

And she was already beginning to tingle again. One rollicking, earth-shaking release was not near enough for a girl used to faking the buggers with every bumbling, unskilled yo-yo she'd ever had the misfortune to sleep with.

Imagined sex or no, Hottie Scottie could shag circles around any one of them. She stared up at the canopy of her bed, blew out a shaky breath.

Just thinking his name undid her.

Sir Alexander Douglas. Even Hottie Scottie.

Perhaps her very own Pleasure Spender.

So long as her Highlander was meant, the name made her sizzle and burn. Mercy, if she could bottle or can such a dream as she'd just had, she wouldn't need One Cairn Village to help her keep Ravenscraig.

"Man-o-meter," she quipped, flipping onto her back and stretching her arms over her head, wiggling her toes. Sweet, lazy tendrils of pulsating warmth still rippled through her, and if she concentrated really hard, she could even imagine she felt a bit . . . sore.

No, she *was* sore.

And in a worse way than when she'd lifted her skirt in the backseat of Donnie Morton's blue Ford and given him her sixteen-year-old cherry.

But then Donnie Morton hadn't been anywhere near as endowed as Hottie Scottie.

Mara's eyes popped open. An impossible suspicion sluiced through her, the horror of it peeking at her from every shadowy corner of the room.

A room that still smelled of her wretched antighost charms, but also of sex.

The hot, sweaty, down-and-dirty kind of sex she'd dreamt about.

Only dream sex didn't make you ache inside. It certainly didn't leave telltale scents in the air.

"Oh, no." Her heart began to pound. "O-o-oh, nooo!"

She shot off the bed, flipped on the nightlight. But even before she looked down, she knew what she'd see. And she did. All over the inside of her thighs—the undeniable evidence of her own arousal, and his.

"Dear God," she cried, trembling all over. "It can't be."

But it was.

Even her bed screamed the truth at her. The sheets were damp. And the pillows. Almost wet, just as everything would be if he'd come to her straight from a shower.

And that was exactly how she'd imagined him.

Full naked, his magnificent body glistening with water droplets. His rich chestnut hair sleek and gleaming, damp and fresh smelling as if he'd just washed it.

Perhaps he had—to make himself more desirable before he'd appeared to her.

As if she wouldn't run a hundred miles to hurl herself into his arms. Wouldn't leap at him, almost knocking him down in her eagerness to be reunited with him.

No matter what condition he was in. So long as it was him, her precious Highlander, nothing else mattered.

But now he was gone.

And she was crying. Mara never-shed-a-tear McDougall was falling apart.

Because she was also Mara straight-thinking McDougall and anyone with even a speck of sense would know that after such mind-blowing sex no man would simply disappear.

Not even a ghostly Highlander.

Unless he hadn't had a choice.

And that possibility was more frightening than she could bear to think about.

Chapter 12

Six ghost-free weeks later Mara sat at the dark oak table in the middle of the library and considered the amazing state of her finances. Or rather, the incredible surge in the state of Ravenscraig's finances.

Not hers personally, but the estate's.

Even so, she couldn't be more pleased.

She snapped shut the ledger she'd been studying and leaned back in her chair. Looking round, she tapped her pen against her chin, her gaze flicking over the many gilt-framed portraits crowding the book-lined walls. Be-kilted and proud looking, every one of her fierce, bushy-bearded ancestors seemed to beam approval at her.

And perhaps with good reason, she allowed.

Never one to tolerate do-nothings and wannabes, she *had* worked hard. And she still was, pouring more time and energy into Ravenscraig than she'd ever devoted to Exclusive Excursions. And although she wouldn't ever admit it, there were days her heart almost burst with pride.

One Cairn Village, secretly dubbed Brigadoon Revisited, was doing amazingly well, its progress astounding her. The lovely MacDougall memorial cairn at its center would soon see completion, as would the special state-of-the-art genealogical center.

Several of the quaint little whitewashed guest cottages stood ready, some even boasting their first starry-eyed occupants. MacDougalls and family history buffs, the most of them. But others, too, and new ones arrived every day.

One Cairn Village bustled, and a dormitory of sorts had even been set up in Ravenscraig's vaulted basement to house any overflow until the grand Victorian-style lodge could be built, most likely sometime next year.

Mara set down her pen and rolled her aching shoulders. Everything should be perfect, and that it wasn't was something she shouldn't be dwelling on.

There were some things even hard work and determination couldn't make right.

Not wanting to go down that road, she slid a glance toward the tall mullioned windows. Wispy clouds trailed across a brilliant late-summer sky, and each pane of leaded glass gleamed bright in the slanting afternoon sun.

She allowed herself a sigh and took a careful sip of steaming mint tea. Truth was, she had every reason to be happy. Deliriously so. The amazing stream of good things coming her way seemed endless. Blessings that sometimes arrived from the most unexpected quarters.

Like the nondescript, incredibly tweedy woman who'd popped up from southern England to research her own vague MacDougall connections. An art teacher and one of their first visitors, she'd surprised everyone by creating a beautiful tartan-ribboned thistle design as a logo for One Cairn Village.

A striking design she insisted was a gift.

The lovely beribboned thistle now graced the packaging of all Ravenscraig craft and gift items, and was even selling well on everything from coffee mugs and coasters to T-shirts and tea towels.

Mara forced a weak smile and took another sip of tepid tea. Never would she have expected Ravenscraig to thrive to such a stunning degree. Wonder of wonders, a portrait of Lady Warfield now hung over the library's large green-marbled hearth, and she had yet to see a visiting MacDougall not stop to admire the old woman's likeness.

Some even smiled.

Mara swallowed and swiped a hand across her cheek, dashing away a trace of foolhardy dampness. "Damn you, Alex," she murmured beneath her breath, blinking hard until her vision cleared. "How dare you make me love you, then disappear?"

But she'd succeeded with Ravenscraig.

Her chances of losing it at the end of a year were now as remote as the moon, her future and the old castle's secure. A certainty that had infused everyone at Ravenscraig with jubilant triumph and purpose.

Even old Murdoch now walked with an added spring to his bandy-legged gait.

And shame on her for letting *moods* get her down. She should be as giddy-happy as everyone else beneath her roof. She stared across the library to the birch fire crackling in the hearth and drew a deep, back-stealing breath. Nothing should be bothering her.

Especially nonexistent nothings.

"Miss, I'm so sorry to disturb you," Ailsa-Agnes said with all Highland politeness, "but your father is on the phone."

Mara jumped, almost sloshed tea onto her lap. "My father?" She blinked at the girl. "He never calls. I always ring him," she said, her heart dipping. "Something must be wrong."

"I couldn't say," the twin puzzled, handing the phone to Mara. "But he does sound in fine fettle."

In fine fettle?

The last time she'd called home, Hugh McDougall was convinced his heart troubles would land him in the hospital any day. He even moaned that he'd been too weak to work on his book about their family history, a never-ending pet project he'd courted for years.

Mara stared at the phone, waiting until Ailsa-Agnes slipped away before she lifted it to her ear.

"Dad?" she queried. "Are you okay?"

"Am I okay?" her father's voice boomed through the line. "Lassie, I've never been better!"

Mara blinked, wondered if someone was playing a joke on her. But it *was* Hugh McDougall's voice.

Even if he sounded . . . different.

As strong and healthy as he had when she'd been a little girl.

"I'm glad to hear you so perky, but I don't understand," she said, her brow wrinkling. "Last time we talked you said you might be going in for bypass surgery again."

"That was then." Hugh McDougall snorted. "This is now. Everything's changed."

He had that right.

Only six months ago she'd been barely scraping by, running her one-woman tour business and just managing to pay her rent, and now she owned a Scottish castle and had worked to meet the stipulations necessary to keep her inheritance, and she'd fallen hopelessly, irrevocably in love.

With a ghost.

A sexy Highland ghost who'd treated her to the greatest sex she'd ever had and then walked out on her. Or whatever it was called when ghosts vanished and never returned.

She frowned. "I'm sorry, Dad. I didn't hear you. What were you saying?"

A laugh answered her.

A great, belly-shaking laugh that made the phone jiggle in her hand and hurt her ear. Muffled words as if someone else were there with him.

Mara held the phone away from her ear, her confusion complete. The garbled voice in the background sounded like a woman's. And her father's laughter was way too jolly to be normal.

Much as she loved him, her dad was a man who

lived quietly. Little interested him beyond digging into his roots. He was also a card-carrying hypochondriac, a bit of a whiner.

Not a thigh-slapping baboon who guzzled beer with the boys and let loose jocular guffaws.

A sudden alertness tightened Mara's lips.

"Are you sure you're all right?" she demanded, her concern only reaping another hoot of transatlantic mirth. "What is going on with you?"

"Something wonderful," her father gushed, sounding almost moony eyed. "Something you will never believe."

Mara braced herself. Hugh McDougall's *something wonderfuls* were usually embarrassing.

Like the time he'd covered their entire house in plaid at Christmas and tied a giant tartan bow to the chimney.

"I think you better tell me what's up," she said.

"I'm coming over to see you, Mara-girl! For the cairn's unveiling ceremony," he sang out, his excitement carrying through the airwaves. "It'll be my honeymoon!"

"Your honeymoon?" Mara almost dropped the phone. "What do you mean your honeymoon? You're not married."

"Oh, yes, I am," he shot back. "Since last Saturday, and it's given me a new lease on life. I'm feeling fit enough to cross the Atlantic to see you and the *Auld Hameland.*"

Mara's jaw went slack. "Why didn't you tell me? Do I know the woman?"

A pause. "I didn't mention it because we had a

small civil ceremony and I know you're busy over there just now. I didn't want you fretting if you couldn't get away."

"But who is she?"

Her father cleared his throat. "Euphemia Ross."

"The shrew?" Mara's eyes flew wide. "That dried-up stick?"

Hugh McDougall coughed loudly and then there was a scuffling noise as if he'd clamped a hand over the receiver.

"Now look here," he said after a moment, his tone conciliatory. "Euphemia is—"

"I'm sorry," Mara spluttered, horrified she hadn't checked her tongue. "You just surprised me."

"Well, I surprised myself," he admitted, sounding mollified. "With you away, I needed someone to help me with my book. Running errands to the copy shop and typing, that sort of thing. A bit of cooking, tidying the house now and then. One thing led to another and—"

"And now you've married her and you're coming here on your honeymoon?"

"That's the way of it," he confirmed, and Mara could almost hear his smile cracking. "Doctors say she's the best thing that's happened to me in years."

"Then I am happy for you both," Mara said, feeling as if she'd just swallowed a glass of vinegar.

A big glass.

"You'll warm to her," her father was saying. "And she's looking forward to researching her Ross ancestors."

"Ross was the name of her third husband," Mara couldn't help reminding him.

The one before him had been Cherokee. Back then the Cairn Avenue shrew had gone by the name Sunrise or Daybreak. Something to do with dawn.

But that hadn't made her a Native American.

Not that it mattered.

"Never you mind all that," her father said. "You'll like her once you get to know her better."

"I'm sure I will."

"Count on it." Hugh McDougall's voice turned gruff. "Have I ever lied to my little girl?"

"No," Mara admitted, a blasted lump rising in her throat.

"Then it's settled. We'll see you soon."

Then her dad was gone. No, not just her dad, but the Cairn Avenue shrew's fourth husband, and with that amazing transformation, she was quite certain the world had finally gone mad.

Totally bonkers.

With her leading the parade.

She set down the phone and pushed back her hair. Then she reached for her tea, only to discover she'd already drained the cup.

She frowned. For once, she could've used a fortifying gulp of the wretched brew.

"Ah, well," she said, mimicking one of Murdoch's favorite phrases.

She'd just have to make the best of it.

So long as her father and Euphemia Ross didn't act like love-struck fools and start rolling in the heather, everything would be okay.

She only wished *her* love life was running as smoothly.

Instead, it was just . . . running.

Away from her, out of control, and to places she couldn't begin to follow.

Not in this life, anyway.

"No kidding," she muttered, pushing up from her chair and pressing her hands against the small of her back.

She tried to swallow her bad temper, but it really just wasn't fair.

She took a deep breath and looked toward the windows, her heart giving a painful thump at the beauty of the bright blue day. No, not fair at all, she decided, her eyes beginning to burn again. If a thin-lipped terror like Euphemia Ross could bedazzle four men into marrying her, why couldn't she at least manage an occasional nightly tryst with Hottie Scottie?

But even that solace seemed beyond her grasp.

She might be wildly, madly, yearningly in love, but apparently he wasn't nearly as smitten.

There could be no other reason for his absence.

"But I still want him," she sighed, her composure breaking, its loss threatening to dissolve her.

Something nudged her leg then and she looked down to find Ben pressing his bulk against her, lending what comfort he could. "You miss him, too, don't you?" she said to him, her vision blurring.

Grateful for his devotion, she reached down and rubbed his ears. But even the old dog's soulful stare couldn't mend the ache inside her.

Or undo the glaring truth.

If her ghostly Highlander possessed the energy to spook around her bed for nearly seven hundred years, surely a few measly weeks shouldn't deter him?

But they had and she was bitter with it, weary of looking and listening for him.

Yet she did.

Every hour of every day.

And her nights were worse. Sleepless and lonely, each one proved an unending stretch of longing. Cold and dark hours filled with an agony that lanced beyond words. She just couldn't believe he was gone.

Even now she wrapped her arms around herself and cast a glance at the hearth, hoping to catch sight of him. Perhaps his tall, broad-shouldered form silhouetted against the glow from the birch fire. The dimmest outline would thrill her. As would just picking up a vibration in the air, the lingering trace of his scent.

Or his laughter. A naughty brush of wind against her nipples, a hushed word at her ear.

Anything would do.

So long as it reassured her that he was still here and existed, even if he couldn't appear to her.

But there was nothing, and the stinging heat jabbing into the backs of her eyes was growing too fierce for even a MacDougall to ignore.

A mere *Mc*Dougall didn't stand a chance.

So she paced the room, not at all surprised that it'd lost its luster. Her world had lost its luster, so why shouldn't Ravenscraig's library go from warm, bright, and cozy to cold, dreary, and empty? No longer smelling of leather, ink, and age, but reeking only of heartache.

Losing her Highlander had done that to her.

She was going barmy.

But at least she was too busy to notice.

And if she paused in her work, the ever-present crowds, goings-on, and noise kept her distracted. Not otherworldly noises. Or even the incessant groan of water pipes and the creak of aged wood, but lively sounds.

Steps hurrying down corridors, the opening and closing of doors. Faint echoes drifting from the great hall, the clatter of cutlery and the scrape of pushed-back chairs. Happy voices and muted laughter as new arrivals enjoyed sandwiches and drams. From every corner came a stir and buzz.

The bustle of living.

Even here, in the comfy mustiness of the library, her onetime haven of peace.

Until just an hour ago, a chatty clutch of older guests had sat conversing before the fire. Cape Breton MacDougalls, they'd sipped tea, nibbled cheesy oatcakes, and repeatedly praised the room's nostalgic charm.

An ambiance reclaimed in recent days by Scottie and Dottie. Once again comfortable in the mausoleumlike room, the little dogs delighted in entertaining visitors. Always underfoot, they excelled in courting attention.

Reaping oohs and aahs.

At the moment, they cavorted in one of the window alcoves, darting in and out of a sunbeam, fighting over a fallen cushion. A frolic they'd never indulge in if they feared Hottie Scottie might suddenly materialize.

But that danger had passed, and nothing more ghostly looking than whirling dust motes disturbed the afternoon. Even the slight stirring of the wind against the shutters sounded annoyingly . . . normal.

As did the *chug-chugging* of a fishing boat making its way up the firth. The whirring of a vacuum cleaner in one of the guest rooms. Only the imagined sounds of medieval war play fell outside the usual afternoon noises.

Mara froze. *Medieval battle noises.* Could they possibly be real?

Her heart lurching, she tilted her head, strained her ears.

The distant clash of steel against steel ebbed and flowed, hovering on the edge of her hearing. A wild and furious clamor coming from afar and peppered with shouts and whoops, a few Gaelic curses.

Definitely real sounding.

But a ruckus too unlikely to be anything but a daylight manifestation of her troubled dreams.

A sign she really was going batty.

Noises far too reminiscent of *him* if she wasn't.

Then the sounds faded and she almost laughed at herself. Instead, she blew out a nervous breath and stepped away from the windows.

She started pacing again, determined to forget the strange din. Noises she'd only heard because she'd overworked herself. Or else she missed her sexy Highlander so much, her ears were playing tricks on her.

Cruel tricks, but ones Ben seemed to have heard as well.

Mara's senses sharpened. Unreasonable giddiness swept her, but there could be no mistaking. The old dog's gentle face wore a distinct look of . . . excitement.

Tongue-lolling eagerness.

"Oh, Ben," she choked, watching him trot toward the door, his plumy tail wagging. "It was nothing. And it's gone now."

Don't let him break your heart, too, she almost called after him.

But something *was* hastening their way.

Hurried footsteps. A rapid approach that made Ben dance and sniff at the door, his swishing tail and doggy smiles giving her hope.

Foolishly, her heart started to pound and a lump began swelling in her throat, but when there came the sound of the latch being jiggled, it wasn't Hottie Scottie but Ailsa-Agnes who put her head around the door.

Even so, Ben gave a yelp and leapt past her, bounding down the passage before the girl could even step inside. All bright eyes and smiles, she hovered on the threshold, one hand pressed to her breast.

"O-o-oh, miss!" she blurted, her cheeks glowing. "You must come at once. *He's* down by the training ground and he's brought all his braw friends!"

Mara blinked. "Wh-what?" she managed, her voice cracking. "Who are you talking about? And what training ground?"

"The medieval practice grounds," the girl supplied, pausing for breath. "Some people call them the lists. It's the big grassy field near One Cairn Village. In olden days, knights used it to train. Your boyfriend is there now, with his reenactment friends. Everyone is there, watching them—"

"My boyfriend?" Mara could feel her jaw dropping. "I don't—"

"Ach, just come along and dinna worry. He's in right good trim." Ailsa-Agnes took her arm, pulled her through the door. "He told Murdoch everything. How you'd fretted what we'd think if we knew you had a partner, but you worried for naught."

She looked at Mara, flashed a smile.

But Mara scarce noticed the girl's pink-cheeked grin. She only heard her words, their impact whirling through her like a tornado.

In good trim? Her partner? She opened her mouth to speak, but nothing came out. Her stomach began to flutter and she swallowed hard, her chest so tight she could hardly breathe.

It couldn't be.

Yet who else could the girl mean?

"Dinna look so fashed. We're more modern than we seem," Ailsa-Agnes was saying. "Even Murdoch had a lady-love for years. You should have seen them dance and jig at the *ceilidhs,* himself with his kilt a-flying. They were both widowed and shared a bed until she died just last year."

She flicked her apron, a touch of pride crossing her face. "Your boyfriend is a Highlander. How could we not like him? Especially since he's come with all his friends to entertain at the unveiling ceremony."

A Highlander.

The word rushed at Mara, whipping round her like a warm golden flood, its sweetness flowing into her, bringing her back to life. Making her *feel* again, but in good ways.

Ailsa-Agnes was still speaking, but Mara couldn't distinguish her words. Her eyes were misting too rapidly and her blood roaring so loud in her ears, she could barely hear her own thoughts.

She could only put one foot in front of the other and follow the girl down the passage, toward the stairs to the entrance hall and . . . hope.

Impossible, giddy hope, but irresistible enough to make her heart soar.

She stopped at the bottom of the stairs, her knees shaking so badly she feared her legs would give out. "Are his friends *medieval* reenactors?" she asked, clutching the banister. "I-I've never met them."

"Aye, sure as I'm standing here," Ailsa-Agnes beamed, her answer cinching it. "And looking like they just walked off the set of *Braveheart*. But much more authentic."

Mara's heart slammed against her ribs.

"Oh, God," she cried, not caring who heard her. "It *is* him!"

Then the world flashed black and white before her eyes and the buzzing in her ears grew so deafening, she wondered her head didn't burst.

"Oh, Alex," she gasped, clapping a hand to her cheek. Her entire body trembled and even the soles of her feet tingled. Her pulse raced with incredible speed, its wild surging sure to break her apart.

He was here. Her ghostly Highlander had come back to her.

"Murdoch thinks he brought his friends so their swordplay will impress you." Ailsa-Agnes's voice came from afar, her words faint. Barely audible through the sparkling joy spinning inside Mara. "He said he'd bet his best sporran that your Alex is here to ask you to marry him."

Her Alex. Mara's heart almost split upon hearing his name.

But she was already stumbling for the door, her fingers shaking as she fumbled with the latch. And then it flew wide and she was running, tearing across gravel paths and the lawn, making for the medieval training ground.

Ask her to marry him, Ailsa-Agnes had said.

The words haunted her, echoing in her ears, teasing and taunting. Urging her on.

Not that they really mattered.

She only wanted to see him.

That, and make certain he never left her again.

Mara ran along the track through gorse and broom thickets, Ben's barking and the spectators' cheers giving her strength. Her lungs burned and sharp pain jabbed at her ribs, each racing footfall costing her. She could feel Alex, sensed him with each ragged breath. His presence beckoned, vibrating all through her and fuelling her desperation to reach him.

She bit her lip, pressed a hand against the stitch in her side. Her heart pounded, a thudding agony in her breast, and thundering so loud even the wild clanking of steel and the excited roars of the crowd dimmed in her ears.

"Almost there," she panted, pushing herself as she ran harder.

Then she was there, the path widening to reveal the whole breadth of the brilliant sky and the wide expanse of the grassy, sun-washed training ground. The latter view blocked by the backs of what appeared to be every soul from within Ravenscraig's walls and their guests.

At the edge of the milling spectators, Ben squirmed beside Murdoch, and Mara could see that the garrulous old steward had a firm hand clasped around the dog's collar. Prudentia's broad, floral-printed backside loomed into view as well, but not much else could be seen.

Except for the tall, darkly handsome knight leaning against a drystone wall a short distance from the path. A true medieval knight, as Mara's slack jaw and goose bumps attested. Every inch of him a ghost . . . even if he did look as real as the day was long.

She just knew.

He appeared to know her as well because as she stood gaping at him, he pushed away from the wall and started toward her, his knightly spurs clicking softly, his gleaming mail brilliant in the afternoon sunshine.

Indeed, the only thing unusual about him was how diligently he held his studded medieval shield in front of his groin.

And it *was* a medieval shield.

A fine Highland targe, round and covered with leather, but not looking anywhere near as ancient as the ones decorating the walls of Ravenscraig's entrance hall.

Mara swallowed, frozen in place.

The dark knight smiled. A slow, lazy smile that would have melted her bones were her heart not soundly given. "Be not afraid, Lady Mara," he said, coming closer. "I am but a friend and wish you well."

"You know me?" she managed, still breathing hard, some sharp-eyed corner of her mind stunned at how easily she stood there conversing with a ghost.

Yet another ghost, she amended.

And a dashed good-looking one, too.

"To be sure, and I know you," he said then, his easygoing manner and the way he made her a little bow putting her at ease. "I am Sir Hardwin, longtime companion-in-arms to your Alex. He speaks of nothing but your beauty, wit, and charm. If we have not yet met in truth, the honor is mine that we may do so today."

"You . . . flatter me." Mara resisted the urge to smooth her hair, knew full well how disheveled she must look after half running, half stumbling all the way down here.

"Not flatter, but praise," he corrected, lifting a hand to ward off any objections. "And quite rightly."

"But not why you were waiting for me beside that wall over there?"

"Quite right again," he said with another smile. "I wished a word with you."

"A word—" Mara left the sentence unfinished, speech failing her as, somehow, he was suddenly behind her, gently turning her toward the line of spectators.

Only now they'd all vanished.

Mara's eyes widened, her heart pounding at the sight before her. Medieval clansmen and knights, for they could be nothing other, engaged in a rollicking mock battle with strapping young Highlanders who, for all their size and enthusiasm, were definitely of the flesh-and-blood variety, and clearly no match for the high-skilled swordery of the *ghostly* combatants.

Of those, a huge bearlike man with a shock of shaggy red hair and an equally wild beard laughed uproariously as he windmilled his blade, deftly holding off any and all attempts the younger men made to come at him.

"Bran of Barra," the dark knight identified the burly Islesman. "A friend, and one of the most great-hearted chieftains the Hebrides ever saw. A man who hasn't left his isle-girt keep in centuries, but came here today as a favor to Alex. He brought a good score of seasoned clansmen with him, and the braw young lads challenging him just now are his grandsons, many times removed. He—"

"And Alex? Where is he?" Mara lifted a hand to shade her eyes, peered hard into the clashing tangle of brawn, plaid, and steel. "I can't see him."

"In time, my lady," the dark knight promised, tightening his fingers on her shoulder.

Mara swallowed, something in his tone making her

wonder if he hadn't zapped away Alex as magically as he'd banished Murdoch, Ben, and everyone else who'd been there only moments before.

But he did seem kindly, so she tamped down her impatience, tried not to fidget.

"And that one there," he went on as if she hadn't interrupted him, "the tall scar-faced knight on the far side of the field, do you see him?"

He pointed, and Mara saw the man indeed.

She stared at him, her breath catching at his skill. "He doesn't look Scottish," she said, noting that he was clad like a medieval *English* knight.

"And he is not Scottish," Sir Hardwin confirmed. "But his heart resides firmly in the Highlands. North of here, in Kintail. He is Sir Marmaduke Strongbow, a Sassunach champion and a great friend to Clan MacKenzie in his day. His sword arm is unequalled in any century. Alex journeyed far to find him, though I doubt he did much arm-bending once he did. Sir Marmaduke is a gallant. He will not have needed much persuasion to come."

"And why did he?" She was almost afraid to ask. A suspicion was beginning to burn inside her, and the glory of it, if true, had the power to undo her.

But she had to know.

"Why are any of these men here? The young ones and the—" she broke off, hot color staining her cheeks.

"The young lads and the ghosts?" Alex's friend finished for her, unfazed. His tone just as pleasant as it had been since he'd stepped into her path.

Mara nodded, the thickness in her throat as great a hindrance as her embarrassment in calling ghosts *ghosts*.

The knight cleared his throat, suddenly in front of her again. "Alex's fall to ruin was bright and deep," he said, his shield still in place. "Those who came here in friendship today love him enough to help him avoid another such disaster."

Mara's gaze shifted to the sword-swinging melee, relief flooding her upon seeing the spectators returned. "But I love him, too," she admitted, straining to see him through the crowd. "I would never turn away from him or—"

"The disaster we wish to avert comes not from you, my lady, but from the circumstances." The knight caught her hand and dropped a kiss on her knuckles. "Alex knows how much you care for him. But he couldn't exactly sally up to your door and announce himself, could he?"

"So you came with him as a foil?"

"Call it what you will." He gave her another slow, easy smile. "You only need to know he spent the last weeks seeking out amenable friends, then searching up their great-great-grandsons. The ones still Highland enough not to keel over when a ghostie relation slips into their dreams asking a favor."

"The favor of posing as medieval reenactors?"

One raven brow lifted. "Can you think of a better way for Alex to return to you?"

Mara couldn't.

She glanced at the training ground again, blinked against the blinding flash of weaving steel. "It was clever, yes. Medieval reenactment shows are popular."

"And something Alex can do to make himself useful." The knight looked pleased. "Once the younger lads are properly trained and our friends return to their respective haunts, Alex can run tournaments, perhaps give lessons in swordery."

He paused, tucked a curl behind her ear. "Do not look so troubled, lady. Alex will charm your guests. He can even offer piping instruction or teach knightly riding. Beguile with Celtic whimsy."

Mara's heart tilted. Hottie Scottie *could* beguile.

And seduce, her rapid pulse and damping palms reminded her.

"I just wish he'd told me himself." She lifted up on her toes, tried to see over the shoulders of the spectators. "He was gone six weeks. I missed him," she added, scanning the field. "I must go to him now."

She started forward, but a firm grip to her elbow stopped her.

"There is another reason I wanted to speak to you," the knight cautioned, once more blocking her way. "Alex is injured, though I am sure he'll try and conceal his pain. You must treat him gently. He—"

"*Injured?*" Mara stared at him, her chest tightening. "How can he be hurt? He's a ghost!" she blurted, then immediately snapped her mouth shut, heat scalding her cheeks.

To her surprise, a hint of color touched the knight's face as well. "There are mysterious forces in the otherworlds, my lady. Things Alex and I haven't begun to comprehend in all our years having to deal with them."

He took her hand again, this time drawing her toward the line of spectators. "Alex was punished for finding *enjoyment* with you. Pleasure he will seek again. As his friend, I ask you to have a care with him."

Mara's jaw slipped. "You mean no—"

"Precisely." He looked at her, the seriousness of his expression frightening beyond words.

But then a hint of his roguish smile returned. "There are many ways for a man and woman to enjoy each other," he said, his dark gaze holding hers. "Explore them until Alex's wounds heal. If he is pulled away again, he might not be able to return."

Mara gulped. "You mean that is why—" she got no further, found herself talking to thin air.

The dashing knight was gone.

Or rather, he now stood midfield, his rakish smile brighter than ever, his gleaming sword slicing the air, his every arc or thrust deflected by the whirling, quicksilver blade of a tall, vigorous man whose bold, high-spirited laugh almost brought Mara to her knees.

"Alex!" she cried, running onto the field.

He spun around and raised his sword in greeting, his devilish grin melting her. And then she was flying across the grass, barely registering the cheers ringing in her ears or how swiftly her love lowered and sheathed his blade.

She only saw the joy spreading across his face, his

arms extending in welcome, and how utterly real and *uninjured* he looked.

The beaming fool standing next to him was mistaken.

Nothing ailed Hottie Scottie.

And the effort of appearing whole and hearty was killing him.

But the triumph of having made it back at all and now seeing her racing at him, her hair streaming out behind her and her eyes sparkling, was a glory far stronger than any searing lightning bolt pain.

Even so, the instant she reached him and flung herself into his arms, it was all he could do to keep from wincing. Instead, he smiled all the broader and dragged her into his embrace, crushing her against him.

"Sweet lass," he soothed, for she was gasping for breath, clinging to him with all her strength, flushed and wide-eyed. "Did I no tell you I'd return?"

"But—"

"No buts. I am here now." He tightened his arms around her, burying his face against her shoulder. Giddy relief sluiced through him that the feel of her pressing her pliant body to his, melting against him, didn't send him spinning back into the darkness.

"Y-you were gone so long," she cried, her voice breaking. She thrust her fingers into his hair, holding him close. "I missed you so, and I feared—"

"My heart was with you the whole time I was away," he told her true, lifting his head and seizing her face in his hands for a deep, devouring kiss.

A kiss he broke all too soon, but his need for her was ferocious and growing more fevered with every hot beat of his heart.

"Wait till I get you alone," he vowed, sweeping his hands over her trembling body, running them up and down her back. "This is no the place with kith and kin—"

"Nay, it is not, my friend," a deep voice warned in the same moment a steely hand clamped down on his shoulder. "You would be wise to show your affection in a more private place. Perhaps One Cairn Village, as it stands deserted just now."

Sir Marmaduke.

Alex frowned, recognizing the scar-faced Sassunach's smooth, low-pitched voice. And the absurdity of the man's prudish warning.

His prudish, *uncharacteristic* warning.

Champion sworder or no, if ever a soppy-headed, romantically inclined knave walked the hills, it was Sir Marmaduke Strongbow. As Alex knew him, he'd be the last man to object to a passionate embrace and a few scorching kisses.

No matter how many onlookers milled about.

Blowing out an irritated breath, Alex made to wheel about and tell him so, but he couldn't move, for his friends had surrounded him, the whole fool lot of them pressing close and buzzing round like wet hornets gone mad.

Even e'er-grinning Hardwick, only he wasn't grinning now.

None of them were.

Some even looked infinitely sad. Defeated.

Others, the younger lads mostly, were dashing about the field waving and shaking their swords, causing a general stir and drawing all eyes.

A glance at his lady showed him why.

He was still holding her face, his hands cradling her jaw and cheeks, her lovely flushed skin clearly visible beneath all ten of his fingers.

He was fading.

And no matter how long his friends meant to dance and cavort around him, hiding the fact from the still-cheering spectators, Alex strongly suspected there wasn't much he could do to keep it secret much longer.

He'd wagered his all and was losing.

Fury welled up inside him, and he clenched his fists, throwing back his head to glare up at the cloudless blue sky, staring at its brilliance until his eyes stopped burning and the hot lump in his throat receded.

Raging at his fate would avail nothing.

But *thinking* might.

To do so he needed a clear head and an iron will. Two things he'd had almost seven hundred years to cultivate.

The good saints be praised.

Chapter 13

Alex paced behind the whins and bracken edging One Cairn Village. The worst possible place for a reunion tryst with his lady, but apparently the only corner of the entire Ravenscraig demesne currently emptied of long-nosed, gog-eyed gawkers.

Everyone else still rimmed the training ground, watching raptly as his sizeable company of Highlanders, ghostly and otherwise, continued to entertain, their flashing, weaving steel holding the crowd in thrall.

All save the wee bit of an ancient female called Innes.

Oblivious to the furor, the tiny white-haired woman bustled about inside one of the craft shops, arranging and rearranging her candles and soaps. But not so diligently that she hadn't hurried outside so soon as she'd caught a glimpse of Alex and Mara arriving at the near-completed village.

Sharp-eyed if dotty, she'd cocked her head and peered at them, twittering on about how well and fit Alex looked.

How dashing in his plaid.

Then she'd ruined it by calling him Lord Basil and declaring she'd never seen him look younger.

A corner of Alex's mouth twitched. If the poor biddie knew he was almost seven hundred years young, she would not have been content to hobble back into her cozy little craft shop. She would have scuttled herself clear to Oban.

So fast as her birdlike legs would carry her.

Alex flinched. The last thing he wanted was to frighten hapless old women.

Especially feeble-minded ones.

Frowning, he cast a look at the back of the low, whitewashed cottage that was the soap-and-candle craft and workshop. Just visible through the gorse bushes and with a curl of blue peat smoke rising from its chimney, the thick-walled cottage was definitely still firmly in the old bird's possession.

Snatches of her reedy voice engaged in a monologue about the surprising appeal of *Lord Basil* in full Highland regalia proved it. As did the occasional flutter of the window curtains.

The wee biddie was spying on them.

Not that he cared.

He'd gladly shout his love for his lady from the summit of Ben Nevis and even smother her with kisses in front of a whole score of age-bent, tongue-clacking women.

So long as he was here to do so, he'd be grateful.

And so long as Innes lingered in the craft shop, he had good reason to avoid One Cairn Village's newly cobbled square and the kick-in-the-shins annoyance of having to stroll past the recently finished memorial cairn.

The whole place made his hackles rise, and the cairn was a botheration he was determined to ignore.

What he couldn't ignore was the horror of seeing his transparent fingers cradling his lady's face.

Or his burning need for her.

Fighting back a ferocious frown, he wheeled about and went long-strided to where she stood beside a patch of springy heather. He seized her hard against him, bracing himself not to wince. No easy feat, for the more fiercely he clutched her to him, the more wickedly his wounds stabbed him with sharp, searing heat.

Even worse pain than had shot through him when she'd flung herself into his arms on the training ground.

But at least this time his hands were splayed across her back, well hidden from view.

Not that hiding them meant he didn't have to warn her.

"Lass, sweet lass," he began, his heart twisting when she slid her arms around him and pressed her cheek against his chest. "Ne'er have I lied to you and I willna do so now. It would seem the fates—"

"The fates have been kind," she gushed, hugging him tightly. "I thought I'd never see you again. Even thought you'd sent a female friend to scare me away. But you came back and now everything is—"

"A female friend?" Alex set her from him, looked down at her in surprise. "I have not had female associations since . . ." He trailed off, jerked a glance at the tall Celtic cross rising from the top of the memorial cairn.

A muscle twitched in his jaw. All that failed was the white-on-blue Scottish saltire flapping proudly against the afternoon sky.

Blessedly, that insult was spared him.

"You haven't had female associations since?" his lady prodded.

"Since before I was sent to wed your ancestress, Isobel," he finished with a shudder. "Even if I had, I would ne'er have sent a ghostie maid to frighten you."

He looked at her, hoped she could see the sincerity of his words.

Apparently she did, because she drew a trembling breath and blinked furiously against tears she couldn't stop from spilling down her cheeks.

Forgetting himself, Alex reached to brush away the dampness with his thumbs, felt a surge of relief when his hands appeared solid against her flesh.

"You are a gift beyond measure, and I would move heaven and earth to keep you," he vowed, undone by the love in her eyes. He stroked the hair back from her face, slanted a kiss across her lips. "You ought know that by now."

She colored. "I do," she admitted, her voice quivering despite the lift of her chin. "But at the time, I didn't know what to think. I saw her just after you . . . *er* . . . vanished."

This time Alex flushed.

He knew the exact moment he'd been swept out of her arms. A moment of wondrous, shattering joy and a triumph he'd dare not risk again lest whatever forces controlling such things separate them for good.

"I am sorry you were frightened." He smoothed his hands down her back to cup her buttocks, allowing himself the pleasure of kneading the plump rounds. "But I canna imagine who may have appeared to you. Perhaps—"

"I think I know who she was. I researched her, just like—"

"Just like you buried your nose in those dusty tomes in the MacDougall library and discovered lies about me?"

She blinked. "I didn't mean it that way," she said, tightening her arms around him. "I no longer care what the books say. You should know that."

Pushing up on her toes, she rained adoration across his face, lighting her sweet, lush lips everywhere she could reach, each soft kiss squeezing his heart and stirring his loins.

Making it next to impossible to tell her what he must.

Alex groaned, set her from him again. "Then who was this woman you saw?" he asked, seizing the reprieve she was offering like a drowning man grabbing at a tossed plank of wood. "Did she appear in the bedchamber?"

Mara shook her head, remembering. "I saw her on the little strand beneath the wall walk. I went out onto the battlements after . . . after you left. She was green and glowing, all transparent and very beautiful. I am sure she looked at me, wanting to tell me something, but then she was gone.''

Shivering at the memory, she looked aside, noticing at once that Ben had joined them. The old dog busied himself on a scrub-grown knoll a few yards away, moving in and out of the heather, his nose to ground as he snuffled after whatever enticements intrigued him. From the looks of it, a cluster of large, lichen-blotched stones.

Another rush of chills sweeping her, Mara turned back to her beloved Highlander. ''You don't think he'll stumble across an adder?''

''Animals are far more wise than people,'' he answered her, a flicker of something indefinable in his eyes as he looked over at the dog. ''Had an adder chosen yon boulders for a sunbath, he would have slithered away well before Ben disturbed him. But like as not, Ben wouldn't have neared the rocks anyway had a snake been coiled there.''

''You are sure?''

''Aye, sweetness. No harm will come to old Ben. Of that, I am certain,'' he said, drawing her back into his arms, needing her. The aged dog reminded him so much of Rory that it made him hurt inside to watch him.

Now wasn't the time to be reminded of those he'd once loved and lost.

Four-legged or otherwise.

Holding on to love was all that concerned him just now, and so he pulled his lady even closer, tucking her head beneath his chin so he could enjoy the feel of her silky hair, its heady fragrance that always delighted him.

"Tell me more of your green lady," he said, caressing her back. "I have ne'er encountered one, though I know they exist."

Just keep talking.

Help me put off the words that will break my heart.

"I think she was the Ell-Maid of Dunstaffnage," she obliged, snuggling into him, her warm softness making him ache in ways that weren't good for him. "A *glaistaig* or, yes, a green lady, according to the information I found. She is said to be a Campbell ghost, haunting Dunstaffnage Castle and appearing as a harbinger whenever doom or good fortune is about to befall the Campbells."

"I have heard of her," Alex spoke true, the thundering of her heart against his chest a bliss that near unmanned him. "No one kens who she is, but I canna think she'd come here. 'Tis Clan Campbell that interests her, and she's ne'er been known to leave Dunstaffnage."

His lady lifted her chin, looked up at him with shining eyes. "The MacDougalls of Lorn held Dunstaffnage long before Robert Bruce wrested it from us in 1309," she said, pride limning her. "And certainly before the Campbells insinuated themselves with the castle's custody."

Alex stiffened, the way she'd said the word *us* hitting him harder than it should have.

But the wickedness of the MacDougalls of that day was renowned, their feats of pillage and rapine legend. Hearing her speak of the waylaying ravagers with such starry-eyed reverence was like looking into the face of his destiny and knowing he'd drawn a dulled sword.

Hearing her mention his king in the same breath, a man he'd loved above his own life and had thought to serve for the course of it, just another reminder of how quickly one's fate could change and how desperately he wanted victory this time.

That there even was a this time was a wonder.

He only hoped he'd use the chance wisely.

And he'd best start by telling her the truth. "Lass, let us walk a bit. There is something I must tell you," he began, taking her hand and leading her into the heather.

Deep into the hush of a birch and hazel thicket, needing the distance from One Cairn Village and the MacDougalls' sacred treasure of a cross-topped cairn before he trusted himself to speak.

"See you," he continued at last, stopping beside a rocky burn. "Just as the Ell-Maid of Dunstaffnage is a mystery, so are there other unexplained *things* in the realms I hope you ne'er have cause to visit."

Her eyes began to widen, so he grasped her shoulders, kissing her hard before he decided to become a less-than-honest man. "There are powerful forces at work in those realms," he said, threading his hands in her hair, caressing her nape. "Elements and consequences most of us will ne'er understand or master. We can only hope to tolerate them, or, in time, perhaps learn ways to lessen their annoyance."

"Dear God!" She broke away from him, all color draining from her face. "I forgot!" she cried, her eyes round. "You are injured. Your friend Sir Hardwin told me. He warned me to treat you gently lest I hurt you."

"*Hardwick*?" Alex coughed. His face darkened and even the sun-bright little wood seemed to fill with shadow. "When did that rogue speak to you?"

Mara blinked. "He was waiting for me by the little stone wall near the training ground. But he said his name was Hardwin."

"And so it is. But Hardwick suits him better."

"I do not understand."

"Nor do you want to," he shot back, his eyes narrowing. "He didn't touch you, did he? Say anything *unusual*? Unusual beyond telling you of my wounds?"

Mara shook her head. She remembered how the dark knight had clutched his shield before him but thought it best not to mention it.

Especially with a nickname like Hard*wick*.

"He was a true friend to you," she said, opting for diplomacy. She was also certain the rakish knight had meant only good. "He did not want me to accidentally hurt you. And now"—she raised a hand to dash at the moistness filming her eyes—"I've been throwing myself at you and likely causing you all kinds of pain."

"I should have expected as much—that Hardwick would seek to warn you," he said, not taking his eyes from her. "He is indeed a longtime friend if a bit of a scoundrel."

"Then you are in pain?"

"The only pain that concerns me is the possibility of losing you." He slid his fingers under her chin, angling her face toward his. "That such a threat exists cannot be denied. The wounds I carry were received in warning. A punishment meted out for taking my ease with you, a flesh-and-blood female."

He paused, drew an audible breath. "If I indulge myself thusly again, there stands the chance I might be whisked away for longer than six weeks. As well, that I might face worse than being skewered by a few lightning bolts."

"Skewered by lightning bolts?" Mara's heart stopped, then slammed hard against her ribs. "Tell me it isn't true!"

"Would that I could." He slipped his hand down her arm, gave her fingers a squeeze. "You may lift my plaid and see for yourself if you like. I don't mind. It is my wish that you understand so that we may fight this together. Fight it and win."

He let go of her and stepped back. "Come, lass, I know you have a bold heart," he said, holding his arms out to the sides. "Ease up my plaid and look."

Mara's stomach turned into a cold, hard knot and her mouth went dry, but she did as he bid, reaching for the tartan cloth and lifting.

"God in heaven!" she cried, staring.

White and gray dots whirled across her vision, her heart clenching at the livid scars slashed onto his muscled thighs. Angry, black welts—they almost looked alive—seeming to throb and smolder beneath her stare.

His *sex* hung proud as ever, its thick length blessedly free of the marks. Nor did she see any too near the wild tangle of his dark chestnut bush.

"Dinna look too closely, Mara-lass, or I willna be able to stand so quietly before you," he purred, his husky burr almost making her forget the scars.

A flash of intense sexual heat whipped through her and she bit her lip, unable to look away as he slowly lengthened and filled.

She sucked in a breath. "Th-that must hurt beyond endurance," she stammered, her heart pounding wildly when his full-stretched shaft began to twitch and jerk.

"Och, aye, it does," he owned, a sensual smile curving his lips. "But not beyond endurance."

"I meant—"

"I ken what you meant and I love you for it," he said, speaking from the heart. Seizing her hands, he stepped close and kissed her roughly, testing the fates by letting his hardness rub against her hip.

"There are times I'd vow I have always loved you, waited forever and aye to find you," he added, slanting a discreet glance downward.

Relief flooded him when he couldn't see the black silk of her skirt through his arousal.

"I love you, too," she cried, beginning to tremble. "So much it hurts at times."

"And that, my love, is what we shall ignore. The hurting." He stepped back from her, his hands already on his sword belt, undoing its latch. "What we canna ignore, we will besiege in other ways."

"Other ways?"

"O-o-oh, aye," he said, his voice tight, thrumming with need. "The saints know I've had enough time to ponder such things."

Mara began to melt inside. "W-what things?"

"You will see soon enough," he promised, casting aside his sword belt.

When he dropped his plaid as well, spreading it on the sun-warmed grass, Mara's breath began to come shallow and her female place turned hot and achy.

Hot, damp, and achy.

There could be only one reason for a Highlander to toss his plaid on the ground.

An incredible yearning ripped through her, but her fear for his wounds warred with her passion, making her feel as if she were walking blind along a cliff's edge.

One false move and she'd plunge into darkness.

Possibly lose him forever.

She eyed the plaid, glanced back at him. "You can't mean for us to . . . to *you know*?"

"For me to take you on my plaid? Here in the heather?" He flashed her a look so sexy she almost wept. "Nay, sweetness, such bliss must wait for another day. Then, when I am sure our couplings won't mean an end to us."

"B-but you said the pain is tolerable," Mara's need made her protest. "And there doesn't seem to be anything wrong with—"

"My shaft?"

She swallowed, could feel her cheeks heating.

He gave her another deadly smile.

Then, holding her gaze, he took the object in question in hand and curled his fingers around the swollen head, squeezing until all hardness receded and its thickness rested once more against his thigh.

Still formidable, but . . . sleeping.

Calmly benign.

"You have the rights of it, lass." He dragged her against him again, kissing her deeply. "There is naught troubling my *need* for you save the exertion it's costing me to keep it at rest."

Mara looked at him, her own need saturating her, its hot drumming making her bold. "Then why are you? Exerting yourself?"

His lips curved in a devastating smile. "Because it is my hope that by doing so, I can safely treat you to other delights."

"Delights that have to do with your plaid?"

"Och, aye," he agreed, stroking his fingers into her hair. "I wish you to spread yourself across it so I can feast on you." His deep voice flowed into her, the intimacy of his words sending hot tingles to her core. "Dinna deny me, lass."

"Deny you?" Mara's breath caught on the absurdity.

Already long liquid pulls of desire coiled through her belly and her throat had gone dry. She knew exactly what kind of feasting he meant and she wanted it. Badly. She couldn't wait to feel his mouth on her, his tongue laving her pulsing, needy flesh.

"But it isn't fair," she blurted, realizing too late she'd voiced the words.

"Not fair?" he echoed, sliding strong fingers

around her arms and easing her onto the plaid, positioning her in a way that made her body thrum with craving.

He reached down to touch her breasts, let his fingers play at her nipples. "What isn't fair when I've a ravening hunger for a certain moist and succulent part of you?"

Mara looked up at him, almost climaxing.

She *did* slide right over that cliff's edge she'd been teetering along.

Only instead of hurtling into darkness, deep languorous heat swirled around her, consuming her. A sensual haze so exquisite she could only swallow against the dryness in her throat and keep staring at the long, thick length of him still dangling so provocatively between his thighs.

Provocatively and deliciously.

She shivered, unable to look away.

He followed her gaze, his breathing as ragged as hers. "I told you, lass, no staring. Or shall I cover myself?"

"No." That much she could manage.

Heaven forbid he hid such well-hung masculine beauty from her.

Looking at him, even relaxed, flooded her with streaming anticipation. Drenched her with such need, it took her breath away and sent the heady musk of her arousal spiraling up around them.

His eyes darkened, the slow curve of his smile making her think he'd noticed it, too.

"That's good, Mara." He moved closer, the smolder in his gaze letting her know he had. "Melt and burn for me. I want the scent and taste of you all o'er me, need to brand the essence of you into my skin so I can carry you with me always, no matter where I go or how long I might be parted from you."

He knelt beside her on the plaid. "You are beautiful, the most desirable woman I have e'er seen," he vowed, smoothing his hands up and down her legs.

Inching her skirt upward, he exposed her naked thighs, the delicate triangle of sheer black lace stretched so intimately between them.

Or rather the delicate black lace that *had* covered her so intimately.

Somehow he'd maneuvered himself between her legs and was using his teeth and tongue to tug down the lacy panties. Mara had never seen anything more erotic in her life.

Nor had she ever been so excited.

"O-o-oh!" she gasped. Tingling warmth streaked across her exposed flesh as he eased the panties over her ankles, sent them sailing with a jerk of his head.

"Oh!" she cried again, intense pleasure rinsing her.

"Oh, *aye*." He flashed her a knowing grin. "Sweet lass, I have burned to do that e'er since I first saw you wearing such a wee slip o' nothingness."

"Doing it cannot have been near so sweet as having it done!"

He arched a brow. "Say you?"

She nodded. "Any sweeter and I would have—"

"Not yet, lovely." He raised and bent her knees, spreading them wide. "You call me Hottie Scottie," he challenged her, slipping a hand between her legs to rub her softness, letting his fingers toy and caress. "Shall we see just how hot I can make you?"

And if this pleasure, at least, can be ours.

Willing it so, Alex kept his gaze on her sweetness, sent up a silent prayer of thanks that the fingers stroking and rubbing her remained solid.

That he could feel her slick heat, the soft moistness of her most tender flesh and the lush pelt of her gleaming, red-gold nether curls was a wonder.

If his entire body pounded with the need to bury himself deep inside her again, a thorough tasting of her would have to suffice.

"You are mine," he breathed, spreading her legs wider. He lowered his head, looking up at her as he touched his tongue to her inner thigh. "I will ne'er let you go," he vowed, licking his way closer to her heat. "You are my salvation, your name engraved on my every breath. Written across my heart."

Drawing a great breath, he released its warmth onto her most sensitive place. "And me, lass," he said, flicking his tongue back and forth across that same spot, "I would be everything you e'er desired in a man. Pull down the moon and the stars for you if only I could."

"You are more! Everything to me." She arched her back, her entire body quivering when he traced a finger down the very center of her, slipped it inside. "I do not want the moon and the stars. Only you."

She trembled then, a great rippling shudder that swept through her so fiercely, its echoes streamed through him as well, the wonder of it spilling clear to his toes.

"Precious lass," he murmured, gliding his finger in and out of her. "Keep enjoying. Let me pleasure you."

"But I can't stand this," she moaned, writhing now. "It's too sweet, too—"

"Shush, and just relax." He opened his mouth over her, sucking gently, her scent and taste making him dizzy.

He closed his eyes and inhaled her essence, letting it saturate him as he drew on her musky, wet heat until he was sure he'd drown in the glory of her.

The saints knew he burned to lose himself in her!

Would that he could . . . truly.

She cried out then, clutching at him, her fingers winding in his hair, pressing him against her. "Don't stop," she moaned, rocking her hips, her breath coming hard and fast.

"O-o-oh, I dinna mean to, ne'er you worry." He pulled back to look down at her, touched a finger to the swollen, pulsing nub at the top of her sex, relief flooding him when that precious little bud disappeared beneath his circling finger.

She was almost there, he could feel it in the tremors washing through her and hear it in her whimpers, the hitching in her breath.

Saints be praised, he was still there, too.

Solid and thrumming with desire, his wounds screamed bitterest outrage, but his hands and every other part of him blessedly solid.

But the wood around them was fading, the birch scrub beginning to shimmer and weave. And strange, whirling clouds threatened to blot the sun. Even the bold colors of his plaid were running together, the grassy earth beneath it rolling like the sea.

Alex squeezed shut his eyes, denial lancing him. Dread gripped his heart, but he continued to drag his tongue over her quivering heat, willing her release. Ignoring the dangers closing in on them.

He kept his finger on her, circling and flicking as he licked her, not daring to peek at his hand.

Not that he needed to.

The darkness was seeping into him, squeezing past his tightly closed eyelids. Taunting him cruelly with each long slide of his tongue across Mara's hot, trembling flesh.

"No-o-o!" he roared, jerking up when his laving tongue met only air. "I feel and taste her!" His entire body tensing, he used his will to defy whatever sought to damn him. "I-am-drowning-in-her-pleasure!"

And then he was, for she clamped her legs around him, grinding her soft, moist heat so firmly against him even the fates couldn't rip them apart.

"Yesss!" Her release exploded through them both, and with it, the madness receded, spinning away as quickly as it had come, leaving only a brief and angry keening of the wind.

And then that, too, was gone.

The wood fell silent again, quiet but for his lady's soft panting and the wild thundering of his heart.

Alex bit back a cry of triumph, his teeth sinking so deeply into his lip he tasted blood.

Shouting victory against such powerful foes wasn't wise, however tempting.

He sat up from between his love's still-spread legs

and raked a shaky hand through his hair, his heart too full for speech.

His shaft was full, too.

Ragingly so.

And aching. But before he could reach down and quell his misery with another hard pinching squeeze, his lady's hands were all over him. Smoothing and stroking, strong, warm, and firm, and pushing him down onto the plaid.

"Lie there and don't move," she insisted, her beautiful eyes glittering as she yanked up her skirt and straddled him. "That was glorious, but unfair. Now it's my turn to pleasure you."

"No!" Alex reached for her, seizing her hips in a tight grip before she could lower herself onto him. "You dinna understand," he panted, unable to keep his shaft from straining for her, bucking hard against the damp, soft curls hovering so close.

"I understand only too well," she argued, wrapping her fingers around him, stroking hotly, then reaching lower to knead his balls.

Balls drawn so tight, he couldn't bear it.

"That's it," she cried, throwing back her head as she rubbed her wet heat up and down his aching shaft, her massaging fingers making him crazy. "Spill for me, Alex. Now."

And he did, loosing a hot torrent of seed right onto her sweetness.

"Holy saints!" He went still, every ghostly inch of him sated and shuddering. Ecstasy whipped through him as the world splintered and darkened, leaving him to spin away into nothingness.

But this time, when he opened his eyes, it was to gaze into his lady's beloved face and not the whirling gray mists that had claimed him when he'd last dared touch her so intimately.

"Mara." He spoke her name like a prayer, would have sobbed with the wonder of her if he didn't want to frighten her.

Instead, he slid his arms around her, pulling her down against him for a long, soul-deep kiss. A searing, claiming kiss, but so soft and tender the sweetness of it spilled through her, making her tremble anew, filling her with indescribable bliss.

Until she remembered the strange words he cried as he'd pleasured her.

I feel and taste her!

I-am-drowning-in-her-pleasure!

Words that had sounded ripped from his soul, but as if he'd been speaking to someone else.

Her brow knitting, she wriggled out of his arms and pushed up on an elbow. "Who were you talking to when you called out?" she asked, smoothing his hair. "Then, when you were—"

"I ken when you mean." He caught her hand and pressed a kiss into her palm. "And I wasn't speaking to anyone. Leastways, nothing that has a face."

She blinked. "I don't understand."

"Praise God you do not." He sat up and pulled her onto his lap, holding her as if he meant to shield her from something she was certain she didn't want to know about. "I meant those *things* I mentioned earlier. The bad kind of things I can't begin to explain but that can plague the damned."

He looked at her, a strange blend of resignation and steely determination on his face. "See you, the pain from my scars is not the reason I canna love you so fully as I'd wish," he said, running his hands up and down her back. "I would suffer any pain under the heavens to lie with you, and completely. Again and again until the light fades or we were both too depleted to move. Whiche'er came first."

"But?" She began to tremble, knew just looking at him that whatever he was about to tell her would rock her world.

And not in a good way.

"What is it?" She had to know. "What else is there that might separate us?"

"Och, lass, it's only the minor complication that when I seized your face to kiss you back on the training ground, I could see your skin right through my fingers. I—"

"You *what*?"

He tightened his arms around her, pressed a kiss to her brow. "It would seem I am fading," he said, the calmness of his voice astounding her. "Growing faint at certain times. Such as when we are most intimate."

Mara gaped at him. White-hot panic sluiced through her. "But you are here now." She shook her head, struggled to breathe. "You didn't fade just now and we were incredibly intimate."

"Exactly," he agreed, slanting his mouth across hers in a triumphant kiss. "I did feel the darkness closing in on us. But I clung to you, refusing to accept its claim."

She slid her arms around his neck, holding fast to him. "You think we can ward off this darkness, this risk of you fading?"

"I do not know," he said, his answer making her heart plummet. "But so long as there *is* a we, I refuse to surrender hope."

And neither would she.

No matter that he'd scared her so badly she feared to let go of him.

"You know this means we must live with certain limitations?" He looked at her, then cleared his throat. "I was not the only one who noticed the fading. My friends saw it, and not just the ghostly ones."

Mara gasped, could feel her eyes widening.

"That's right, lass. And I willna see you or Ravenscraig turned into a spectacle," he said, in a tone that brooked no argument. "If the young flesh-and-blood Highlanders noticed, so will other mortals."

"If it happens again." She lifted her chin, blew a curl off her brow. "Maybe it won't."

To her surprise, he laughed. "You are a bold lassie," he said, pushing to his feet and pulling her with him. "If you are strong-hearted enough, we can share whate'er small joys the fates allow us."

Mara forced a smile, the best and brightest she could muster. "I'm strong-hearted enough to face anything—so long as I have you at my side," she said, putting back her shoulders. "And I would call the *joys* we share anything but small."

"Och, lass," he beamed, catching her to him for another kiss. "Do you have any idea how much I love you?"

"Yes, I do," she shot back, his high spirits and the beauty of the day making her bold. "But I am all ears if you wish to tell me."

He gave her an equally bold grin and chucked her under the chin. "Then be warned that I am so crazy-mad in love with you, I'd go down on my knee before your da to ask for your hand—even if the man is a MacDougall."

"He's a *Mc*Dougall," Mara corrected, knowing he wouldn't hear the difference. "And he—"

She broke off, her cheeks flaming.

She didn't have the first clue how to tell him about her father's imminent arrival.

Her father and his second wife, the Cairn Avenue shrew.

A combination she wasn't sure Scotland was ready for.

Especially with all Hugh McDougall's airs and eccentricities.

"What is it?" He put his hands on her shoulders, a shadow flitting across his handsome face. "You've ne'er mentioned your da before. Is he . . . if he's gone, pray forgive me, lass. I didna mean to grieve you."

Mara bit her lip, searched for the right words. "He's not dead," she finally blurted. "He's very much alive and in better health than he's been in years. Such good health, he's coming here next week for the memorial cairn's unveiling ceremony."

"But that's a reason for gladness," he said, looking puzzled.

Mara swallowed, still not believing what she was

about to say. "The trip will also be his honeymoon. He's recently married."

"All the more reason to celebrate." Hottie Scottie grinned. "Or is there something else you're not telling me? Are you afraid he willna like me?"

She almost choked. "Heavens, no. He'll worship the ground you walk on."

"Then what's the problem?"

"I can't stand his wife," Mara admitted, glancing aside. "She's a soured-up old shrew. The kind of female you'd probably call a long-nosed tongue-wagger."

She looked back at him. "Maybe even worse."

He hooted another laugh. "Then we'll just ready a welcome sure to sweeten her," he declared, sweeping her off her feet in a bone-crushing hug. "I've waited too many centuries for happiness to let it be marred by one ill-tempered woman."

And Mara had to agree.

Even if she hadn't waited a fraction as long.

It'd still taken the whole of a lifetime to find her one true love. And looking at him now, feeling his arms strong and tight around her, his sweet, golden warmth surrounding her, she knew without doubt that she was blessed.

Life could hardly get any better.

Chapter 14

Could life get any worse?

A three-hour arrival delay for any transatlantic flight certainly qualified in the worst-things-that-could-happen category. A delayed overseas flight with Euphemia Ross onboard was a recipe for disaster.

That her father seemed to have chosen the busiest day of the year to land at Glasgow International Airport didn't help matters.

His arrival would surely cause a stir whether ten or hundreds of people milled about the smallish airport's none-too-large arrival area.

Hugh McDougall of One Cairn Avenue wasn't just flying to Scotland for the first time, after all.

He was going home.

To the *Auld Hameland.*

As he'd repeatedly emphasized by phone every day of the preceding week.

Mara glanced at Malcolm the Red, felt a shivery twinge of déjà vu.

Had it really been only a few short months since he'd startled her by plucking her carry-on out of her hands outside the Oban rail station?

Amazingly, it had. And then, as now, she couldn't help but smile at the sight of him.

Well gifted with Highland courtesy and patience, the strapping young man stood with his hands clasped in front of him, his red cheeks glowing as always, and his even brighter red hair gleaming in the airport's stark, artificial lighting.

He turned to her then, looking quite unfazed for having wasted most of the fine summer morning in the crowded arrival hall. "Shall I fetch you another cup of tea?" he asked, his dimpled smile hard to resist. "But it willna be much longer now."

Mara shook her head. "Thank you, but no."

If she drank any more lukewarm Scottish tea, she'd find herself in the loo just when her dad and the shrew strode out of Customs and Immigration.

And Malcolm the Red was much too nice to deserve such a fate.

Not sure she was ready for it herself, she leaned back against an unmanned tourist information counter and closed her eyes.

"A right shame your Alex couldn't come with you," Malcolm allowed, joining her.

Mara's eyes popped back open.

"But I doona blame him wanting to stay down-bye," Malcolm added, making himself at home against the counter. "He'll want to be certain everything is done proper at Ravenscraig."

Mara looked down to smooth her skirt, deliberately avoiding the young man's eyes.

Without doubt, Hottie Scottie would be in the thick of things back at Ravenscraig. Elbow to elbow with old Murdoch, tripping over Dottie and Scottie, and flustering Prudentia, as they all readied what Mara secretly thought of as the Great Reception.

But that wasn't the reason he hadn't joined them on the drive south to Glasgow.

Hottie Scottie was simply not yet keen on riding in cars.

Not that she'd share his reservations with Malcolm the Red. "I don't mind that he didn't come," she said, speaking truthfully. Remembering how many appeals Alex had made to his Maker the one time she'd persuaded him to ride into Oban with her. "There'll be plenty of time later for him to—"

She got no further, cut off by a great stir and commotion near the arrival screen. A hullabaloo that could mean only one thing, she realized, surprised by the sudden hot swelling in her throat.

It was time.

Forget the Cairn Avenue shrew.

After sixty-nine endless-seeming years of longing and yearning, Hugh McDougall had finally arrived in the land of his ancestors.

There, be-kilted and moony-eyed, in the crush of the passengers pouring into the arrival hall. A soppy smile on his face and a chieftain's eagle feather bobbing from the blue tam-o'-shanter perched jauntily on his head.

He pushed a trolley piled high with bulging, tartan-patterned luggage and seemed oblivious to both the pinched-face scowl of the minuscule woman crowding his side and the drop-jawed gawking of the teeming throng.

"Your da?" Malcolm glanced at her.

Mara nodded, speechless.

The tops of her ears were burning and she was quite sure that if she had a mirror to hand, she'd see that they'd turned bright red.

"Looks like he's right pleased to be here," Malcolm said, starting forward.

But he only went two paces before turning round and grabbing Mara's hand, pulling her along with him. "Come, lass," he said, squeezing her fingers. "Dinna fash yourself o'er what others might be thinking. The brightness o' your da's eyes is all that matters."

Mara agreed, suddenly finding herself blinking back the brightness in her own eyes as her father spotted them and a broad grin spread across his tear-dampened face.

"Mara!" he cried, snatching off his tam-o'-shanter and waving it in the air. "My little girl!"

"Dad!" Mara let go of Malcolm's hand and elbowed a way through the jostling passengers. "It's so wonderful to see you," she said when she reached him.

Then she threw her arms around him and hugged

him tight, vaguely aware of Malcolm clapping a welcoming hand on his shoulder. Her heart swelling, she gave him a smacking kiss, no longer caring who in the terminal might wish to stop and stare at them.

"This is Malcolm, a friend," she said, glancing his way as she introduced him. "He was kind enough to drive me here. Alex is busy at Ravenscraig but is looking forward to meeting you."

Hugh McDougall thrust his hand toward the younger man. "By God, if you don't remind me of myself in younger years," he enthused, pumping Malcolm's hand. "Back when I had a bit more brawn to fill my kilts!"

Turning to Mara, he added, "As for your young man, I've brought him something special—two whole boxes of saltwater taffy from the Jersey shore and a bag of Lancaster County soft pretzels."

Mara smiled, well aware of just who would be eating the most of both.

"Oh, Dad," she said, her voice thick. "It *is* good to have you here. A-and you look great!"

"Don't I now?" He beamed at her, swiped an age-spotted hand across his cheek. "Bought a new kilt special for you. And"—he looked down and plucked at his full-sleeved shirt—"this here's a *Jacobite* shirt! Just like our forebears wore at Culloden."

"If you'd changed into a T-shirt to sleep in on the plane as I'd suggested, it wouldn't be so wrinkled." The tiny dark-haired woman at his side sniffed and reached small hands to fuss at the shirt. "My tartan sash has nary a crease."

And it didn't.

Looking impeccable as always, the Cairn Avenue shrew's ladies dress sash of Clan Ross tartan was draped stylishly over her right shoulder with neither a wrinkle nor speck of lint visible anywhere.

"Euphemia—welcome to Scotland," Mara blurted before her tongue refused to greet the woman. "And congratulations on your marriage. I wish you both every happiness."

The shrew gave her a tight little smile. "Our honeymoon would have had a more auspicious start had security in Newark not caused us such a long delay."

"But you're here now and the day is bonny," Malcolm put in, taking charge of the overburdened trolley and guiding them out into the sunshine.

"I expected to see mist," Euphemia said, sounding peeved. "Mist and castles."

"Och, you'll see plenty o' both," Malcolm promised, flashing her a blinding smile. "Dinna you worry 'bout that."

"I hope so." Euphemia cast a skeptical glance at the cloudless sky.

Malcolm winked at her. "If you'd like to stop for tea along the way, I know just the place guaranteed to give you a good glimpse o' some real Highland mist."

To Mara's surprise, the shrew smiled.

"I'd love to stop for tea," she said, hooking her arm through her husband's. "So long as we don't arrive at the castle too late. Hugh needs his sleep. He wearies easily."

But it was Mara who was soon wearying as they made their way north on the A-82, a narrow and winding ribbonwide bit of road and one of Scotland's most scenic routes into the heart of the Highlands.

Indeed, the sparkling waters of Loch Lomond shimmered through the trees to their right and the wooded, sheep-dotted slopes rising so steeply on their left could've been straight out of *Rob Roy.*

But the only things catching anyone's attention were Euphemia's repeated shrieks and exclamations of doom each time they had a close encounter with an RV or tour coach that happened to be heading in the opposite direction.

"O-o-oh, I don't believe this!" she shrilled, clapping her hands over her eyes as they squeezed past yet another superwide recreational vehicle. "And they're all going so fast."

"Ah, well, that's no bad thing," Malcolm owned, his eye on the road. "See you, we're almost nigh to Crianlarich, where we'll turn west to Oban, and up just ahead is our tea stop, the Drover's Inn."

But when they pulled into the popular inn's car park a few minutes later, Euphemia eyed the place and frowned.

And the Drover's Inn seemed to glare right back at her.

A three-storied pile of old stone with a colorful past, the somewhat tumbledown droving inn hugged the road, a scatter of empty picnic tables stretched along its front and a rise of great, moody hills looming to its rear.

Mist-hung hills.

Just as Malcolm had promised.

"Look, Phemie! There's your mist," Hugh McDougall cried, pointing to where tendrils of drifting gray mist hung down the hillside. "Highland mist just for you."

"Those are rain clouds if ever I saw one," his wife quipped, hardly looking. "And if this place isn't haunted, Philadelphia doesn't have the Liberty Bell," she added, brushing at her tartan sash. "I'm not sure I want to go in there."

"Och, I ne'er drive past without stopping here, and I've yet to see any spirits save the kind served in wee dram glasses," Malcolm assured her, opening the inn's door. "Though there's surely some that do call the place haunted. Most tourists like the idea."

"Not this one." The shrew shivered and set her mouth in a hard, tight line.

"Oh, come, Phemie, you know there's no such thing as ghosts." Hugh McDougall took her hand, patting it. "We'll just have a quick look inside. Only long enough for your tea."

"They have kilted servers and give you shortbread with the tea," Mara put in, trying to be nice.

"Shortbread is fattening," Euphemia said, peering into the inn's main taproom, a dark-paneled low-ceilinged pub that reeked of ale, peat smoke, and dogs. "And I doubt they can serve tea good enough to get me in there."

Shuddering, she cast one last contemptuous look into the smoky little room.

"This entrance hall is even worse." She folded her arms, glaring round at the clutter of discarded, broken furniture shoved into the corners, the many stags' heads on the walls. "No, I don't want tea here. They probably don't serve it with ice cubes anyway."

"Ice cubes?" Malcolm's brow furrowed. "I thought you meant hot tea."

Euphemia looked at him. "No, I wanted a tall glass of iced tea with lemon, and now I just want to go," she said, turning toward the door so quickly she almost collided with a moth-eaten standing bear. "I am sure Ravenscraig will suit me better."

"But, Phemie, this place is like peeking into the past. Just look at those smoke-blackened hearthstones. You know each one would have a tale if only they could speak!" Hugh McDougall threw a longing glance at the glowing peat fire on the far side of the dark little pub. "You drink hot tea, too. Come on, five minutes."

But the Cairn Avenue shrew was already out the door.

"I'm sure you'll be able to do plenty of past peeping at your daughter's castle," she called over her shoulder. "I won't stay anywhere that smells of mold and mildew and looks like it might have ghosts."

Mara slid a glance at Malcolm as they crossed the car park, but his face showed no sign that he'd guessed the true nature of Alex and his reenactor friends.

Blessedly, neither did her father or the shrew when, about two hours later, they drove through Ravenscraig's massive gatehouse and Alex's stalwarts came into view.

They lined the drive, standing proud in their plaids and mail.

Excepting a few that Mara knew especially well, even she was hard-pressed to say who was a ghostie and who was a flesh-and-blood Highlander.

"Now *there's* your past peeping." Euphemia leaned forward to poke her husband's shoulder. "They must've robbed a museum or paid a fortune to have such authentic costumes made."

Mara bit back the urge to tell her just how real most of the costumes were.

And the swords.

Not that she really cared whether she frightened Euphemia Ross or not. The look of awe on her father's face was well worth suffering the woman.

With luck, a good stout wind might even blow her into the firth. Considering she didn't even top five feet and looked to weigh no more than eighty pounds, Mara figured the possibility had chances.

"By golly!" her dad exclaimed then, rolling down his window. "Will you look at that wild-eyed devil over there on the left? The big burly one with the bushy red beard. If he doesn't look like he just stepped out of a history book, I'll eat my tam-o'-shanter!"

Mara smiled. "That's Bran of Barra," she was glad to supply. "He's one of Alex's closest friends and a genuine Hebridean chieftain."

"I can sure see that," her father said, his eyes almost popping out of his head.

"And over there on that rise, the tall piper with his plaid lifting in the breeze, that's Alex." Mara waved at him, her heart catching when he flashed her a grin and started playing "Highland Laddie."

"Piping is just one of Alex's talents," she added, glancing back at her dad. "I hope you'll like him."

"Like him?" Her dad slapped his knee. "Any young man who wears a kilt, pipes, and puts such a twinkle in my little girl's eye is a young man I'd be proud to call son."

Mara felt happiness tighten and burn her throat, sting the backs of her eyes.

Swallowing hard, she fought the sensations before the first tear could fall. She wasn't going to get emotional in front of Euphemia Ross. She just hoped her dad would still feel the same about Alex if ever their secret leaked out.

Not that she intended to let that happen.

With so many guests, ghosties, and friends attending the welcome reception planned for the evening, if Hottie Scottie *did* start to fade at some point during the celebrations, enough of his men would be on hand to shield him from view until the fading spell passed.

There'd been at least a dozen such incidents in the last week, but Mara refused to think about them.

Leastways not tonight, on the eve of the memorial cairn's unveiling ceremony.

A traditional Highland *ceilidh* with all the bells and whistles.

And, she hoped, no unexpected surprises.

A hope that lasted until the evening's entertainments of music, singing, and storytelling were in full swing and she spied her father's teeny tartan-swathed wife heading her way. High color stained Euphemia's usually pallid cheeks and her thin lips were pursed so tightly that she looked like she'd just bit into a persimmon.

Even worse, a likewise tartan-sashed Prudentia sailed along in her wake.

Neither Mara's dad, nor Alex, nor even Murdoch was anywhere close by. Much to her dismay, all three men were presently making *gentlemanly* across the vastness of the jam-packed great hall. Resplendent in their dress kilts and silver-buttoned Prince Charlie jackets, they stood before the hearth fire, sipping drams and having a blether. And, from the looks of it, eating her dad's brought-along soft pretzels.

And the shrew was bearing down on her.

Mara straightened and put back her shoulders, waiting.

It didn't take long.

"I can't spend a night beneath this roof," Euphemia announced, drawing up in front of her. "Everything smells musty and old and—"

"Ravenscraig *is* old." Mara took a sip of her own single malt, Royal Brackla, then placed the dram glass on a plaid-covered trestle table. "And there are some here who might be offended if you call the place musty."

She looked at Prudentia. "Wouldn't you say Ailsa and Agnes do an excellent job keeping up the castle?"

The cook had the grace to look chagrined, but she recovered as quickly.

"She means the dog smell," she said, sending a pointed look to where Dottie, Scottie, and Ben were making hopeful rounds, begging tidbits and savories from guests. "That, and all the ornate ancestral portraits everywhere."

Euphemia nodded. "They're downright creepy." She glanced at a particularly large one hanging above the great hall's enormous hearth. "I'm certain I saw one that had a nasty-looking chieftain in it whose eyes followed me when I walked past."

Mara folded her arms. "If you did, I imagine the painting was done by a highly talented artist."

The shrew sniffed. "You won't change my mind. Your father and I will not be staying here. And"—she paused to glance at Prudentia—"*she* told me the place is riddled with ghosts."

"Ghosts?" Alex slid a black-jacketed arm around Mara's waist, dropped a kiss onto the top of her head. "What's this about bogles? Has someone seen one?"

Prudentia turned to him. "Anyplace where time has stood still is a place where sensitive souls can feel the past."

Alex took Mara's hand, lacing their fingers. "And are you such a sensitive?"

The cook narrowed her eyes. "I always ken when a spook is about," she said, looking superior. "The very air in a room changes, giving you a chill that goes right to the marrow."

"Indeed?" Alex arched a brow. He was sorely tempted to conjure an icicle from behind his back and offer it to her like a rose.

"And you, fair lady?" He gave the small, sour-faced woman his most dazzling smile. "You do not wish to spend the night here? In the castle?"

"Most definitely not," she snapped, apparently unimpressed by medieval Highland charm. "I, too, can sense ghosts. I feel them everywhere here."

"Well, then—"

He broke off, his words drowned by the sudden skirl of pipes as Erchy, another of Alex's *special* friends, strutted into the hall, blowing his pipes with red-cheeked gusto. A piper of some renown from the days of the '45, he marched right past them, drawing nary a flicker of alarm from either of the spirit-seeing women.

"Well, then," Alex continued when Erchy and his screaming pipes reached the far end of the hall, "if you are concerned about sleeping where you suspect ghosts are underfoot, perhaps you'd prefer one of Mara's cottages down at One Cairn Village."

"You mean out near the memorial cairn?" Euphemia worried her lip. "I don't know. It's pretty isolated out there, isn't it?"

"To be sure." Alex smiled at her. "But the cottages are newly built and modern even if they look old and quaint on the outside. And"—he discreetly stepped on Mara's toe—"many of my reenactment friends are housed in the cottages or they camp nearby. They'd surely come to your aid if you needed them."

"Well . . ." She looked hesitant.

"They're all here just now, celebrating." Alex waved a hand, indicating the milling Highlanders, corporeal and otherwise. "Braw lads, as you can see. I can guarantee you nary a one of them is afraid of ghosts."

Mara almost choked.

She did turn aside, unable to watch and listen.

Stepping up to the plaid-draped trestle table, she helped herself to a piece of saltwater taffy and waited until the shrew hurried off to inform her husband that they'd be sleeping elsewhere.

"I can't believe you did that." Mara whirled around, not at all surprised to find Alex wearing a self-satisfied grin. "My dad was looking forward to sleeping in a castle."

"That wee besom wouldn't have given him a moment's peace no matter what room you might have given them."

Ben joined them then, pressing against them and nudging their hands with his cold, wet nose until Hottie Scottie reached down to fondle his scruffy head.

"Even so, the empty cottage isn't very inviting," Mara said, taking another piece of taffy. "It'll be cold. Someone will have to go down there and ready it for them."

"We'll do it." A mischievous twinkle lit Alex's eyes. "You, me, and Ben. We'll slip away now and no one will be the wiser."

"Us?" Mara blinked. "But the dancing is about to start. Didn't you see the fiddlers setting up? Or your friends helping to clear away the trestle tables?"

"Och, aye, I saw." He looked down, the light gone

from his eyes. " 'Tis a reason I'd rather be off with you now, before such merriment begins."

"You don't like dancing?" she asked, sounding so disappointed he bent his head and kissed her.

"Och, sweetness." He rested his hands on her shoulders, gave her another quick kiss, this time on her brow. "On my soul, I would dance with you all night and ne'er have enough. But—"

Her eyes widened. "Are you fading again?"

"Not that, either." He shook his head. "But my lightning bolt scars are troubling me more than usual this e'en, and while I'd gladly suffer the discomfort to dance with you, I've no wish to whirl around the hall with the other women here tonight. If we stay, Highland courtesy demands I do just that."

"Oh." Color flared on her cheeks. "I didn't think. And I'd forgotten about the scars. You just seem so—"

He pressed his fingers to her lips. "Precious lass, for the two of us, I *am* real," he vowed, willing it. "So real as this fool MacDougall sporran I donned just for you."

"MacDougall sporran?" Her gaze flew to the thing, her jaw dropping as astonishment washed her lovely face. "You are wearing a clan sporran," she gasped, looking back up at him. "Why? I m-mean . . . wherever did you get it?"

"Why?" He cocked a brow at her. "Can you not guess? I wear it to honor the day. And my lady."

Mara swallowed, unable to speak.

She couldn't stop staring at the proud MacDougall

clan crest on the sporran's gleaming silver cantle. A fine dress sporran, it looked to be of best-quality leather and fur with tasseled diamond-cut chains.

Then the beautiful sporran swam before her eyes and Alex's arms were reaching for her, dragging her against his warm, blessedly solid chest.

"Y-you don't know what it means to me to see you wearing that," she said, the words choked. "But w-where did you get it?"

"Och, lass," he soothed, rubbing her back as he held her. "I fashioned it by will. The same way I conjure my plaid or sword or anything else I desire."

He set her from him then, the light back in his eyes. "I conjured a duplicate for your da. He's wearing it now. 'Tis why we spent so much time having a good *craik* o'er by the hearth. I thought such a gift might please him, and increase my chances when I ask him for your hand."

Mara stared at him, her jaw slipping again. And then the world disappeared for a heartbeat only to reappear in bold and thrilling colors.

Everything looked freshly washed and bright.

New and wonderful.

She swallowed, dashed at her tears. "You mean to ask for my hand?" she asked, glancing across the hall at her father.

Sure enough, he was wearing an identical sporran.

Beaming, he appeared to be showing it to anyone whose eye he could catch.

She looked back at Alex, her throat so thick she could scarce speak. "Does this mean what I think it means?"

He grabbed her hand, started pulling her toward the door. "That I wish to marry you?" He slanted a glance at her as they paused on the threshold, waiting for Ben. "Of course, that's my intention. If—"

"Oh, Alex!" She flung her arms around his neck, kissed him hard and deep. "I never thought—"

"Dinna let your heart swell too quickly," he cautioned, breaking the kiss. "I meant to say I wish for us to marry if e'er we can find a way to enjoy a more normal union than the present circumstances allow."

"Oh." Mara's elation vanished like a pricked soap bubble.

"No frowning." Alex captured her face in his hands, dropped a quick kiss to her down-tilting lips. "We have much to relish together even if we can ne'er truly be man and wife. For the now, a pleasant walk through the *simmer dim* to One Cairn Village."

He opened the castle's main entry door, led her out into the luminous, silver-washed night. "And," he added, as they made their way along the gravel path toward the distant line of woods, "a fine four-legged companion to accompany us. Such joys are worth much. Let us be glad for them."

He looked down at the old dog trotting so happily beside them. "I ne'er told you, but it pleases me greatly to have won Ben's affection," he said, his own heart catching this time. "He reminds me of Rory. A dog I had . . . *er* . . . shall we say, a very long time ago?"

"We shall," Mara agreed, smiling as Ben bolted off across the grass.

When he disappeared into a thicket of rhododendrons, she turned to Alex, throwing her arms around him again and hugging him until her breasts hurt from being crushed against him.

She reached down between them, slipping her hand beneath his MacDougall sporran, then smiled when she felt the thick, hard ridge of his desire.

"O-o-oh, Alex, I want and need you so!" she cried, curling her fingers around him, squeezing. "And I love you so much I can't breathe without feeling you somehow. Holding your hand, kissing you, just . . . touching you. So long as we touch I am alive."

"And if we do much more such touching, you'll have me lifting my kilt right here on the garden path—in clear view of all our guests."

"Oh!" Mara said for the third time that night. "I forgot some of the hall's windows look out onto the lawn."

"Then come, let us be away to ready that cottage for your da and his wee spitfire of a wife." He offered her his arm, smiling when she took it. "Who knows what pleasures the night may yet bring?"

A good hour later, in the very heart of One Cairn Village, Mara closed the door of her dad and the shrew's soon-to-be love nest and gave a great sigh. She glanced at Alex, her heart dipping at how handsome he looked in the soft silver-blue light of the late summer's evening.

A quiet evening.

A night full of beauty with a slender moon shining in the heavens and a gentle wind stirring the hushed air.

Not a sound from the *ceilidh* could be heard this far from the castle, and with all of One Cairn Village's current occupants enjoying the revelry, the silence felt thick and heavy. And just a touch eerie.

Almost otherworldly.

Shivering, she pushed the thought from her mind and looked back at the quaint little cottage with its bright blue door and low, romantic lights gleaming through the thick-silled windows. Not real candlelight, but electric lamps fashioned to look and burn like candles, they cast the same flickering golden light.

"Oh, Alex. Do you think they'll be pleased?"

"The besom?" He scratched his chin. "That one, to be sure. But, snug as the cottage is, I suspect your da would've preferred the tower room you'd selected for them. Which one was it? The Islesman?"

Mara nodded. "Yes, that was it."

"Aye, he would have liked that one," Alex agreed, winking at her. "It would've reminded him of Bran of Barra. Your da seems quite taken with him."

Mara laughed. "Dad would have appreciated the views from the room, too. But he'll like being right across from the memorial cairn."

She glanced at it then and frowned.

A great blue cloth had been swirled round the cairn's base, covering the stone and the large brass memorial plaque. Much to her horror, Ben had an edge of the cloth clamped between his teeth and was pulling on it.

"Ben, no!" Mara cried, running toward him across the little village square. "Stop that!"

But Ben only tugged harder, his tail swishing wildly when the cloth ripped. He froze for a moment, looking stunned by his own triumph, a good-sized piece of the blue sheeting dangling from his jaws.

And then, almost smiling, he streaked off into the heather, the blue cloth whipping behind him like a knight's banner.

"I didn't know he could run that fast." Mara threw a startled glance at Alex.

"Looks like he's headed to that scrub-grown knoll again," Alex said. "I'd wager there's a rabbit or some other wee creature that makes its home in that cluster of rocks he was snuffling at the other day."

He slung his arm around Mara's shoulders, gave her a squeeze. "Come, let's go fetch him," he said, leading her toward Innes's soap-and-candle craft shop and the thicket of gorse and whins just beyond it. "He's clearly caught the scent of something."

Sure enough, when they finally reached the base of the heathery knoll, there was Ben scrambling excitedly over the tumbled, lichen-blotched stones.

He looked at them and barked, then resumed leaping about the knoll, thrusting his nose into one rabbit hole after another, his tail wagging furiously.

Then he disappeared.

"Ben!" Mara ran forward, dropping to her knees in the heather where Ben had been but a moment ago.

Alex hurried after her, scanning the hills as he ran.

But Ben was gone, nowhere to be seen.

Fear for the old dog tightened Alex's chest. Seeing his lady ripping at the heather, searching for Ben, tore his heart.

"The blue cloth!" she cried then, whipping it into the air, waving it at him. "It was stuck in a crack between two of the boulders."

"Don't move!" Alex warned her, ignoring how his wounds were beginning to twitch and burn. "Don't even breathe. Ben must've fallen into one of those heather-covered crevices I warned you about."

"Yes, he has! I can hear him whimpering." She twisted round to look at him, her eyes wide with fear. "Oh, what can we do? We have to get him out."

"We'll get him. Dinna you worry," he called to her, the words sounding distant. "Just be still until I can get to you."

"Oh, no! Something's wrong with you, too!" She stared at him and clapped a hand to her cheek. "You're so pale."

"It's the lightning bolt scars," he said, his voice sounding even fainter. "The pain will pass."

But he needed all his strength to climb the knoll. Claws of fire raked him with each step, searing and slashing at his innards as if his scars had grown talons and were ripping him, tearing him apart.

He forced himself to move, kept putting one foot in front of the other until he made it to his lady's side.

Then he threw back his head and looked up at the liquid-silver sky, drew a deep, lung-filling breath to strengthen him. But when he grabbed Mara's arm and yanked her away from the stones, the effort near brought him to his knees.

It *did* make him dizzy.

But he couldn't risk her falling into an underground crevice or cave. And Ben needed him, too. The old dog was barking now, bless him.

Sounding more excited than anything.

Certainly not injured.

Such relief swept Alex that he almost felt himself again. "Ben's well," he called to his lady as he yanked at the heather covering the crevice. "He'll be fine so soon as I make an opening large enough for me to scramble down inside there and get him."

But Mara said nothing.

Understanding her fear, he kept tearing at the heather and bracken, tossing aside loose stones. "It must be an underground cave," he said, working faster now, his strength returning. "I can see Ben's eyes looking up at me."

Ben's eyes, something bright and glittery, and old, moldering bones.

A rusted sword and bits of what looked to be a shirt of mail.

"Jesus wept!" His eyes flew wide. "It's not a cave. Ben's fallen into a tomb. My own sainted grave!"

The earth tilted and spun, the beautiful night blurring around him, its silvery-blue hues turning an ethereal green that swirled and caressed.

Soothing caresses that took his pain but also sharpened the sound of Ben's loud barking.

And Mara's silence.

He twisted round to face her. "Did you not hear me? Ben's fallen into my tomb! There can be no mistaking. My own old sword is down there. And the Bloodstone of Dalriada. I saw its glitter winking up at me!"

But she only stood frozen, staring at him.

Not saying a word.

And, Alex finally saw, not looking at him, but past him.

Whipping round, he saw what lamed her.

"It's my green lady," she said then, her voice glazed with fear.

Beautiful and glowing, the apparition shimmered on the far side of the knoll, the whole of One Cairn Village clearly visible through her luminous green gown.

"That's not a green lady, lass." Alex pushed to his feet, humbled. "She's one o' the fey. I'd bet my life on it."

"And so you did once," the woman said, her voice a song. Like sweet, tinkling music on a breeze. "And so you shall wager again, if you come to this side of the knoll and retrieve your poor dog."

"Ben!" Mara grabbed Alex's arm, gripped tight. "He's there, with her."

And he was.

Bright-eyed, dirt-streaked, and swishing his tail.

"I'm not sure I want to come close to you, lady of the fey." Alex eyed her, too wary of the tricks of the sidhe to approach the woman without caution. "I'd be grateful if you unspell our dog and let him come over here."

"You are a prudent man, Sir Alexander. And a good one," she said, releasing Ben. "I but wished to show you the most conspicuous way into your tomb."

"And why would you do that?"

"Because you might have cause to seal it." She smiled when Ben loped across the rocks toward them. "Or would you wish your children to fall into such a place?"

"My children?" Alex's blood began to hammer in his ears. "Children with Mara?"

The fey beauty glowed a shade brighter. "If you so choose."

"If?" Hope near split Alex. "I desire nothing more fiercely. Save having and keeping my lady."

"Oh, God!" Mara looked at him. "What is she saying?"

"Simply that the choice is his." She held up a magnificent ruby brooch. "The Bloodstone of Dalriada carries three wishes," she said, suddenly standing before them. "Long ago, he cursed himself with the second wish. But a—"

"A third remains?" Alex stared at the brooch, the roaring in his ears deafening now.

The woman nodded. "Make your wish, Sir Alexander, and I shall take the brooch back with me to my own realm. We have waited long for its return."

"As I have waited—" Alex snapped shut his mouth, looked at his hand.

The brooch rested in his palm, its pulsing warmth sending chills all through him.

Chills and hope.

"Mara." He turned to her, saw the same dream beating all through her. "It might not work," he cautioned. "Dinna be sad if it doesn't, if something happens to me."

A tinkling laugh chided him. "Only what you desire will happen. The Bloodstone's magic is strong—as you ought know!"

And that decided it for him.

He did know.

So he pulled Mara into his arms, holding her tight, his heart squeezing when Ben pressed against them, his fool tail still wagging.

A tear rolled down Alex's cheek and he looked down at the dog, for one split second seeing not Ben but Rory.

And then he made his wish.

But nothing happened.

The hills didn't shake and the heavens didn't split wide. Nor did the world spin and contract as it sometimes did.

Everything felt perfectly normal.

Ordinary.

And then he understood.

"Mara, look!" He unclenched his hand, stared down at his naked palm. "It's gone. The brooch is gone and your green lady with it."

"And you are whole again!" she sobbed, yanking up his kilt, staring not at her favorite part of him, but at his scar-free thighs. "The scars are gone, too."

But Alex was undoing his shirt, opening it wide to look at his chest. It, proved free of the scars. His pain had vanished, too.

Every last bit of it.

All that remained was his happiness.

And the woman he loved more than a thousand

eternities. He could now make her his in truth. In name, as well as body. But she'd moved away a bit, stood with her shoulders slumping.

He went after her, catching her to him. "Mara, sweet Mara, what is it?" He rained kisses on her face, smoothed back her hair. "Are you not happy for us?"

She looked away, her lip quivering. "I-I have never been happier," she said, her voice breaking. "But I am shamed for not believing you in the beginning. Tomorrow is the unveiling ceremony, and"—she broke off to swipe at her tears—"my dad will read words from a memorial tablet honoring the very people who damned you!"

She hugged herself, almost convulsing. "I will stop the ceremony," she vowed. "I'll have the cairn dismantled and the plaque thrown into the firth."

To her surprise, he laughed. "You will do no such thing. I forbid it."

"You what?" She blinked.

"I said, I forbid it," he repeated, taking her hand and leading her off the knoll. "Only unlike that time in Dimbleby's when I tried to forbid you from buying my bed, this time I mean it."

"But how can you?" She hurried to match his long strides. "Knowing what we do now."

"Exactly." He stopped, kissing her hard and swift. "The ceremony goes on as planned because of what we know. How hard you've worked. How many innocent people are looking forward to tomorrow. And how happy the day will make your da."

He started walking again. "Do you think I would have given him a MacDougall sporran if I hadn't put the past to rest? Nor will I deny him his day to shine."

"So you're doing it for my dad?"

"And for myself." He slid a glance at her. "Dinna think I am so selfless."

"Then what do you mean?"

He flashed her a dazzling smile. "Simply, that when we return to the *ceilidh* and if I can catch him alone, he'll have a very special announcement to add to his duties tomorrow."

"Oh, Alex!" she cried, her heart bursting. "You're going to ask him for my hand?"

"In the right and proper Highland way, aye." He looked at her, a mischievous gleam in his eyes. "As if you didn't know."

But she couldn't answer him.

This time it was her world that careened and spun. And the wonder of it took her breath away.

The next morning, Mara stood in the very heart of One Cairn Village surrounded by so many MacDougalls, McDougalls, and other assorted Highlanders, ghostly and otherwise, that she strongly suspected she might dream in tartan for many weeks to come.

Not that she would mind.

She'd come to love the Highlands with a passion she would never have believed possible. Just hearing the soft lilting voices and rich, rolling laughter of the clansmen and friends come to celebrate the memorial cairn's unveiling filled her with warmth and joy.

As did the praise of her London solicitor, Percival Combe, when he'd arrived earlier that morning to witness the ceremony and assure her that Ravenscraig was hers, all stipulations well met and satisfied.

And that, many months before the required year had run its course.

The day's weather blessed her, too, for another cloudless blue sky smiled down on the celebrants. And a soft wind sighed across the heather, sweetening the air with the pleasant scent of birch.

Even Euphemia had spared her a cordial word, claiming she'd rested well in her thick-walled cottage, secure in knowing Alex's friends were but a help cry away should her sleep have been disturbed by ghosts.

One less ghost now haunted Ravenscraig, and Mara could not remember ever being so happy.

Hottie Scottie looked happy, too.

And surprisingly at ease in MacDougall tartan, his handsome clan sporran catching all eyes.

She reached for his hand as her father droned through the cairn's dedication.

". . . in reverent memory of Sir Colin MacDougall and the Lady Isobel, those who went before and laid a path for those who came after . . ."

She closed her ears to the words, hearing instead the happiness in his voice.

". . . more proud than I have words . . ."

". . . will burst my heart to see him place his ring on my little girl's finger . . ."

She whirled to face Alex. "What did he say? I wasn't really listening."

"I can see that," he said, smiling.

Then he was pulling her toward the cairn, where her father, Murdoch, and Percival Combe stood beaming like peacocks. He sank on one knee, but rather than reach for her hand, he unclasped his sporran, producing a topaz and diamond ring.

"Mara MacDougall, I told you I meant to ask for your hand in true Highland tradition and I am doing so now," he said, lifting his voice above the cheering. "With your father's blessing and these witnesses, I am telling you that I want you for my own."

His eyes brimmed with love. "Will you have me, Lady of Ravenscraig?"

"Oh, yes!" Mara watched him slide the medieval-looking ring onto her finger. "I will love you this day, this night, and for all our tomorrows unending, *Laird* of Ravenscraig."

The skirl of Erchy's pipes ended the poignancy of the moment when he materialized beside them, a twinkle in his eye and his red cheeks puffing. Amidst the stir, no one noticed his unconventional arrival or that Alex and Mara seized the opportunity to slip away.

"So," Mara said a short while later on a less-frequented path to the castle, "where did you get this ring?"

"You do not like it?"

"I love it," she said. "But it looks medievaly. Is it?"

He nodded. "Conjured at the *ceilidh,*" he admitted, looking pleased. "I fashioned it the instant I knew your da would be pleased by our union."

"You really do like him, don't you?"

"Och, aye," Alex admitted. "It was good to see him in such high fettle. He has big dreams and sees with his heart. A true Highlander even if he wasn't born on Scottish soil."

He glanced at her. "You were kind to call me *laird*. He'll weave tales about that. A Highland laird as a good-son!"

"But you *are* Laird of Ravenscraig," she said, sounding as if she meant it. "Did your king not give you a charter granting you this land and its holding?"

"Och, lass." He drew her into his arms. "That is done and by with. Forgotten."

"Well, I haven't forgotten it." She pulled away to retrieve a slender packet from inside her jacket. "My betrothal gift to you."

"Lass! What is this?" Alex's hands began to shake, his vision blurring as he opened the packet and withdrew an official-looking parchment of modern making, but fashioned to look of his day. Complete with red wax seals and ribbons.

It was a deed.

The same as his medieval charter—granting him full rights and titles to Ravenscraig and its lady.

Alex's heart split. "All saints, Mara, what have you done?"

"Only what should have been done nearly seven hundred years ago." She lifted on her toes and kissed him. "It's quite legal. Why do you think Solicitor Combe is here? He made the arrangements."

Alex crushed her to him, his world more complete

than he would have ever dreamed. "I don't know what to say."

"Then don't say anything." She slipped her hand beneath his sporran and squeezed. "Just love me."

His eyes darkened. "That I shall do."

"Forever?"

"O-o-oh, aye," he promised. "For all our days and then some."

She pulled back to peer at him. "On your plaid? In the heather?"

"That, too," he agreed, tightening his arms around her. "So often as you desire."

And then he closed his eyes and smiled.

Life had become indescribably good.

And he couldn't wait to start living it.

Epilogue

One Cairn Avenue
Philadelphia, a Year Later

The launch party for Hugh McDougall's self-published book on his family history, *Tartan Roots,* was in full swing by the time Alex managed to drag himself from bed and join the fine cracking revelry going on belowstairs in his father-in-law's plaid-hung living room.

Plaid-hung and plastered with so many likenesses of the book's cover, the startling vision had made Alex dizzy when he and Mara arrived from Scotland late last night.

Still feeling a bit queasy, he pressed firm fingers to his temples, knew now that he was suffering from something called jetlag. A malaise that didn't surprise him at all, considering how harrowing the journey had been.

He couldn't believe he'd allowed his beloved wife to persuade him to undertake such a nightmarish adventure. And although they were staying a full fortnight, he was quite sure he'd not change his mind about air travel by the time the fourteen days passed and they were left no choice but to board another flying machine.

Not that he'd let his dread show.

But he suspected Mara knew.

After all, she'd kindly refrained from commenting on his white-knuckled grip on her hand all through the travails of the Atlantic crossing.

But at least now he'd never again complain about the drive into Oban. Dodging sheep on the road in nowise compared to sailing through the clouds!

Och, aye, now he knew there were much worse things in his Mara's world than automobiles. But wonderful things, too, like the beautiful roundness of her swelling belly.

Alex stopped halfway down the stairs and swallowed hard. Then he pinched the bridge of his nose until all threat of possible misty eyes vanished.

He wouldn't embarrass his father-in-law by striding into the man's *ceilidh* looking teary-eyed. Mara had warned him that her father told everyone his good-son was a fierce Highland laird, and Alex didn't want to disappoint him.

"Here he is! Come straight from the *Auld Hameland*!" Hugh McDougall grabbed Alex's arm the instant he reached the bottom of the stairs, pulling him into the dining room, where a giant likeness of *Tartan Roots* served as a table centerpiece.

Looking like he might burst with pride, Hugh McDougall threw his arm around Alex and raised his voice, "Sir Alexander Douglas, Laird of Ravenscraig Castle, and *my* son-in-law," he boasted, beaming round at the circle of his impressed-looking friends and his somewhat tight-lipped wife. "And"—he cast a glance at Mara—"soon to be father of my first grandbaby, *Hugh Colin McDougall Douglas*!"

A chorus of happy-sounding *oohs* and *aahs* rose at that, and Erchy, rotund, red-cheeked, and be-kilted as always, underscored the moment's glory with a fine rendition of "Highland Laddie." Claiming to be an old friend on tour with a group of traveling Highland musicians, the Jacobite piper had arrived last night, touching Alex deeply.

As did Hardwick's and Bran of Barra's presence, though Alex knew he was the only one able to see those two. They hadn't chosen to materialize as Erchy had and simply stood against the wall, arms crossed and smiling, observing the day.

"Alex?"

He turned, found his lady at his side. "You really don't mind the name?" she asked, one hand resting on her middle. "We can still change it, you know."

Alex touched her hair, slid his fingers through the silky strands. They seemed to gleam even brighter these days, as did her beautiful eyes. Mara MacDougall Douglas wore motherhood well and he simply could not get enough of her.

Truth be told, he'd even fly clear around the world with her in one of her ghastly flying machines if the notion pleased her.

She meant that much to him.

Naming his first son after her da and their ill-winded ancestor was a small thing in the grandness of it all.

The peace and happiness she'd brought him.

"Hellfire and damnation," he muttered, dashing at the tear he hadn't realized was trickling down his cheek. "See what you do to me."

"Hottie Scottie," she said, using the nickname that never failed to make him smile, "methinks you have a soft heart."

Alex pulled her against him, brushed a kiss across her lips. "When we are alone again, I shall show you just how *soft* your Highlander is, lassie."

She flushed prettily, looking pleased. "Then you really do not mind the name?"

Alex hesitated, glanced at the giant likeness of *Tartan Roots*. One Cairn Village and the memorial cairn stared back at him from the book's cover, and he knew his own name and the name of his soon-to-be-born son were scrawled across the book's first page in a flowery dedication so touching it would have made a medieval bard weep.

And, some mischievous corner of his heart knew, would have Colin MacDougall turning in his grave.

But his lady was waiting for a response, doubt beginning to cloud her beautiful eyes.

"Our son's name is perfect," he gave her his answer, sealing it with a kiss. "It pleases me greatly."

"It pleases you?"

"Oh, aye." He kissed her again, deeper this time, and not caring who saw them. "Though I can think of two very good friends whose names I'd like to give our next-born son, if I may do the choosing."

"Of course," his lady agreed.

And across the room, Hardwick and Bran grinned like fools.